W9-BYL-664

continued . . .

"Rarely does a book with its own magic and idealism have such a message for the world today: to respect and revere all life, to protect our fragile environment, and to end the divisiveness that is escalating between individuals, families, communities, and nations. Once again, T. A. Barron has produced a new volume in which readers young and old will see the battle lines drawn between the forces of greed, arrogance, and evil, and those of sharing, of compassion, and of the will to do good."

—*Vermont Country Sampler*

SHADOWS ON THE STARS

"In the tradition of high classic fantasy, this is a lengthy novel of the battle between good and evil . . . Barron touches on many worthy themes: the power of one person to make a difference, trusting in one's abilities, the fragility of our environment, the need to honor all forms of life."   —*School Library Journal*

"Aficionados of Arthuriana and T. A. Barron get a double treat in the form of *Shadows on the Stars*."   —*Publishers Weekly*

"Adventure and mystery. [A] riveting tale." —*The Clarion-Ledger*

"An elaborate, richly detailed world . . . This sequel to *Child of the Dark Prophecy* continues the saga in a fine and multilayered fashion . . . Barron infuses the story with humor as he shares both the wonders of his lovingly created world and his appreciation of nature . . . This dynamic fantasy adventure will leave readers wanting more."   —*Booklist* (starred review)

THE ETERNAL FLAME

"A satisfying conclusion."   —*Deseret Morning News*

"A fitting finale . . . written in the grand tradition of epic sagas of the battle between good and evil . . . Barron leaves himself an opening to revisit his Arthurian realm yet another time."

—*Booklist*

"Combines adventure with a deep appreciation for nature."

—*The Oregonian*

MERLIN'S DRAGON

T. A. BARRON

ACE BOOKS, NEW YORK

THE BERKLEY PUBLISHING GROUP
Published by the Penguin Group
Penguin Group (USA) Inc.
375 Hudson Street, New York, New York 10014, USA
Penguin Group (Canada), 90 Eglinton Avenue East, Suite 700, Toronto, Ontario M4P 2Y3, Canada
(a division of Pearson Penguin Canada Inc.)
Penguin Books Ltd., 80 Strand, London WC2R 0RL, England
Penguin Group Ireland, 25 St. Stephen's Green, Dublin 2, Ireland (a division of Penguin Books Ltd.)
Penguin Group (Australia), 250 Camberwell Road, Camberwell, Victoria 3124, Australia
(a division of Pearson Australia Group Pty. Ltd.)
Penguin Books India Pvt. Ltd., 11 Community Centre, Panchsheel Park, New Delhi—110 017, India
Penguin Group (NZ), 67 Apollo Drive, Rosedale, North Shore 0632, New Zealand
(a division of Pearson New Zealand Ltd.)
Penguin Books (South Africa) (Pty.) Ltd., 24 Sturdee Avenue, Rosebank, Johannesburg 2196,
South Africa

Penguin Books Ltd., Registered Offices: 80 Strand, London WC2R 0RL, England

MERLIN'S DRAGON

An Ace Book / published by arrangement with the author

PRINTING HISTORY
Philomel hardcover edition / September 2008
Ace mass-market edition / September 2009

ACE
Ace Books are published by The Berkley Publishing Group,
a division of Penguin Group (USA) Inc.,
375 Hudson Street, New York, New York 10014.
ACE and the "A" design are trademarks of Penguin Group (USA) Inc.

PRINTED IN THE UNITED STATES OF AMERICA

10 9 8 7 6 5 4 3 2 1

Dedicated to my children Ben and Larkin
and their friend Lucile—
who asked two simple questions:

"What really happened between
The Lost Years of Merlin and *The Great Tree of Avalon*?"

and

"Who was Merlin's most bizarre friend?"

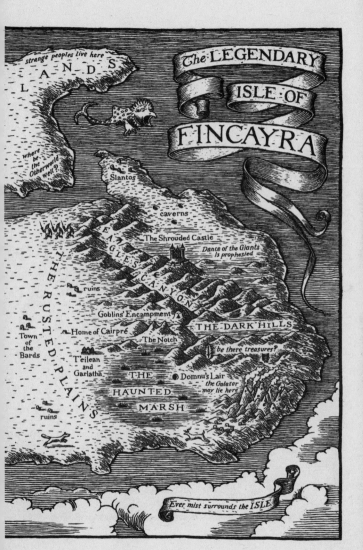

The LEGENDARY ISLE OF FINCAYRA

strange peoples live here

L A N D S

where be the Otherworld well?

Slantos

caverns

The Shrouded Castle

Dance of the Giants is prophesied

EAGLES' CANYON

ruins

Goblins' Encampment

Home of Cairpré

The Notch

THE DARK HILLS

Town of the Bards

be there treasures?

T'eilean and Garlatha

Domnu's Lair
the Galator may lie here

THE HAUNTED MARSH

ruins

THE RUSTED PLAINS

Ever mist surrounds the ISLE

The Seven Root-Realms
of the Great Tree of
Avalon

Born of Merlin's Magical Seed Planted in Lost Fincayra

T.A.B. '03 2003

GOBSKEN FORTRESS

OVERNIGHT PEAKS
Beware of the Deathravens

Vale of Echoes

LASTRAEL
(SHADOWROOT)

CAVERNS of the FLAMING JEWELS

DARK ELVES
Be here

LOST CITY
of LIGHT

RHANNAWYN
(FIREROOT)

VOLCANO LANDS

EAGLE FOLK Be here

CRATER of the CROOKED TEETH

RIVER of FIRE

High Realm

CLOUD GARDENS of the FAERIES

LIGHT HILLS of the FIRE DRAGONS

FLAMELON FORGES

Hoolahome

DANCING GROUNDS of the MIST MAIDENS

ANCIENT HOME of MUSEO?

PALACES of the FLAMELONS

MALÓCH
(MUDROOT)

Y SWYLARNA
(AIR ROOT)

the Haplands

Mud Hills

ISLE of the BIRDS

PLAINS of ISENWY

MISTY BRIDGE

the SOUNDSCAPES

MUDMAKERS be here?

VEIL of ILLUSION

Realm of the Wind

SECRET SPRING of HALAAD

HALL of the WINDS

AIRFALLS of SILMA

CLIFFS PERILOUS

GNOME LANDS of the LOWER MALÓCH

Blxthpxt SYLPHS

CRAFTED
from the BEST
AVAILABLE SOURCES
YEAR of AVALON
1002
By the
EOPIA COLLEGE
of MAPMAKERS

BEWARE of SINKLERS

CONTENTS

Prologue

The Pebble

*Look here, I know it sounds far-fetched—impossible,
even—that such a huge story could have such a tiny,
unremarkable beginning. Call me a liar if you like.*

*But that's how it was. I know, believe me. Just as I
know more than most about the surprising nature of
beginnings. For I just happened to be right there, at the
start.*

Three years before the birth of Avalon

A pebble, half buried by other pebbles, sat beside the
river. Even though it was surrounded by thousands of
bland, forgettable pebbles, this one was more forgettable
than most. There was nothing at all special about it.

Nothing.

Except, perhaps, that this pebble attracted plenty of
abuse. Much more than its share. Even before the unfortunate seagull incident, it seemed to be a magnet for all sorts
of indignities.

More than any other pebble on the shore, this one had

been scraped by claws, poked by beaks, and squeezed by jaws of hungry creatures who had mistaken it for an egg and then spat it out in disgust. One small beetle, attracted by the pebble's mottled green color (which nearly matched its own), had tried to lay its eggs right on top of it. But the beetle's body kept slipping off the smooth surface. Finally, with an angry hiss, the beetle kicked the pebble hard— several times—and scurried off.

On this particular morning, a rather chubby seagull with splayed wingfeathers waddled along the bank of the River Unceasing, looking for something. His beady black eyes flitted about, scanning the tumbled mass of pebbles that lined the water's edge. Heavy mist clung to the river and its banks, making visibility difficult. But one particular pebble—mottled green in color—caught the gull's attention.

With a clack of his beak, the seagull waddled over. He studied the pebble, inspecting its rounded shape, polished contours, and greenish hue. Squawking with approval, the bird moved closer, sat his plump bottom on the pebble . . . and dumped a large, gooey mass of guano.

Without so much as a backward glance, the bird rustled his wings and waddled off. Meanwhile, the reeking gray excrement oozed across the pebble.

TWO YEARS BEFORE THE BIRTH OF AVALON

Darker than the heavy mist along the river, a shadow formed on the opposite bank. Slowly, the blurry shape approached, slogging through the chill water. As it drew closer to the pebble's side of the river, the shadow hardened into a thin, two-legged figure. It seemed to be an old man, bent with age, not at all frightening—except for the huge, curved blade he carried. And the look of grim, messianic certitude on his face.

Reaching the bank, he stepped onto the water-washed stones. But he didn't pause to notice their glistening colors or varied shapes. His boot crunched hard on them, though his toe only grazed the side of the green pebble.

He grasped his deadly weapon with both hands. Even in the swirling mist, the blade gleamed ominously. Stealthily, without a sound, he raised it high above his head—

And swung.

The blade slashed deep into an enormous egg, as large as a boulder, which rested a few paces away from the pebble. The egg had only just started to crack open. At the instant of impact, there was an explosive *craaack!* as shards of shell and drops of thick, silvery liquid scattered across the riverside. From inside the egg came a painful whimper, more a whisper than a cry. The strange orange glow that had been radiating through the jagged cracks suddenly went dark.

The baby dragon within the egg released another whimper, then died.

Giving a grunt of satisfaction, the old man pulled out his blade, still dripping with the newborn dragon's silvery blood. He squinted, scanning the shore: There were, in all, nine of these enormous eggs here by the river—the only offspring of Fincayra's last dragon.

"An' now there be only eight," he said with a quiet cackle. "Evil creatures ye be, as evil as yer festerin' father." He spat on a broken bit of shell by his feet. "That's what I say to yer mis'rable face, Wings o' Fire!"

For a moment he glowered at the severed egg, where one lifeless claw protruded from an opening. He knew that this egg, like the others, had rested here by the river, undisturbed for centuries. Many centuries. For though he understood very little about magical creatures, he did know this much: The more magical the being, the longer it took to be born. And nowhere on this island of Fincayra was there any creature more magical than a dragon.

Yet this glimmer of knowledge—that he'd just killed something that had taken so long in its quiet incubation, its preparation for life—didn't trouble him in the least. Quite the opposite.

"No hope for ye now, ye wicked little beast," he growled. "When yer scaly body dies, yer wicked magic also dies! An' soon, this island will be rid o' yer kind forever."

Lifting the blade again, he strode over to the next egg. Even as he neared, a hole opened in the shell. Through it pushed a twisted, gangly arm, covered with iridescent purple scales. Then came a bony shoulder, dripping with lavender-colored ooze, and a crumpled fold of skin that vaguely resembled a wing. Finally, a head poked out, supported by a thin neck flecked with scarlet scales.

The newborn dragon blinked her two triangular eyes, adjusting to the misty brightness. Orange light poured from them, as if they glowed hotter than fire coals. Then, raising one of her claws, she tried to scratch the bright yellow bump on her forehead. But she missed and poked her tender nose instead. Whimpering, she shook her head, making her long blue ears flap against her face. Strangely, when she stopped, her right ear didn't droop down again. Instead, it stuck out sideways—more like a horn than an ear.

Suddenly, sensing danger, she froze. Right beside her stood another creature, whose own eyes flashed menacingly. Above the creature's head, something sharp glinted.

The blade slashed down. Another agonized whimper, almost a screech, echoed along the bank. The river continued to flow, its surface now tinted with thin streams of silver.

Not far away, down by the water's edge, the small green pebble quivered slightly—almost as if it had somehow sensed the baby dragons' agony. From deep beneath its hard surface came a thin, plaintive cry.

For it, too, was a kind of egg.

1: A Living Bridge

Memory can be hot as molten lava, or cold as a frozen glacier. But it's rarely reliable. Even when it comes back to you, clear and true, it can vanish on the next gust of wind.

Sometimes, it's not really even a memory. Just a hint, or a glimpse, or a mirage. Yet strange as it sounds, that sort of memory can be the truest of all.

One year before the birth of Avalon

Spring rains drenched Fincayra's western hills. Torrents poured down for weeks without end. The skies rained relentlessly, soaking every field and forest, every cliff and valley, until the very island seemed ready to drown.

Water tumbled down gulleys, streams, and rivulets. Once-green valleys started to resemble muddy lakes. Birds fluttered helplessly in the downpour, searching for safe places to build their soggy nests. What became of smaller, more delicate creatures—the fragile mist faeries, the lavender-winged butterflies, and the mysteriously glowing light flyers—no one could guess.

So powerful was the ongoing storm that the giants' ancient city of Varigal, nestled high in the hills, flooded completely. As the ground shook from the pounding footsteps of displaced giants, herds of wild unicorns galloped away from the rising waters that now filled their cherished glades. Spirited men and women who lived in the Town of the Bards, so recently restored after the brutal reign of King Stangmar, tried to organize a water-themed opera— but even the most passionate performers finally gave up when the whole stage (together with a good part of the town) washed away. Even the immense white spider known as the Grand Elusa was forced to abandon her underground cave that glowed with magical crystals.

The River Unceasing swelled, rising higher than anyone could remember. Waves roared down the river channel, ripping out trees by their roots, rolling along boulders, carrying the remains of bridges and fisherpeople's huts—along with a few young giants who whooped with delight at their exciting ride. The muddy waters raced seaward, toward the Shore of the Speaking Shells: the spot where, not long before, someone called Merlin had washed ashore.

The little green egg, swept up in the flood, rolled far downriver. By the time the floodwaters finally diminished, it had traveled many leagues from the place where the baby dragons had been slaughtered. At last, it came to a stop in the tangled grasses under a rowan tree whose graceful branches still sagged from all the rains.

Just as the egg ceased rolling, a gray-streaked river otter spied it. Sensing that it was, indeed, an egg, the old otter scampered over. Anticipating a small but tasty meal, his long whiskers quivered with excitement. In these days of theft, murder, and gathering armies—when an invasion by the wicked warlord from the spirit realm, Rhita Gawr, had grown increasingly likely—any morsels of food were highly prized.

Just as he grabbed the egg in his furry paws, a falcon shrieked and plunged from the sky. The otter spun around, losing his balance and dropping the egg. He rolled down the slippery bank, landing in the water. Two seconds later he lifted his face above the surface, just in time to see the falcon rising swiftly skyward, talons clutching the precious egg.

Westward flew the falcon, over the enchanted trees of Druma Wood. She sailed just above the branches of the forest's tallest tree, the ancient oak Arbassa, where the young woman Rhia—famous for her ability to talk with trees, rivers, and even living stones—had long made her home. Without warning, one of those gnarled branches lashed out, clawing at the falcon's wing. She screeched angrily, nearly dropping the egg. But she held on, beating her wings furiously to gain altitude. As she flew off, the oaken branch swiped at the air, crackling in frustration.

Veering south to avoid the forest, the falcon rounded the coast of Fincayra, then flew over the lost homeland of the treelings, strange people who lived now only in legends. Ahead, across the water, she spied the long, rugged peninsula whose cliffs held her nest. She clucked with glee: Nearly home now, she'd soon be feeding this egg to her brood of hungry chicks. Five of them, to be exact—always crowded in her nest upon the ledge, always squawking at each other, and always hungry.

All that remained of her journey was the simple crossing of the channel that divided her peninsula from the main island. She'd done it hundreds of times before with ease.

Nothing could interrupt her flight now. Even when ocean currents roiled the waters of the channel, no waves could reach as high as that cursed branch!

Glancing down at the channel, she noticed something odd. An extraordinary boat, looking for all the world like a huge upside-down hat, bobbed on the water. How had it come to float there? If some giant had tossed his enormous hat into the sea, he was nowhere in sight now.

The bird noticed that the great vessel was drifting toward an immense wall of waves that bordered the only island in the channel—a place so remote and hostile that it was called the Forgotten Island. Here, as every seabird knew, no people had walked for centuries. For the island's sheer cliffs held untold dangers and many mysteries— including the truth of why Fincayran men and women had lost their wings long ago.

Battered by the churning wall of waves, the floating hat started breaking apart. Its sides, made from woven boughs, started to collapse; its hull groaned and split apart. The vessel began to sink, dropping lower and lower in the water.

Suddenly the falcon heard a terrible shrieking sound. Fearing attack from another bird of prey, she banked sharply to the side, diving lower to evade her pursuer. At once she realized her mistake. That sound was coming not from above, but from below. And it wasn't the sound of any bird. No, it came from children. Human children!

Above the din of bursting boughs and splintering wood, many children wailed in fear. They climbed out of the rupturing bowl of the hat and onto the rim, trying desperately to cling to wood, rope, each other—anything that might float. Many of them toppled into the sea, shouting in terror as they fought to keep their heads above water.

As a mother herself, the falcon shuddered at this ghastly

scene. Yet she couldn't do anything to help. All she could do was continue her flight across the channel, bearing some food for her own children. She beat her wings faster, squeezing the green egg in her talons.

Just then another strange sight caught her eye—this one so astonishing that she almost dropped the egg. With all her concentration, she peered at the water below to make sure this wasn't an illusion. But no. This was real.

Mer folk! From far beneath the waves, their sleek, glistening forms broke the surface. The falcon circled overhead, amazed to see them—creatures so rare and secretive that even the sharpest-eyed hawk might only see, in a lifetime, one fleeting glimpse of an iridescent tail fin or shoulder. And the mer folk's numbers continued to swell. Several of them appeared, then dozens more, rising out of the deepest sea. Here, a scarlet-scaled torso twirled, flashing bright. There, a graceful fishtail slapped the waves, creating a luminous veil of spray. And there, a pair of muscular bodies leaped high, breaching, before falling back into the sea with a double splash.

The mer folk swam toward a single spot, where a new, enormous wave was steadily lifting out of the sea. Higher it rose, water streaming off its colorful crest. Watching from above, the falcon clacked her beak in surprise when she realized that this wasn't a wave at all—but a bridge. A luminous, living bridge.

The mer folk had entwined themselves together! Interlocking tails and fins and arms, they were forming a great, radiant archway. Swiftly it rose higher, gleaming with watery hues. Part solid, part liquid, it vaulted out of the depths.

Before long, the living bridge reached from the sinking vessel, over the crashing wall of waves, all the way to the shore of the Forgotten Island. Like a rainbow of the ocean, glowing with the colors of sea rather than sky, the archway gleamed. Small seabirds started to gather—terns and skimmers, kittiwakes and murres—piping and cooing and whistling as they soared around the magnificent bridge.

As the falcon watched in awe, her thoughts returned to the children struggling in the water. Would they find the bridge in time? Would it lead them into some greater danger on that forbidden island? Curious, she veered toward the island's coast, just for a brief look.

As she sailed across the jagged line of sheer cliffs at the island's edge, a fierce gust of wind suddenly struck. Slamming into her body with the force of a gigantic, invisible wing, the gust hurled her backward. Screeching with fright, she dropped the egg, which fell toward the rocky cliffs below.

Before she could regain her bearings, another gust struck so hard that it flipped her completely upside down, tearing two feathers out of her tail. Crying out in panic, she spun helplessly through the air. Finally she managed to flap her wings so vigorously that she righted herself. When, at last, she could fly again, she fled from the evil island at top speed.

As she flew toward her nest on the peninsula, her talons empty, she never even considered going back to that accursed place. She had no desire whatsoever to search for her lost egg, to see if it had been smashed on the cliffs. Just as she had no desire whatsoever to find out why those terrible gusts of wind had carried the vaguest scent of cinnamon.

2: MIRACLES

*An egg. A seed. A newborn child. They all hold secrets.
And they all hold magic.*

*At the moment an egg cracks, its magic, at last, is
released into the world. Or is it the other way around?
Is the world, at last, allowed inside the egg?*

THE YEAR OF AVALON'S BIRTH

Downward the green egg fell, plummeting toward the
rocky cliffs. Its green surface gleamed darkly, a last
hint of its potential for life—before being utterly smashed.

Below, the Forgotten Island lifted out of the sea like
a ghastly, broken crown. Sheer cliffs ringed the island's
coast, broken by only a few meager wedges of sand. Into
the shallow waters by one of those beaches, the miraculous
bridge of mer people reached. Already, several children
had clambered across and flopped down in exhaustion on
the sand; a few others scampered playfully in the shallows,
no longer thinking about their near escape from drowning.
One young man, wearing a tattered brown tunic, carried

two smaller children in his arms. As young as he was, he moved with the sureness of a wizard . . . and the grimness of someone who needed more than one miracle to save his world.

Above the cliffs lay the wreckage of an enormous burial mound. Broken timbers, blocks of granite, iron cauldrons, and huge sarsen stones lay scattered over the grassless slope. Strewn among them were treasures of all sorts— jeweled swords, broken-stringed harps, sounding horns, silver chalices, decorated masks, heavy shields, upturned wagons, and more. Bones, too, lay everywhere. Cracked skulls, ribs, leg bones, and a few intact skeletons were all that remained of whatever people had once lived here. Who they had been, and what had happened to them, no one knew—just as no one knew the truth about this mound. Originally, it must have been gigantic: the burial place not of a person or a family, but an entire city. But now, thoroughly destroyed, it looked like nothing more than a huge, violated grave.

Air whizzed past the falling egg. It spun slowly in the afternoon light, twirling, a brief but graceful dance that would soon come to a sudden end. Straight toward a sharp pinnacle of rock it plunged. Closer it came, and closer, just a few final seconds from destruction.

At that instant, a new gust of wind blew across the cliffs, scattering dirt across the ruined barrow. Like the wind that had knocked the egg from the falcon's grasp, it appeared quite suddenly. But unlike those gusts, it blew more gently this time, surrounding the egg with a cushion of air. This wind broke the egg's fall and carried it sideways, so that it missed the pinnacle and instead skimmed across the soil of the slope. Finally, it rolled down a small ravine toward a pile of bones bleached white by time.

The egg came to a stop, at last, in the outstretched fingers of a skeletal hand. Buffeted by the gentle wind, the bones of the hand almost seemed to close around its new treasure. Then the lifeless fingers relaxed again. The green egg rested like a precious ring upon one finger.

Then, as if its work were now complete, the mysterious wind vanished. It left behind a living egg that now adorned a long-dead hand. And it also left, afloat on the air, the slightest smell of cinnamon.

Hours passed. The young man in the torn tunic scaled the cliffs to explore the ruined burial mound. His coal-black eyes, glinting with magical sight, scanned the area. He took in every detail, searching for something that had eluded everyone else. Something that could help him save the world he loved. Something that would be visible only to a wizard.

Yet he couldn't find it. Biting his lip in frustration, he wandered about, poking at crushed shields and broken vases with his gnarled wooden staff. At one point he followed the contours of a small ravine, examining the wreckage around him. Something crunched under his boot: a bleached, bony hand. On one of its fingers lay something green—the stone, perhaps, of a ring.

The young man bent down to look more closely. Was it a stone—or an egg?

Abruptly, he halted. Not far away lay an object even more unusual: a glowing wreath of mistletoe, its golden leaves quivering in the breeze. It adorned a fallen statue carved from black obsidian. Intrigued, he left the green egg and stepped over to the statue.

Moments later, he exclaimed, "That's it! I've found it!"

To which another voice, deep and wrathful, answered: "Found your death, you mean."

Whipping around, the young wizard faced his challenger, a foe so ruthless he was known by the name Slayer. "You! You followed me here."

"That's right, Merlin. Come to end your meddling, I have. Once and for all."

A fierce battle ensued, so violent that the very ground shook. Nestled within those lifeless fingers, the green egg rocked with the vibrations, rattling against the bones.

All through that day and the long night that followed, the two enemies fought. Sword and staff, fist and knife, magic and counterspell—these were their weapons. Under the silver arc of the moon they battled, and into the next day's dawn.

At last, young Merlin prevailed. He stood shakily, holding his sword over his rival's chest, ready to end this brutal ordeal. A mighty wave crashed against the island's shore, sending a blast of spray onto the cliffs. Merlin swallowed, tasting the salt of the sea mixed with his own sweat and blood. And another taste, as well—one also richly imbued with blood. Revenge. He braced himself, then raised his sword, as a single drop of seawater rolled down his cheek, stinging the scars under his eye.

He squeezed the hilt of his sword, even as Slayer glared up at him, taunting him wordlessly. Yet . . . the scars on Merlin's cheek reminded him of a terrible blaze long ago— and the terrible anguish of his past. Anguish that his enemy had shared.

"I could kill you," he proclaimed.

"Then do it now, whelp."

"I could," repeated Merlin. He drew a deep, ragged breath. "But I won't."

To his foe's astonishment, Merlin lowered his sword and

slid it into its scabbard. "Too much blood has stained this soil—and our lives—already."

All at once, the whole island trembled. Distant thunder sounded, then swelled louder and louder into a deafening rumble. The quaking grew suddenly stronger, knocking the young wizard to his knees. The green egg rattled vigorously against its bony cage, until one of the fingers finally broke off. Free again, the egg rolled down the ravine and only stopped when it smacked into Merlin's boot. But the wizard didn't notice. Something else filled his mind with wonder.

Even as the quaking grew more violent, the water surrounding the island grew strangely calm. All the way across the channel, no waves rolled, no surf pounded. The sea itself seemed to be holding its breath.

A new breeze kicked up, fluttering the sleeves of Merlin's tunic. Bracing himself against his staff, he managed to stand. But the sight that met his gaze almost caused him to fall over again.

Moving. The island was moving! Like a shard of driftwood blowing across a pond, the small island slid toward the western coast of Fincayra. Cliffs on the opposite shore drew steadily nearer. The channel narrowed by the second. For a timeless moment, Merlin gaped at the sight, the breeze tousling his dark hair.

A sudden, grinding crunch erupted—pitching Merlin, and the egg by his feet, into a shallow pit. The egg bounced off his arm, nearly falling into the pocket of his tunic. But just at the last instant, it rolled away, dropping to the ground by his side. Merlin glimpsed it, recognizing its color. But he didn't pause to examine it. For his mind was teeming with thoughts of miracles.

The Forgotten Island had, at long last, rejoined the mainland! Just as the prophecy had predicted, *the land long forgotten* had returned to its shore. Unlikely as that feat was, though, it was perhaps no more unlikely than the wondrous sight of mer folk rising from the depths to make a radiant archway. And no more unlikely, thought Merlin, as he glanced over at the huddled form of his old enemy, than an unexpected act of mercy that spared someone's life.

Merlin nodded, pondering all this, even as he wondered whether more miracles were yet to come. Miracles that just might enable him to defeat the immortal Rhita Gawr, whose craving to conquer this magical realm had never slackened. Would this world—or some new world— survive the coming battle?

His gaze turned to the shiny green egg at his feet. Was his own destiny just as hidden, just as mysterious, as the contents of that egg? Would the miracles he hoped would come—rising from the courage of children, the loyalty of friends, and the depths of magic—be enough to prevail? Would they open up a new future for this world, just as new life emerges from an eggshell?

An idea struck him. Right at that spot, he knelt down. Placing his palms flat on the ground, still moist from sea spray, he felt the soil's gift for renewal. He considered how the land beneath him, returned at last to Fincayra's shore, finally felt complete. Much as his own heart, which had so recently spared his enemy, also felt complete. And then, reaching into his leather satchel, he carefully removed something precious.

A seed. A magical seed. Held in his palm, it beat slowly, like a living heart.

The young wizard studied this seed, recalling the mysterious person who had given it to him. Although that person had refused to reveal what the seed would become, he had told Merlin that it would grow into something marvelous. Truly marvelous.

Instinctively, Merlin knew this was the right time and place to plant it. And so, only a hand's width away from the green egg, he dug a small niche in the ground. Carefully, he placed the seed into the sea-dampened soil. He covered it, gently patted the spot, and then rose to his feet.

Moments later, he departed. Concentrating, he summoned the wondrous power of Leaping—magic whose strength came from what the great spirit Dagda, lord of the Otherworld, called *the great and glorious song of the stars.* At one instant, Merlin was there, standing on the soil atop his newly planted seed; the next instant, he was gone. Soon, on the far side of Fincayra, he would confront his enemy, Rhita Gawr—and face his destiny as a wizard.

For a few seconds, that spot fell as still as if it were frozen in time. No wind stirred the soil; nary a whisper broke the silence. A few grains of sand fell from the cliff ledges nearby, the individual grains sparkling like diamonds in the waning light. But nothing else moved or breathed. The land itself seemed to be waiting. Just waiting.

Of all the creatures who lived in Fincayra—and of all those who would one day live in the new world of Avalon—only one witnessed the very first sign of change. It was not someone who could see clearly. Or even see at all.

It was the creature who lay hidden inside the egg. Although it couldn't peer beyond the shell, or smell the hint of new life, or hear the crackle of electricity in the air—it could feel the first subtle stirring of the soil.

For from that tiny niche in the ground, hollowed out by Merlin's hand, emerged a thin, frail shaft of something green. As sparks crackled all around, flashing in the air, the shoot began to swell. And swell. And swell some more. Cracks appeared in the soil, radiating out from the base of the plant like dark bolts of lightning.

The ground started to shake. The little green egg rolled once again, skipping over a clump of soil to lean against the fast-growing shoot that was rising from Merlin's magical seed.

As the shoot grew taller, expanding into a sapling, the egg caught in the fork of one of the first branches. Still bigger the sapling grew, carrying the egg upward. Soon the egg disappeared into the layers of greenery that burst from every side. With relentless vigor, the young tree kept growing, bearing the egg ever higher.

For this was no ordinary tree, born of no ordinary seed. Rooted in the ancient soil of Fincayra, which would soon merge with the immortal mists of the spirit realm, this tree would continue to grow. It would reach upward and outward and inward as well. It would expand with majesty and mystery and complexity beyond description. It would, in time, grow so vast that it would become a world of its own—a world that would embrace all things mortal and immortal, a world that would rest between the realm of the spirits and all the other realms of the universe.

It was the Great Tree of Avalon.

3: LITTLE WANDERER

Of course, I have a special fondness for smells. All sorts—the more exotic, the better. But there has never been, and never will be, a smell that I treasure as much as the scent of cinnamon.

YEAR OF AVALON 1

There came a day when an immensely strong gust of wind blew across the highest reaches of the Great Tree of Avalon, now fully grown into a world between worlds. Enormous branches, pathways to the stars, quivered from the wind's force; the constellation that would someday be called the Golden Bough seemed to shift its place in the heavens. Out of the fabled River of Time roared this remarkable wind, over the gracefully curled branch that one day would be the wizard Merlin's favorite stargazing point, across the pristine lakes of Starlight's Palette, and, at last, into a narrow canyon where a certain mottled green egg lay in a cluster of ferns.

The wind, smelling vaguely of cinnamon, circled the

egg—not just once, but three times, as if it were examining it closely, making sure that this was indeed the very
egg it sought. Then, with renewed vigor, it gusted strongly,
lifting that little egg high into the air. Far, far away it bore
its prize, which spun slowly in the starlight as it moved.
Finally, at a place chosen by the wind itself, the current of
air suddenly ceased.

The egg fell.

Faster and faster it plummeted, speeding downward.
Past the Great Tree's branches, past the promontory that
future explorers would call Merlin's Knothole, past the
trunk that already held within itself such wonders as the
Spiral Cascades and the Great Hall of the Heartwood, past
the bizarre little body of water to be named the Swaying
Sea—all the way down to the westernmost root, the forested realm of El Urien, that would someday be known as
Woodroot.

If the creature inside the egg could have known, it might
have felt genuinely glad that of all the places in Avalon's
root realms to land, it was heading toward one of the most
wondrous. For the egg was dropping directly into Woodroot's deepest grove, home of trees so rich with magic that
even the slightest breeze that stirred their branches produced achingly beautiful melodies. Unfortunately, the creature's gladness would have been somewhat tempered, since
the egg was falling so fast that it would soon be crushed,
utterly obliterated on impact.

Already the air around the falling egg had thickened,
full of the rising mist from forest glades. Resins, both
sweet and pungent, wafted above the trees. Spray from
Woodroot's waterfalls thickened the air even more, and a
few tiny droplets of water formed on the egg's surface.

Just seconds remained before the egg finally smashed

to the ground. If the creature inside had any premonition that its free fall—and its life—were about to end, it showed no sign: Not a whimper of sound, not a trace of movement, came from within.

At the final instant before impact, a new gust of wind erupted, bending the tops of the trees. Like the earlier gust, it smelled of cinnamon; and also like the earlier gust, it seemed to know precisely where it wanted to carry this small green object. The egg flew slightly to the side, just enough to hit the thick branches of a massive cedar. Caught by the swaying boughs, the egg dropped slowly downward, from one layered canopy to the next, until it fell into a deep cushion of moss in the tree's roots. The wind abruptly ended, its cinnamon scent mixing with the resins of the forest.

As the egg landed—it cracked. Seconds later, the crack opened wider, as something pushed from within. A narrow nose, glistening green, poked out through the opening. Again the crack widened, breaking off shards of green shell.

The nose crinkled slightly, sniffing the rich aromas all around. Then, all at once, the whole head pushed out, crashing through the eggshell. Two tiny bright eyes, as green as emeralds, sparkled in the misty light. A pair of cupped, batlike ears, so big they dwarfed the rest of the face, rode atop the head like sails. As the head pushed farther, more pieces of shell toppled onto the bed of moss. Finally, the remaining shell split in two—and a minuscule green lizard with big ears crawled out of the debris.

Although the creature was no larger than a child's smallest finger, he moved with unusual confidence—almost a swagger. Perhaps he sensed somehow that, even before emerging from his egg, he'd taken a rather remarkable journey. Perhaps he knew, in the hidden depths of his mind, that he alone, among all the mortal creatures of this world, had witnessed the birth of Avalon. Or perhaps he simply felt glad to be able to move, at last, by his own power. In any case, he stepped with surprising sureness into this new phase of life.

Climbing up onto one of the cedar tree's roots to inspect his surroundings, he held his small, triangular head high. His thin tail, which ended in a knob the size of an apple seed, tapped against the root, drumming steadily. Against his back, a pair of crumpled wings lay tightly folded. The lizard's green eyes glowed bright as he surveyed his surroundings, never blinking.

A tender, warm breeze swept around him. Smelling of cinnamon, the gentle wind flowed over him like a living breath. And then, with an airy voice, the wind spoke.

"Hhhwelcome into the hhhworld, little hhhwanderer."

The lizard ground his tiny teeth and tensed every muscle in his legs, back, and tail. With a sudden movement he leaped into the air, spun completely around, and landed back on the root facing the other direction. Small though he was, the impact broke off some flakes of lichen, which drifted down into the mosses below. His eyes glowed brighter than ever as he scanned the forest for the source of the mysterious voice. Seeing nothing, he leaped and spun around again.

"No need to hhhworry, little hhhwanderer." The voice spoke soothingly, ruffling the edges of his cupped ears. "I am Aylah, a hhhwind sister, part of the people some call hhhwishlahaylagon. And hhhwhile you cannot remember meeting me before, little hhhwanderer, I have touched you several times, and have alhhhways been your friend."

The lizard listened intently, cocking his ears forward. But he said nothing.

Again the warm wind blew, filling his nostrils with the scent of cinnamon. "Like my sisters, little hhhwanderer, I must move as freely as the air itself, never sleeping, never stopping, never staying anyhhhwhere for long. That is a hhhwind sister's hhhway."

The breathy voice seemed to come closer, to whisper right in the lizard's ear. "But the spirit lord Dagda came to me in a vision, many years ago. He spoke hhhwith me, hhhwanting me to look after you until the day you finally hatched. He never said hhhwhy, my little hhhwanderer . . . but he did say that your life hhhwould be hhhwell hhhworth saving."

At this, the small fellow shifted himself on the root and tilted his head thoughtfully. For the first time, he blinked his eyes. Then he spoke his very first words, in a voice that crackled quietly, like a tiny twig that had burst into flame.

"Thank you . . . friend."

"You are hhhwelcome, little hhhwanderer, you are hhhwelcome." She blew all around him, gently stroking the edges of his ears. Then, with her airy voice, she sighed and spoke again. "I do not know hhhwhether you and I hhhwill ever meet again, little hhhwanderer. The hhhworlds hhhwhere I travel are many and the distances between them are hhhwide. But I certainly hhhwish you hhhwell."

Aylah swept closer, brushing the scales of his back and tail, a whirling circle of wind that tousled the cedar's boughs. "And nohhhw I must go. For I, too, am a hhhwanderer—as hhhwatchful as the stars, and as restless as the hhhwind."

4: NO ESCAPE

*Eat or be eaten, they say. Not very encouraging words.
And not very accurate, either. For I discovered early on
in life that it's perfectly possible to eat a lovely, delicious
meal—and then, when it's time for dessert, to get eaten.*

YEAR OF AVALON 2

C'mere, you runt!" The enraged fox charged through
the underbrush, snapping twigs and crushing newly
opened meadowsweet flowers under his paws.

Spotting the tip of his prey's tail as it vanished under
a cabbage plant, the fox shook his own tail angrily. That
knocked loose some of the thistles, needles, dead leaves,
twigs, and thorns he'd gathered during this frustrating
chase. How could a thief so small move so fast? And so
cannily, with almost as many tricks as a fox?

Saliva dripped from his jaws. "I'll teach you to steal my
meal, runt! That makes *you* my next meal."

Just ahead raced the thief, whose sharp little teeth still
gleamed yellow from the yolk of the pigeon's egg he'd

taken from the fox's cache. Now one year old, he looked like a cross between a small green lizard and a bat whose wings had been ruthlessly crumpled. Those wings, flapping against his back as he ran, resembled tattered shreds of skin more than anything that could someday fly. Wheezing from exhaustion, he wished those wings could take flight—here and now.

He dashed through the forest glade, sliding under fallen branches and crashing through thick clusters of fern, trying desperately to keep ahead of his pursuer. Hearing a gust of wind sweep through the trees overhead, his mind flashed briefly on Aylah's words: *He never said hhhwhy, my little hhhwanderer . . . but he did say that your life hhhwould be hhhwell hhhworth saving.*

But now, as he raced to stay alive, those words seemed hollow, fraught with irony. *My life worth saving? To be somebody's next meal, perhaps. But that's nothing special!*

Indeed, his first year after hatching, much of which he'd spent being chased, had taught him one basic rule of life: *Whatever is bigger than you wants to eat you.* And this fox was no exception.

Worse yet, the fox had already proved much more determined than most of the enemies the lizard had made in a year of scrounging meals from badgers' dens, birds' nests, and squirrels' hideaways. This chase had continued now for most of the morning—and the fox showed no sign of losing interest. While they had covered only a small fraction of Woodroot's forests, it felt as if they had traversed the entire realm. Truth was, this time the lizard's pursuer wanted not just to eat him, but to eliminate him. This chase was less about getting a meal than about getting revenge.

The little fellow clambered onto a rotting tree limb, swathed in turquoise-tinted moss. Then, spying a hollow trunk nearby, he darted into it, hoping to confuse the fox. Out the other side he ran, right into a thick patch of red-topped mushrooms. Dank and woodsy they smelled, emitting perfume so potent that the lizard started feeling dazed, almost giddy, as he dashed among the trunks of this miniature forest. But not so giddy that he forgot that he was running for his life.

As he was about to race out of the mushroom patch, he sensed something above him. Veering sharply to the right, he scurried into the open—just as the fox pounced on the exact spot where he would have been if he hadn't changed direction. Too close! Frantically, he hurtled across a bed of pine needles, sticky with resins, then tore into a clump of ferns.

Glancing behind, he saw the enormous forepaw of the fox about to slash at the ferns. Changing direction again, he sprinted down a leaf-covered slope that dropped into the bank of a splattering stream. Suddenly—a shadow moved over him. The fox had pounced again!

Little legs whirling, the lizard turned sharply. He shot sideways, careening on the bank. But the soil, so slippery from spray, wouldn't hold his feet. He skidded, then flipped over, rolling helplessly down the slope.

The fox, sensing victory at last, landed on the bank and instantly lunged at his prey. Eager to tear this bothersome thief to shreds, he opened his slavering jaws and waved his bushy tail like a flag of triumph. He stretched his neck toward the rolling lizard, slammed his jaws shut, and—

Missed.

The lizard dropped into a dark hole. Down he plunged,

into the moist soil of the stream bank. Even before he landed with a splat on the muddy bottom, the meeting point of several tunnels, he heard the fox's angry cursing and stamping.

"I'll get you, lizard. Get you and eat you and then vomit you up and eat you all over again! I'll chew your ugly little head, pop out your eyes, make bird bait from your heart. I'll squash you, stomp you, maim you, mangle you, and pummel you! I'll . . ."

On and on the fox ranted. Meanwhile, the little green lizard, panting in the darkness, sat back on his tail and lifted his face toward the hole above his head. His green eyes glowed with new radiance, something close to satisfaction.

"Too bad, you fat old furball," he called in his small, crackling voice, still out of breath from the chase. "Maybe next time you'll move faster than a boulder rolling uphill!"

This sent the fox into a spasm of uncontrolled rage. He lifted his head and roared with frustration. His paws pounded the turf, digging madly at the hole. Dirt, pebbles, and spittle rained down on the lizard below. But he didn't care. His foe's fit of agony was, for him, more lovely than the song of a meadowlark.

The lizard chortled happily. "What a delightful outing! I should do this more often."

"Yesssss," hissed a menacing voice behind him. "Yesssss, you mossssst definitely should."

Whirling around, he found himself facing a wide, triangular head with two yellow eyes, each slit vertically by a shadowy, quivering pupil. The head did not move, but a thin black tongue danced around the edge of the mouth.

The eyes slowly widened, beckoning. And the lizard found himself paralyzed—partly with fear, partly with some other feeling he couldn't name.

"Ssssso glad you came," hissed the river snake. "Ssssso delicioussssssly glad."

Still, the lizard couldn't make himself move. No amount of will could even lift one of his legs. Something in the shimmering eyes of this creature made him want to stay right here, for all time.

A chunk of dirt tumbled down the hole, kicked loose by the still-ranting fox up above. It struck the lizard squarely on the top of his head. Instantly, he awakened, freed from the snake's hypnotic gaze.

Just as the snake hurled himself forward, deadly jaws opened wide, the lizard darted out of the way. The snake skidded past, coasting on the mud. Seizing his chance, the little fellow dashed down one of the tunnels—hoping it would lead somewhere more friendly than a predator's gullet.

Racing as fast as he could, the lizard rounded a bend. His tiny feet slapped on the muddy floor, even as the immense bulk of the river snake slithered behind him. Ahead—a fork. He dived into the left branch, which sloped sharply downward. Barely able to control his momentum, he slammed against one wall, bringing down a shower of dirt. Right behind him, the snake hissed with annoyance and readied for the final lunge.

Hurtling down the tunnel, the lizard saw shredded rays of light ahead. An opening! Covered by a thick mesh of river grass, the bright spot wavered, shifting with shadows. Though he couldn't see what lay beyond the opening, he knew it couldn't possibly be more dangerous than what lay on this side. Or could it? This day had grown worse by the minute.

The snake's wrathful hiss echoed inside the tunnel. Feeling the sinewy reptile's cold breath upon his tail, the lizard gathered all his remaining strength and threw himself into the opening.

Whoosh. Grasses, wet from spray, slashed at his face as he flew past—and into the light. He rolled down a pad of sopping leaves, right to the bank of the stream.

Just uphill, the fox heard something stir by the riverbank and pulled his face out of the hole where he'd been digging furiously. His dirt-coated snout trembled with rage. The instant he saw the lizard roll to a stop by the water's edge, he didn't hesitate a single heartbeat. He simply pounced.

Right on the back of the snake! The reptile had emerged from his tunnel just as the fox leaped. The two of them rolled farther down the bank, locked in combat even before they stopped their slide. Roaring and hissing, tearing at fur and scales, they fought wrathfully. While the snake coiled around the fox's neck, squeezing tight, the fox snapped his jaws on his assailant's tail, ripping away flesh. Flecks of mud, along with wet leaves, sprayed everywhere.

Immediately below the battlers, the little lizard with the cupped ears cowered at the water's edge. Blocked by the stream below and unable to swim, he had nowhere to escape. Unless both predators died in their fight, he would still end this day being someone's meal.

The fox, struggling to breathe, clawed frantically at his foe. Then, with one powerful shrug, he threw off the snake, whose long body splatted against the ground. Before the snake could slither away, the fox leaped over and bit off the reptile's head. Dark, bluish blood seeped out of the severed form, staining the wet soil.

Even as he spat out the snake's head, the fox turned to face his original prey. His eyes smoldered like fire coals. The lizard swallowed, knowing that he'd run out of ways to escape. Except possibly . . .

At the instant the fox pounced, the lizard did something utterly unexpected: He jumped into the rushing stream. While the fox looked on, seething with frustration, the small green body submerged in foam and disappeared into the swirling currents.

5: BASIL

Did I make that wish? Or did the wish make me? To this day, I can't say for sure.

Rushing currents carried the little lizard downstream. Pounded relentlessly by water, flung against river stones, whipped by eelgrass, and spun around by eddies, he grew weaker by the second. And colder, as well, from the icy stream.

Hard as he tried to churn his tiny legs, stiff from cold, he couldn't push himself onto the bank. The ragged folds of skin on his back, so unlike wings, merely dragged him down like the sopping sails of an overturned boat. So did his oversize ears, which filled with water and weighed down his head. Breathing was nearly impossible: His few instants above the constant swirl came without any warning and with barely enough time to cough before he was submerged again.

Finally, the stream swung around a sharp bend where auburn reeds grew thickly under a sheer cliff. Caught by the reeds, the half-drowned lizard was tossed out of the surging current and into calmer shallows, where he lay motionless for several minutes. At last, he forced himself to move again and weakly paddled toward the shore. Fortunately for him, a dense patch of basil grew along the bank. When he reached the leafy herb, whose green color almost matched his own, he collapsed.

His head spun; his chest ached. He coughed, vomited water, and coughed some more. The smell of basil—so strong it seemed to shout—wafted over him. He wished the smell, both sweet and tart, were even stronger, knowing that it would provide the best possible camouflage against enemies. Then everything went dark.

He lay there, unconscious, for the next two days. Occasionally he would awaken for a few seconds—barely long enough to lift his head and smell the heavy scent of basil that shrouded him. Then he'd drop his head and fall into darkness again.

Once, in a brief moment of consciousness, he stirred, as a heavy wind whipped through the basil leaves. Just for an instant, he thought he heard, in a familiar, airy voice, those words from distant memory: *a life hhhwell hhhworth saving.*

A life well worth saving! Ridiculous! His whole life he'd spent hiding, being hunted, or trying to steal somebody else's food. Unlike many of Avalon's creatures he'd seen, he wasn't magical. Not at all. Even a lowly sparkworm, who could glow dimly at night, had more magic than he did. Why, he couldn't even fly! Nor even say what kind of creature he really was—just a scrawny lizard with round ears and useless wings.

All he knew with certainty was that he wasn't the least bit worthy of Aylah's words. Those words, like her acts of kindness toward him, were as fleeting as a breeze. The sweetness of basil now tainted by something more bitter, he lost consciousness.

In this state, he never knew how many predators crawled or slithered or flew nearby. Disguised by the herb's color and, even more, by its smell, he evaded the hungry river otter who swam past, the yellow-tailed fisherhawk who swooped above the shallows, and the tan-coated bear cubs who splashed through the reeds. Even the vengeful fox, still stalking his elusive prey, passed just a tail's length away—but didn't notice him.

Finally, he awoke. Vaguely aware that he needed to find some food, he concentrated on a damsel fly hovering lazily just above his snout. At just the right moment, he reared up and snapped his jaws. But as weak as he was, he moved far too slowly. The fly easily evaded him, darting out of reach.

Dejected, hungry, and weak, he crawled slowly to the edge of the herb patch. There he found a small pool, no more than a puddle, which still held a bit of water from the spring floods. The potent smell of basil still surrounded him, so he felt safe enough to crawl into the open, sliding onto the sand beside the pool.

Maybe, he thought, he'd find some slow-moving grub or drowned beetle in there—something he could eat. Yet as soon as he raised his head to look into the pool, the only creatures it held—a flock of spray faeries with bright silver wings that flashed like liquid stars—lifted off immediately, wings humming.

The lizard watched the delicate, silvery creatures rise into the sky, climbing in unison as if they were raindrops pouring upward. Then, all at once, they called on their particular faery magic and melted into the air, completely invisible. *So beautiful*, he thought, gazing at the sky. *So magical.* Then, glumly, he shook his head. *And for me, so impossible.*

Lowering his head, he gazed into the pool. But for the gentle ripples caused by the faeries' wings, the water sat very still. And beautifully clear. Light from the stars of Avalon, which brightened every dawn and dimmed every evening, sparkled on the surface.

Suddenly, without any forethought, the little reptile felt compelled to make a wish. Leaning over the edge of the pool, so that he could see the full reflection of his face, he said in a small, reedy voice: "Hear me, stars of Avalon. Hear me, if you can. I want to be . . ."

He paused, hesitant to say the next word. And then he spoke it, as ardently as he had ever spoken anything.

"Special. Just . . . special. Not big, or powerful, or anything like that. But someone who, well, *matters.* The same way a new day matters. Or a fresh rain. Or even . . . a faery's magic."

At that instant, something fell on him, as fast as lightning. A beak! Catching the lizard firmly by the tail, the slender, gold-colored beak lifted him high into the air, where he dangled helplessly.

He hung upside down, writhing madly to free himself. But whenever he twisted, the beak merely gripped his tail more tightly. Meanwhile, two yellow-rimmed eyes above the beak studied him with obvious interest. Recognizing those eyes and the plume of white feathers rising over them, the lizard froze. Struggle, he knew, was useless. For he'd been caught by one of the realm's most feared hunters, a bird known for deadly, ruthless efficiency. A great blue heron.

This is what I get for making a wish, he grumbled to himself.

Still inspecting her catch, the enormous bird hunched her head down on her grayish-blue shoulders. Then, with one deft motion, she flipped her beak upward, hurling him into the air—and kicked out one of her long, bony legs. Immediately she caught him again, this time in the tight grip of her foot. Standing on one leg in the reed-choked shallows, the heron continued to peer closely at him. As she turned his scaly little body from side to side, her plumed head tilted in puzzlement.

"By the deep gaze of Dagda, what do we have here?" The heron's hoarse squawking rose above the splatter of the stream. Still content to stand on one foot, she hopped a bit closer to the bank, never relaxing her grip on her catch.

"You be not a bird," she squawked, "though you do have some sort of wings. If you call these floppy feather-less things wings! You be not a lizard, with those ears the size of holly leaves. And you be not a bat, at least no bat worthy of the name. What be you, then? Some sort of ugly insect?"

An insect? Insulted, the lizard ground his teeth angrily. Trying his best to sound imperious and terrifying—not very easy to do when imprisoned by your enemy's foot— he declared: "Actually, I am—well . . . I am an extremely dangerous . . . *dragon faery*! Yes, yes, a dragon faery. Capable of eating you in a single bite! Release me at once, good bird, if you value your life."

The heron clacked her beak and then, from deep in her throat, released a loud chuckle. "Whatever you be, it be something funny."

"My good bird, I am not joking! Hear me, I command you! I am merely giving you fair warning before I slaughter you without mercy." To emphasize his point, he grimaced, showing a mouthful of microscopically small teeth.

The heron laughed, so vigorously that her head seemed to bounce up and down on her hunched shoulders. "Well then, dragon faery, you be funny, yes indeed. And also," she added with a curious look in her eyes, "you be smelly. Very smelly."

Surprised, the lizard sniffed himself. Sure enough, he smelled powerfully—of basil. It wasn't just a lingering aroma, what he might expect after staying so long among those fragrant leaves. No, he smelled as if he *himself* were a patch of basil—as if he, too, were made from the herb. But how could that be?

The heron scrutinized him, turning her foot to view him from another angle. After a moment, she announced, "You be somewhat magical, I believe."

"Er . . . me?" asked the lizard, surprised. "You must be mistak—" Suddenly realizing the bird had given him an unexpected opening, he caught himself. "Of *course* I'm magical," he declared. "All extremely dangerous dragon faeries are—"

"Hush," commanded the immense bird. "By my father's feathers, I do believe you have the ability to make smells! Strong smells. A rare talent, yes indeed! One I have not encountered before. And judging from your startled look just now, it seems you be not aware of your own power."

Caught completely off guard, the lizard remained silent. Could this really be true? Or was the heron merely toying with him before making him her next meal?

"Such a waste," she said with a ruffle of her blue-tinted wings. "To have a gift and not know about it! My guess be that you produced the smell of basil to help you hide among those herbs. Consciously or not. To keep you safe—at least until a superior hunter came along."

With that, she chuckled, her head bobbing again on her shoulders. But the lizard she clutched didn't quite see the humor, and kept quiet.

"This calls for an experiment," she squawked decisively. "If I be right—and, by the wings of the wind, I be almost always right—you can make other smells, too."

"Wait," protested her captive, still not at all sure that his basil smell was anything more than residue from the herb patch. "I'm not—"

"Therefore," she continued, ignoring him, "here be the terms. Listen up, now. Your little life depends on it. If you can produce another smell—preferably something pleasant—then I shall release you. Yes, release you! I shall set you free . . . at least for the rest of this day. If, however, you can't do anything but basil, then I shall eat you. In one gulp—a tasty little gulp, I expect. Scented with basil."

The heron chortled at her little joke, then demanded, "Do you accept the terms? Say yes, and I will grant you this chance to demonstrate your power. The threat of impending death, I find, can bring out the best in creatures. Or the worst. In any case, this be your opportunity to do something truly remarkable. Say yes, and you be spared. Say no—and it be time for supper."

To emphasize her point, she jabbed her beak into the shallows at her foot. Half a second later, she pulled out a wriggling minnow, then swallowed it whole.

What to do? The lizard's thoughts raced madly. Why in the name of Avalon did this crazy bird think he possessed magic? And even if she were somehow right, how could he possibly make that magic work?

Clack. Clack. The heron's beak tapped impatiently.

Think smelly thoughts! the lizard told himself. With all

his concentration, he conjured up mental images of slimy fish eggs. Rotten apples. Piles of boar dung, crawling with maggots.

Hopefully, he sniffed the air. Nothing. Not even the smell of basil reached his nostrils.

Clack. Clack. The heron watched him, eyes narrowing.

Hurriedly, he tried other pungent ideas. He imagined a parade of moldy pears, a grove of pine trees dripping with sap, a pile of crushed beetles, some newly opened daffodils, a family of stinking skunks, and a whole field of rotten eggs.

Nothing.

Clack. Clack.

The heron's eyes strayed to the small fish swimming by her foot. Clearly, she was getting hungry. And clearly, she wouldn't wait much longer.

Harder and harder the lizard tried, picturing the smelliest things he could remember. The week-old carcass of a fallen deer. The sulfurous bubbles rising out of a hot spring. The first bush of lilacs to blossom.

Clack. Clack.

I'm running out of time. All those images, he thought ruefully, *but no smells.* Wait! He caught his breath. Maybe the trick was not to picture pungent things in his mind—but to *smell* them. Aromas, not images. Smells, not visions.

Clack. "Your time be up, regrettably." The heron shook her feathered head. "I be sad you disappointed me. So very sad. Fortunately, though, eating something always brightens my mood."

Even as her beak bent toward him, the lizard tried furiously to concentrate. *Think smells!* But how? He wasn't used to doing that. He wasn't even sure he *could* do that.

The beak approached, nearer and nearer. It started

to open. Inside, all he could see was a gaping chasm of darkness.

Think like a hunter! he commanded himself. *Like the heron—smelling out her prey.* He tried his best to imagine how she would catch the scent of every fish before catching the fish itself. Even a big, meaty trout that might leap out of the stream, she'd probably smell first: its oily scales, its fishy breath. Then she would—

Snap. The heron's beak closed hard.

But not on the lizard. She had whirled around to clamp her beak on the fish she had smelled right behind her. And yet, to her astonishment, there wasn't any fish at all.

"What?" she squawked, turning her head to and fro. "I be sure I smelled . . ."

"A trout?" the lizard asked. "A nice juicy one, maybe?"

The heron's head spun back around. Judging from her expression, she was greatly annoyed. Rarely, if ever, had she been fooled—certainly not by someone she'd already caught. The lizard swallowed anxiously. Would she go back on her bargain? Had she never planned to keep it?

The heron's foot tightened around her prey—then abruptly released him. He fell with a splash in the reedy shallows. Quickly, he swam to shore.

"Congratulations," she declared with a flap of her broad wings. "You have an unusual life ahead, I predict. A most unusual life! Perhaps even a long one." She glared down at him. "Unless," she whispered, bending low, "you ever make the smell of a trout near me again."

The lizard stiffened. Instantly, his fishy smell vanished from the air. Still, he didn't feel entirely comfortable with the heron's beak so close to his face. She might still be thinking about the appetizing fish she'd almost eaten. In a flash, he knew what to do. Closing his eyes, he concentrated on a new smell.

"Basil," said the heron, nodding with amusement. Pulling her head back to her bony shoulders, she observed, "You have learned two important lessons today, my little mystery beast. How to use your power. And how to distract your enemies."

The lizard stared up at her, his green eyes aglow. "True. But I disagree with one thing you said."

The heron cocked her head inquiringly.

"You may have been my hunter," he explained. "But really . . . you're not my enemy."

The heron waded a bit closer. "You could be right, little one. At least for today. Tell me now, before we part. What is your name?"

The lizard blinked, suddenly aware that he didn't *have* a name. "I . . . I really don't know."

"Don't know?" The huge bird shook her grayish-blue wings in amazement. "Don't know your name? Well then, allow me to give you one."

With a loud clack of her beak, the heron announced: "Your name, from this moment on, shall be . . ." She paused, sniffing the air. "Basil. Yes indeed, Basil."

Warming to the idea, the lizard gave a nod. "And your name is?"

"Gullpiver," she declared. "Gullpiver, the great blue heron."

"Pleased to meet you," he replied, rearing up on his hind legs to give her a cordial bow. "And I am Basil. The extremely dangerous dragon faery."

6: MY WORLD

I learned something valuable that day—a lesson I've never forgotten. It's worth listening well to what you hear. No matter how bizarre the story . . . or how bizarre the storyteller.

Furtively, Basil darted out of the sheltering leaves of cabbage and onto a root at the base of a towering hemlock tree. As he'd done many times before, he scurried up the root to the tree's massive trunk, where he spied his favorite hideaway, a tiny protected cavern formed by a burl in the tree's bark. Though his wings felt uncomfortably stiff, as if they were hardening right into his back, he managed to squeeze into the cavern's narrow mouth. As usual, he brought a meal with him—this time, a slightly bruised but meaty yellow mushroom he'd stolen from the den of a sleeping badger.

"He won't miss this one," said Basil, settling into a comfortable position on the cavern's smooth floor. Then he nodded, agreeing with his own remark. Conversing with himself, he'd found, could be a surprisingly pleasant pastime. And besides, with all the time he spent dodging predators, he had almost no opportunities to talk with anybody else.

"Fat old chump," Basil went on, "he could use a bit less to eat anyway."

He took a big bite of the mushroom's stem and chewed slowly, savoring the rich woodsy flavor. His eyes surveyed the dark grain of the cavern walls, glistening with hemlock resin. "Mmm, I sure do like eating in here. So quiet, restful, and alone."

Yet even as he spoke the words, he knew that they were a lie. Sure, he liked the privacy of this hidden niche. But why? Not for its restful isolation. For its *safety*. From outside the hemlock, this place was virtually impossible to see or sniff (thanks to the potent smell of hemlock resin he always released upon entering). The truth was, he lived alone not because he liked it—but because he feared living otherwise, out in the world inhabited by other creatures.

Taking another bite, he chewed thoughtfully. Ruefully, he wondered, *Will I always live alone? Always live in hiding?*

He scowled, which made his cupped ears flop over onto his snout. Shaking his head, he sent the ears back to their usual upright position. Then he did something he'd never expected to do. Something he'd never done before.

Dropping the mushroom on the cavern floor, he crawled back outside. Slowly, hesitantly, he pushed his nose out into the humid air of the forest. Then, carefully checking for anything that might like to eat a lizard—and for any signs of an angry, overweight badger—he turned and started climbing up the tree.

Cautiously, he scaled the rough ridges of the trunk. Ignoring the stiffness of his wings, which made him less flexible as a climber, he concentrated on another, more serious danger. Predators. He released his strongest hemlock smell, hoping to disguise himself, but he knew that his vibrant green body shone like a flame against the dark brown bark. His heart pounded within his ribs, drumming incessantly, for he knew this was risky. Foolishly risky. Yet still he continued to climb.

"I need to see this forest," he whispered as he worked his way higher. "Not just run through it, seeing only whatever might eat me."

He scooted around a protruding knot, trying not to think about how exposed he was to birds, snakes, magic-tongued tarantulas (who could sing their prey to sleep in seconds), and other tree-dwelling hunters. "I want to know where I live," he panted. At least I can see it—really see it—just once."

With a deft maneuver, he swung himself onto a wide branch and scurried out to its nearest cluster of needles. At the same instant he ducked into the greenery, a great horned owl swooped past, silent as a feathered cloud. But the owl kept flying; neither Basil's bright scales nor his thumping little heart had given him away.

Seconds later, Basil settled into a bowl-shaped knot on the branch. Obscured by hemlock needles, he could see much of his surroundings without being seen by others. He swung his head to and fro, taking in the rich complexity of forest life.

Not far away, on a neighboring cedar, a purple-crowned woodpecker probed for insects in the bark. A pair of squirrels leaped from one bouncing branch to the next, while a family of bright-eyed raccoons watched from their hole in a chestnut trunk. Golden-winged butterflies fluttered past, while honeybees buzzed and teams of ants marched across the roots of a plum tree heavy with fruit. A few eyes glittered that Basil didn't recognize, although a pair of ruby slits, he felt sure, belonged to a tree-climbing adder. With a start, he realized that the thickened branch of a vine-draped oak tree was actually the body of a resting puma. Her belly, swollen from a recent meal, moved slowly up and down with every breath; her feline paws occasionally swatted insects who dared to fly too close.

More than the sights, though, Basil relished all the sounds and smells. Songbirds piped, thrummed, and whistled from branches above and below. Squirrels cracked open nuts, chattering to their neighbors. Sprigs of honey-fern, newly unfurled in the morning light, shivered softly with each breeze. And as they vibrated, the ferns gave off a scent so ebullient that it tickled Basil's nose as well as his mind: Trying to stay quiet, he had to bite his tongue so he wouldn't laugh out loud. Spiderwebs smelled dank and musty, while every kind of moss or lichen released an aroma of its own—sometimes as sweet as rivertang berries, sometimes as tart as lemongrass.

Suddenly, from the branch just above him, he heard a new sound. A loud rustle of feathers, as several birds landed at once. Then came voices—rough and cacophonous.

A flock of crows, Basil concluded, seeing a flash of black wing tips through the needles. *Five or six of them, maybe more.*

"Giants, caawww, huge and ugly," croaked one. "Climbin' up from the mists, they were, comin' to make their new home here in the root-realms. Bigger than hillsides, each one, with mouths that could swallow a lake! Saw them myself, I did."

"Caawww, I thought all that migratin' had stopped by

now! The isle of Lost Fincayra must be empty as a buzzard's brain, with all the birds and beasts movin' up to Avalon." The crow clacked his beak for emphasis. "Wish they'd stop comin' here and leave us alone."

"Where do you think *you* came from then, you saggy-tailed lump of coal? Everybody came here from Fincayra—all but those creatures made from the magic soil of Malóch."

"You believe that nonsense, do you? Why, not even a pack of dog faeries, stupid tongues a-waggin', would fall for that story."

Above a barrage of caws, the crow continued: "Nobody in Avalon is makin' creatures from dirt, I tell you. Nobody! Maybe Merlin, powerful wizard that he was, could do magic that big—but he ain't around no more. Gone to see that other place, far beyond the mists."

"He's comin' back, I hear," cawed a hoarse voice that, to Basil, sounded distinctly female. "When he's had enough of Earth, he'll come home to Avalon." Over the sputtering squawks of her companions, she declared, "He's got a reason to return, a very good reason."

"What, to check on the size of the tree he planted? Ca-ca-caawww! Merlin the gardener!"

"No, acorn head." She flapped her wings, waiting for the flock to quiet down before she delivered her news. Gradually, the crows fell silent. Even Basil, on the branch below, lifted his head so he wouldn't miss whatever she was about to reveal.

"Merlin has a mate! I know, I saw them together, just before he left. A woman with big doe eyes. Ca-ca-caawww! Named Hallia. I promise you, he's comin' back to her."

"Why?" croaked a skeptical companion. "Does she owe him money?"

"No, beetle brow!" The female crow's voice softened to a rough whisper. "He's in love."

"Merlin? In love? Caawww, no chance!"

"Caawww, I thought he was smarter 'n that."

"Just goes to prove that even a wizard can be stupid."

With that, the crows started laughing, so rancorously that their voices blended into one big cacophony. Now it was impossible to hear more than snatches of words here and there. But Basil didn't mind. He had heard enough to be enthralled.

How could he have lived for years in this forest realm—and know so little about its creatures, its magic, and its stories? And what about those other realms the crows had mentioned? Where exactly were they, and what mysteries did they hold? Would he ever get to see them, even if he couldn't fly? And if he could someday fly—a wish so ardent he could barely think about it—just where would he go? Would he hear more tales about Merlin? Was the wizard really going to return to Avalon?

All these questions and more surged through his mind like a spring flood. He listened some more to the crows overhead. They had finally gone back to gossiping. He promised to come back to this spot, as often as possible, in case they ever returned. And, in addition, he promised to find more places where he could witness more of his world—preferably without getting eaten.

"It's worth the risk," he whispered beneath his veil of hemlock boughs. "After all, this is my world, too! An amazing world. I want to know it better."

A sudden surge of doubt flowed over him. Was it *really* his world if he didn't know where he fit in it? Why, he couldn't even say what kind of creature he was! Let alone what might make him special.

He growled, making his slender throat vibrate and his ears tremble. "It *is* my world," he resolutely declared. "It belongs to me, just as much as it belongs to the crows. The puma. Or even the wizard."

Casting aside his doubts, he thought about his new awareness—and his new appreciation for gossip. The forest began to darken, until the golden light of starset filtered through the groves, stretching luminous beams between sky and soil. Though he knew he should find somewhere more protected, he vowed to stay right here on this branch and experience the new sounds and smells of night.

A bat flew just above him; the jagged wings came close enough to make the hemlock needles over Basil's nose quiver. But he didn't notice. He had fallen into a wary, uneasy slumber.

7: DAGGERS

Who was it who warned, be careful what you wish for? Whoever they were, I'd like to crush them under a mountain of boulders. Tear out all their innards. Roast them over searing hot flames. And then . . . I'd tell them they were right.

High in the branches of the hemlock tree, Basil slept fitfully. Whether from the unsettling experiences of the day, the discomfort of his useless wings, or the overriding fact that he lay high above the ground—exposed to nighttime attackers, unseen terrors, or sudden storms that could knock him to the ground at any moment—he barely slept at all.

Dozing under the gauzy blanket of needles, he rolled and kicked and moaned. And throughout all this, he dreamed. Yet the images seemed too vivid, and the pain felt too real, to be just a dream.

He lay on his back, on a bed of hemlock needles. But the needles weren't lying flat, as they do on a forest floor. No, these needles stood straight up, like daggers, jabbing into the scales of his back. Hard as he tried to flip over, he couldn't budge. All he could do was writhe painfully on the blades.

"Stop!" he cried into the darkness that shrouded him. "Set me free!"

No one heard him. No one came. He was utterly, completely alone.

The pain of that realization stabbed deeper than any dagger. Not in his back . . . but somewhere within.

"Stop!" he cried again, more weakly this time.

No answer.

No help.

The more he writhed, the greater the pain. And the greater his pain, the deeper his loneliness.

Hours passed, filled with struggle and torment. Nothing he did seemed to matter. Nothing he said reached anybody else. He might have been disconnected from the universe, suspended in a private realm of his own. Only the visceral reality of his pain, and the ever-present smell of hemlock, convinced him that he was still alive.

But why stay alive? Just to struggle? To ache for something else, something more?

No answer.

No help.

Until . . . at last, a figure strode out of the surrounding gloom. He carried a glowing flame—a torch. Upon his shoulders hung a cape, strewn with glittering stars. And on his face, under a thick black beard, his mouth curled in a grim but gentle smile. Even before Basil looked into his eyes—dark eyes, blacker than the spaces between stars—he knew exactly who this was.

"Merlin!" he cried. "You're back. You're really back!"

The figure said nothing. For a long moment, they stared

silently at each other. Basil started to wonder if he'd been wrong. And yet . . .

Quietly, uncertainly, he said, "Merlin, can you help me? With your magic?"

The wizard stepped nearer. As one of his hands raised his torch, the other reached out toward Basil. Closer it came, and closer, until the fingertips nearly met Basil's nose. In another second, they would help him, free him, that much Basil knew. He waited, quaking, for the touch of that magic.

Just as Merlin touched him—

A deadly creature, darker than darkness, appeared! Waving huge, batlike wings, it viciously attacked Merlin— pummeling and biting, eager to kill. Hard as the wizard fought back, he was clearly overwhelmed.

"No!" shrieked Basil above the terrible din. With all his might, he battled to break free of his invisible bonds. At last, wrenching his whole body, he broke loose. He rolled off the dagger points and fell on top of Merlin's assailant.

Furiously, Basil fought—whipping his tail, snapping his jaws. Even his own pitiful, ragged wings seemed to move at his command. Though the beast was many times larger than himself, he battled furiously. Yet all Basil's strength, and all the wizard's, were no match for the batlike creature. Its powerful wings, hooked at the joints, folded over them . . . squeezing . . . smothering them completely.

Merlin fought less vigorously. He moaned, the sound of someone's life fading away. The wizard kept writhing, as did Basil. Yet as the deadly wings squeezed tighter, the captives' movements slowed. Basil felt the wizard's hand brush against his ear. Then, with sudden finality, the hand went limp. The wizard fell still.

"No, please!" Basil cried. "Don't stop. Don't die!"

The wizard stirred again—only to shudder one last time.

"Wake up!" shouted Basil, banging his head against Merlin's chest. Hard he slammed, once, twice, three times.

And then Basil awoke. He lay not on the dying wizard, but on the hemlock branch. Rather than bashing his head on Merlin's chest, he'd been hitting the branch, which accounted for his sore jaw—and for the flakes of bark that floated downward, glinting in the starlight.

Distressed as well as dazed, the lizard lay on the branch, panting with exhaustion. *The dream! So real . . . so true.* He shook himself, but his head still spun.

What kind of creature had attacked Merlin? And why? Those huge, jagged wings—more like a bat's wings than a dragon's, yet far more frightening than either. What sort of creature had wings like that?

More questions haunted him. What did that dream—or that vision—really mean? Was Merlin, in fact, returning to Avalon? Was he here already? Then Basil's thoughts darkened: Could the dream foreshadow Merlin's death? Would some terrible fate await him if he returned? And why had the dream come to Basil?

All those questions rattled Basil's brain. They rose out of the darkness and pounced on him, much as that bat-winged creature had pounced on Merlin. Then they receded, unanswered, only to attack again.

He ground his teeth anxiously. For there was one more question, more frightening than all the rest, that wouldn't leave him alone. Hard as he tried, he couldn't banish it—just as he couldn't answer it. Was that perilous creature something out there in the wild, something Basil might have to face in the future? Or was it really . . . Basil *himself*?

He stared into the blackness, wondering. Just then, from

the edge of his vision, he caught sight of a shadowy shape—long and flexible, slithering toward him on the branch. A snake! This time what he saw was no dream. That snake was real—as real as the deadly glint in its eyes.

Basil stiffened. What could he do? Where could he go? The snake, nearly as large around as the branch, blocked his way back to the trunk. Sensing his awareness, the serpent sped up, gliding quickly, mouth already starting to open. Starlight gleamed on a pair of curved fangs. In just seconds, Basil knew, those fangs would reach him.

The snake slid nearer. And nearer. Basil watched in horror, his entire body frozen except for his wildly galloping heart. A loud hiss echoed in the night—and the snake struck, biting hard.

But the serpent's jaws closed on empty air. For Basil, at the very last instant, did the unimaginable: He jumped off the branch—

And he flew. Thrust open by the sudden rush of air, his wings spread. They widened, supporting his falling body. Newly stiffened by the growth of bones and sinews—which had swelled so painfully while he'd slept—the wings showed at last what they could do.

Flying! thought Basil, amazed to feel himself riding the air, which rushed past his snout and fluttered his ears. Slowly, he drifted downward, skirting the edge of a cedar bough, then sailing so close to a young squirrel he could have licked the animal's soft whiskers. He felt free—even graceful.

Which is not to say he knew how to steer—let alone land. Stunned by the double shock of escaping the snake and now flying, he couldn't begin to focus on anything beyond this new experience. But what did that matter? He was, after all, airborne at last.

Slam! He crashed into a tangle of mistletoe clinging to a branch, tumbled helplessly downward, and fell with a flourish of needles through a dense stand of saplings. Down he plunged, smacking every twig it seemed, until he landed in a mass of cabbage leaves. Tearing through the leaves, he finally hit the ground with a thud—hard enough to daze him momentarily, but gentle enough to spare any bones from breaking.

I . . . flew, he thought, as his eyes regained their ability to focus. *I really flew.*

Just to make sure, he crawled out from under the canopy of torn cabbage leaves . . . and spread his wings as wide as he could. He gazed at them, so full and sturdy, their leathery skin shining in the scattered light from the stars. He waved them back and forth, feeling the rush of air against his face—a sensation he'd never known before. And then he noticed something that doused the flame of his delight.

The wings, jagged and bony, looked all too familiar. They resembled those of a bat—or those of a creature he'd once seen in a dream.

8: A RASH IDEA

Size is more elusive than I ever guessed. It's less something you see, more something you feel. The same person can feel as huge and enduring as a mountain, or as small and transient as a breath.

*W*hoosh.

Just above Basil's head, an enormous wing slashed through the air. If the wing had been even a hair lower, it would have hit him with the force of a hurled stone, knocking him right out of the sky. As it was, the sudden rush of wind blew him completely onto his back, so that he plunged helplessly downward.

He knew, without even seeing the deadly talons scraping at the air just above his head, that he'd been attacked by a dactylbird—one of Avalon's most vicious predators. And unlike most predators, these birds killed not just for food—but for sport.

Flying, ever since that first astonishing discovery, had

never felt entirely joyous. Too many times he'd lost control in a sudden storm; too many times he'd caught a branch with his wing tip. And then there were those memories, impossible to push aside, of a vivid dream where batlike wings—his own, perhaps—had attacked the great wizard Merlin.

Yet despite its flaws, flying offered plentiful advantages. He could, thanks to his wings, avoid trouble. Evade predators. And maybe even stay alive long enough to make the greatest discovery of all: what sort of creature he really was.

Until the dactylbird spied him from above—and plunged down for the kill.

Basil fell, spinning wildly. With great effort, he extended one bony elbow and finally steadied himself. Spreading his small, ragged wings, he regained control at last. He swooped, flying over the pointed tops of spruce trees that grew so densely that they looked, from the air, like a giant patch of deep green moss covering the land.

At that instant, the dactylbird shot again out of the clouds. He raised his dagger-sharp talons, plunging straight at this creature who had eluded him one time too many. His heavy-lidded eyes gleamed a dull red, smoldering with anger. For he'd already wasted too much effort on this miserable little thing who looked less like a bird than like a shriveled bat with a lizard's body.

Basil's cupped ears stiffened at the sound of whooshing air. Without even taking the time to look, he raised one wing and banked sharply to the left. Simultaneously, the dark shape of the dactylbird shot through the very spot he'd been flying half a second before.

The attacker shrieked in rage, a piercing cry so loud that it echoed among the spruce trees below. Within those branches, many a squirrel and hummingbird and snake froze, paralyzed with fear, dropping the acorn or blade of grass or tasty beetle they had been carrying. A dactylbird's approach meant only one thing: Some creature was about to die.

Above the treetops, Basil swung around, veering out of the killer bird's path. What to do? How to escape?

Anxiously, his eyes scanned the area, searching for any possible cover. In theory, the dense green boughs of the spruce trees might work. But as high as he was now, even the tallest of them were too far away. He could never fly down fast enough to reach them before the dactylbird's talons sliced him to shreds. Except for one dead spruce, whose crown rose above the rest, no tree was near enough to shield him. And the dead spruce's branches didn't even hold a single green needle.

At once, his eyes glowed with an idea. A rash, utterly desperate idea. Though it was almost certain to fail, it was his only hope. And if, by some miracle, it worked . . .

The dactylbird shrieked again. Flapping his huge, angular wings, he flew straight at Basil. His murderous talons slashed at the air; with every powerful beat of his wings, he seemed to leap closer.

Releasing a shrill, terrified cry, Basil spun around and flew with all his might toward the dead spruce. His oversize ears, flattened against his head by the wind rushing past, could no longer hear his enemy's wingbeats. Yet all Basil's instincts told him that the killer bird was gaining swiftly.

Furiously flapping his scrawny wings, he drew nearer and nearer to the dead tree. His slim chest heaved with the effort, working so hard that every muscle felt ready to burst. Yet he kept going, flying faster than he'd ever flown before.

Not fast enough, though. Right behind, the dactylbird bore down on him. The attacker's beak snapped at Basil's scaly tail, nearly biting the little knob at the tip.

As rapidly as he approached the dead tree, Basil knew he'd never get there in time. Just as he knew that its empty branches couldn't protect him. Yet none of that worried him—for none of that was part of his plan. He had other things to worry about, such as when to make his next move.

Just as the treacherous beak opened again to bite off his tail, Basil suddenly spun around in midair. Face-to-face with the enormous bird who was hurtling toward him, he then did what his foe least expected.

Basil charged.

With a high-pitched shriek of his own, the little batlike creature flew right into his enemy's face. Caught completely off guard, the dactylbird squawked in surprise. Unable to slow down, he smashed into Basil, whose tiny tail whipped hard and struck his eye.

Squealing in pain, the dactylbird lashed out with his talons. But Basil glided just out of reach. Even as the predator's momentum carried him onward, he turned back to glare with his one good eye at Basil, who hovered in the air, smirking confidently. Anger boiled through the dactylbird's body, vibrating every feather, as he—

Slammed full force into the dead tree.

A sharp, spiky branch pierced his chest, spearing him through the heart. Blood—for the very first time, his own—seeped into his feathers. Another branch tore into his wing, ripping through muscle and bone, scattering brown feathers that drifted lazily down into the forest below.

With a last gurgling squawk, the much-feared dactyl-bird hung there, swaying in the branches like a torn, dead leaf. A talon lifted for the last time, raked the air, then fell limp. The eyes' inner fire went dark.

And so those eyes never saw a small, batlike creature fly slowly around the tree, inspecting the carcass, to make absolutely sure that the killer bird was dead. At last, convinced that the skies were truly a bit safer now, Basil drew a deep, satisfied breath. In that moment, he felt something he'd never felt before, something he'd never fully believed could happen to him.

He felt big. For a precious few seconds, he savored the sensation: Somehow, he seemed much bigger than his body.

Then he heard a distant rumble. It swelled, pounding rhythmically, until it filled the air like explosive bursts of thunder. But where did it come from? Basil turned in the air, hovering above the dead tree, as he scanned the sky. Yet, apart from a few wispy clouds, he saw nothing.

The pounding grew louder. Basil's cupped ears trembled with every repeated *boom, boom, boom.* At the same time, vibrations rippled through the spruce forest, so strong that they shook loose twigs and needles and clumps of moss. Soon the whole forest began to quake. Broken branches snapped off and crashed to the ground. Beneath Basil, the dead tree started to sway to the rhythm, waving the dead dactylbird like a tattered flag.

All at once, he understood. The thunderous pounding wasn't coming from the sky, but from the land. He opened his green eyes to their widest, surveying the horizon. There! Far to the west, shrouded in mist, he glimpsed a hulking shape.

Towering above the tops of trees, the shape drew closer.

A giant! *Bigger than a hillside*, that gossiping crow had said. Rightly so!

Basil, captivated by the sight, had to force himself to remember to keep flapping his wings. The huge figure strode from the western side of Woodroot, each of his footsteps slamming into the ground with the force of a landslide.

As he watched, beating his crumpled wings, Basil swallowed. *And I thought I was big?*

The giant strode heavily, step by pounding step. Something immense lay across his gargantuan shoulders: a stone pillar, large enough to fill a small lake. As the giant stomped closer to the spruce forest, his profile revealed a huge, bulbous nose and a shaggy mane of unruly hair.

Between the rhythmic strides, a deep voice rumbled. Cocking his ears toward the giant, Basil caught part of a song, borne on the spruce-scented breeze:

> *Well, pinch me nose, I don't suppose*
> *I am a flapsy bird:*
> *Me songly croon's so out o' tune*
> *Like none you've ever heard!*
> *I withers every word, a songly sound absurd.*
>
> *Just who am I? Me gladly cry—*
> *A giant, bigsy tall.*
> *But would you know, by my big toe,*
> *I once was oddly small!*
> *No highlyness at all, as tiny as a doll.*

Basil blinked in astonishment. For he now recognized this giant, who was even bigger in reputation than in size. Basil had heard about him over the past two years, and not just from a yammering flock of crows. He'd also heard stories from a pair of far-flying owls, with the mist of Fincayra still fresh on their wings. From a bedraggled faery, blown all the way from Waterroot in a gale. And, most recently, from a wandering bard, who had been bursting with songs and stories about the wizard Merlin and his friends.

This was Shim! Of all the giants who had lived in Lost Fincayra, he was by far the most celebrated—a close friend of Merlin the wizard. Though once very small, Shim had grown truly enormous, and had played a crucial part in the famous Dance of the Giants, the decisive battle that banished—for the time being, at least—the evil spirit warlord Rhita Gawr.

Descending, Basil alighted on the topmost spire of the dead tree. From this perch, he watched the giant lumber through the distant hills of the forest. The huge stone pillar on Shim's shoulders reminded him of something the bard had said: Merlin's mother, Elen of the Sapphire Eyes, had just founded a new order to spread harmony among all the creatures of Avalon. Even now, her followers were building a great compound in Stoneroot, using a sacred circle of stones from Lost Fincayra. Could that pillar be one of those stones? Had Shim actually carried it all the way through the mists into Avalon?

Sitting atop the dead tree, which creaked and groaned every time one of Shim's bare feet slammed down, Basil's batlike face crinkled in a grin. Imagine being large enough to carry a stone pillar! To shake the ground with every step. To fear nothing, short of a wrathful dragon, ever again.

Clinging to the barkless tree, Basil sighed wistfully. Size didn't mean everything, of course. But it certainly had its advantages! Why, even a fire-breathing dragon had recently done Shim's bidding, according to the bard. When Shim had donated his own belt buckle to make a great bell

for Elen's compound, there was a problem: No fire was hot
enough to melt down something so big. So Shim, to Elen's
amazement, asked a dragon to blast it with flames. The
dragon obliged—and then, to everyone's relief, departed.

Basil shuddered at the thought. A giant was one thing—
huge in size, but normally peaceful. A dragon, though, was
quite another. They were rarely peaceful, and then never for
long. Compared to them, dactylbirds seemed utterly tame.
Dragons savored every chance they could find to destroy
lands and devour creatures. Especially little creatures.

Stay away from dragons, thought Basil. *Another useful
rule for life.*

Just then he heard another verse of Shim's rumbling
song:

> *So who am I? A proudly sigh,*
> *And I'll say who I be.*
> *Just strips me nude, and you'll conclude*
> *There be no mystery:*
> *Bigly now I be! My size is truly me.*

9: GREEN FIRE

Change. What a paradox! The more you do it, the more you don't. The farther you seek it, the nearer you find it. The less it's in your world, the more it's in you.

YEAR OF AVALON 27

"Time for a rest," sighed Basil. Wearily, he climbed onto an oak branch and nestled into the hollow of one of its leaves. His tiny body—from his batlike nose to the tip of his lizard's tail, from the edge of one little wing to the other—fit snugly on the oak leaf.

"What a day," he muttered, yawning. "Chasing those rascally insects over eighty leagues, through marshes, lakes, rivers, mountains . . . changing speed and direction constantly. Changing tactics, too, as well as my smells. Guess that's one thing I'm good at—how to change."

Noticing a slender cocoon suspended from the leaf beside him, his words seemed to wither, like a pond lily in the heat. He peered at the cocoon—in which a plodding little caterpillar was now growing wings—and shook his head. How to change? Compared to that caterpillar, he knew almost nothing.

Glancing at his small, scaly torso, he scowled. Though now more than twenty years old, he wasn't even a hairsbreadth longer than he'd been on that day he first crawled out of his shell and heard the whispering voice of Aylah, the wind sister.

As if in answer, a subtle breeze blew through the oak branches, rustling them gently. But, of course, it carried no scent of cinnamon. It never did anymore.

Studying the cocoon, he could see the traces of thousands of threads, woven together with considerable skill. Maybe that little fellow in there wasn't so plodding after all. Maybe he was more than he appeared?

What about me? he wondered. *Am I any more than I appear?*

He rolled over on the cradling leaf, suddenly restless. Did change always mean a new shape? Growing wings or getting bigger? The most important changes in his life hadn't been visible to anyone except himself.

Not that those changes amounted to much. Here he was, still living a staid, predictable life, catching insects in one part of Woodroot. He'd never traveled anywhere else! The only journeys he'd ever taken were through the stories told by others. The only lasting friends he'd ever made were—well, himself. And the only real adventure he'd ever had, the only experience that was special somehow, was an intensely vivid dream that he couldn't forget.

Hearing the faint buzz of an approaching locust, he decided, halfheartedly, to have another bite to eat. Not that he felt hungry. Just bored—and tired of thinking. Besides, as small as he was, the locust was even smaller. So why not eat it? He'd always enjoyed the satisfying crunch of a locust in his jaws, even if it tasted like charcoal.

Without stirring from his niche, where his own green color matched perfectly the color of the leaf, he cast a small but potent smell into the air just above his face. Instantly, the fragrance of yellow meadowsweet flowers—irresistible to any locust—wafted from the spot.

As expected, the insect flew heedlessly toward him. Basil watched out of a half-closed eye as the insect flew closer and closer.

Chomp. He snapped his jaws—on air.

How could I miss? he chided himself, as the locust whirred away, heading deeper into the forest. *Too much thinking, not enough doing. Pull yourself together, my friend, or you'll soon be someone else's meal!* He frowned, then added, *Even if it's a very small meal.*

His eyes narrowed in annoyance as he watched the locust disappear into a grove of hemlocks, elms, and lavender-hued birches. "Think you got the better of me, do you?"

He leaped off the oak tree and into the air. Flapping his leathery wings, he zipped after the insect—eager to regain his food, as well as his pride. Through the leafy boughs he raced, searching every hiding place he could see.

There! He spied the locust, diving into a thick bush of thornberries. *Ha!* thought Basil. *As if a few little thorns could stop me.* He swerved in midair and dropped down at the other side of the bush, just as the insect emerged.

Before Basil could pounce, though, the locust veered sharply and flew out of reach. Wings abuzz, the tiny beast escaped into a thick stand of tall, rust-colored grasses whose stalks resembled fountains spewing sprays of grain.

Basil, in hot pursuit, flew toward the grasses. Right before plunging in, however, he halted. Hovering just in front of the stalks, he watched the insect depart . . . and didn't follow it. All the while, his cup-shaped ears quivered, for a new thought had filled his mind.

I'm chasing him not because I'm hungry, but just because I'm bigger. Wincing, he realized that he was acting no differently than so many of the mean-spirited brutes who had pursued him over the years. Didn't dactylbirds act just the same way?

He flapped harder, lifting himself over the grasses. Green eyes aglow, he vowed, "No more of that for me! I'll fight when necessary, and eat when hungry. But I won't chase someone just for the fun of it. Not even a bothersome little locust."

With that, he nodded his head at the rusty grasses and flew off. Weaving between the birches and elms, he spotted a pair of large, oblong boulders that he'd never noticed before. He flew closer, curious about the strange crackling sound that seemed to come from the stones themselves. As he approached, he saw flickers of eerie green light shimmering along the sides of the boulders.

Flames! Between the stones, a circle of green flames danced enticingly. As Basil studied the strange green fire, its light reflected in his eyes, merging with the remarkably similar light that already glowed there.

Unsure why, he felt drawn to this green fire that crackled so vigorously. Although he couldn't see any fuel burning or smell any smoke at all, he felt no fear. Instead, he felt a strange kind of kinship to those flames. And a comforting warmth that penetrated deeper than the heat of a normal fire. Slowly, he flew nearer, entranced by this amazing discovery.

"Hold it, greenie."

Basil stopped in midair, and turned toward the gruff, baritone voice. It had come from somewhere on the ground in front of the flames. But nobody was there, not even a caterpillar: just a scattering of golden grass, a moldberry shrub (whose fruit, he'd learned, was not the best eating), and a slim, yellow-petaled flower. Turning back to the alluring flames, he continued to fly closer—when the voice spoke again.

"I said hold it, if you'd like to live another day."

The yellow flower! Its face had turned toward him, following his flight. Swooping down, Basil peered at it. What he saw made him curl his tail in amazement. In the midst of the petals sat a round amber eye!

The eye blinked. "What are you staring at, greenie? Never seen a flower before?"

"Not, um . . . like you." Cautiously, he flew a bit closer. "And until now, I'd never heard one, either."

"Honestly?" The flower shook its head, making the slender leaves on its stem tremble in unison. "You must live a sheltered life."

Basil didn't respond.

"So then, greenie, are you thinking of flying into that?" The flower bent toward the fire, then snapped back upright. "If so, better think again."

"Why?"

The flower's eye widened until it reached the encircling petals. "You really don't know?" Shaking its stem and leaves in dismay, it declared, "Lucky for you, then, I planted myself here last spring."

"Why?" he repeated, hovering directly above the amber eye. "What's so wrong with those flames?"

"Nothing at all," drawled the flower. "Unless you get too

close." Gazing straight into Basil's skeptical face, it blurted, "That's a portal, greenie! A pathway to other places—the seven root-realms, the hidden lands inside the trunk, maybe even the starward realms."

Crinkling his long nose in disbelief, Basil glanced at the flames. As he watched them crackle so invitingly, his skepticism began to soften. *Travel*, he thought. *To other realms! This could be my chance.*

Still not sure whether to believe any of this, he said, "That doesn't sound so bad. Why did you say I wouldn't live another day?"

The flower's ring of petals drooped. "For somebody so small, you can be a huge idiot! That fire is élano, the very essence of the Great Tree—and the strongest magic in all of Avalon."

Cocking his head toward the flames, Basil asked, "So? What's that got to do with living or dying?"

Quaking as if caught in a sudden storm, the flower replied, "Because those flames transport you by magically disassembling you—pulling you completely apart—and then reassembling you when you arrive." Its gruff voice lowered. "*If* you arrive."

"What do you mean, *if* ?"

"Put it this way, greenie. Unless you concentrate clearly on *exactly* where you want to go, your pieces go wherever the portal decides! I saw one lucky traveler, a goblin, come out of this portal just last week. He looked a bit confused . . . especially when he realized his legs had gone to Fireroot. And right after I came here, a pile of orange scales came through—but without the snake they used to cover."

Basil groaned, missing a whole wingbeat, at such a gruesome thought. But he glanced again at the fire, rising so mysteriously between the stones, and the temptation returned. *Just a closer look*, he promised himself. *No harm in that.*

Without even willing himself to do it, he started drifting closer. The flames seemed to tug on him, pulling him nearer, as a fire swallows a hapless moth. The green light burned in his eyes, glowing deeper than any reflection.

"Wait, greenie!" called the flower behind him. "Didn't you hear what I said? Or is your head made of solid stone?"

Basil only half heard, so captivated was he by the enticing flames. The words *solid stone* echoed inside his mind. *Stone . . . solid stone . . .*

At that instant an arc of green flames leaped out and grabbed hold of him—snout, tail, wings, everything. Frantically, he beat his wings, suddenly aware of his peril. The flames' enchantment vanished, leaving him only with terror—and the dim echo of the flower's voice.

How could he know that the voice, and the image it gave him in those final seconds, would save his life? He couldn't. Just as he couldn't guess, as the flames gathered more densely around him, drawing him into the portal, that he would soon be sent—body, mind, and spirit—to the distant realm of Stoneroot.

Despite his fear, Basil suddenly realized that the flames surrounding him made him feel warm, but not burned. Swallowed, but not destroyed. He felt strangely lighter, as if he were disintegrating, floating away from himself.

In that moment, he plunged into the veins of the living Tree of Avalon. He merged with its brightest fires; he rode on its purest rivers. Deeper into the Tree he traveled, and still deeper, through realms without names, regions beyond count.

He wasn't merely borne by the fire of élano. He *was*

that fire. He had become a spark of light, surrounded by millions more sparks of light, distinct from each of them yet connected to all of them. A rich, resinous smell overwhelmed him—the smell of a thriving woodland, a sprouting seed, a rippling stream: the smell of life, with all its magic and mystery. He felt at peace, at home, as never before! Infinitely small, yet infinitely large.

He tumbled out of another portal, landing on a flat, lichen-covered rock. The impact caused the rock, precariously balanced on a mountainside of jumbled boulders, to teeter. Dazed, Basil rolled weakly to one side. With a grinding crunch, the rock slid off its perch, taking its passenger.

That rock hit other rocks, jarring them loose. Those rocks smashed into others. In seconds, the entire slope roared with cascading boulders. A violent landslide had begun—with Basil in the middle of it.

10: RUDE AND SASSY

Wisdom, like those who possess it, comes in all shapes and sizes. That much I've learned, often the hard way. Yet despite all their differences, truly wise people share this same understanding:

No matter how much you know, you still have a lot to learn.

Falling!

Basil tumbled down the mountain slope, rolling and twirling so fast he felt dizzy and nauseous, unable to make himself think, let alone fly. All around him, rocks slid loose and boulders bounced, crashing into each other with explosive impact, sending up sprays of smashed rocks, shredded lichen, and pulverized stone. The entire mountain roared with the landslide.

One flying rock grazed his side, scraping against his scales. Then another rock, the size of a sparrow, struck him hard under the jaw and sent him reeling backward. Hopelessly out of control, he spun wildly, bouncing down the mountain as if he were just another pebble in this cascade of stones.

Splat. He landed on a broad, flat ledge. Head spinning, he weakly focused his eyes and gazed around. Suddenly he realized that something had drastically changed. He wasn't moving anymore! This ledge, protruding upward from the slope, reached above the chaos of shifting rocks. It was, in fact, a rare island of stability in this stormy sea. Could it be that his luck had finally turned?

That was when he noticed the moving shadow. It darkened the ledge, covering him swiftly. Basil looked up—and saw an enormous, jagged-edged boulder falling straight at him. Frozen with fear, he watched the boulder drop closer, closer. In another heartbeat he would be completely crushed.

A swooshing sound—and something grabbed Basil by the tail, plucking him off the ledge. An instant later, the boulder smashed down. Fragments of rock exploded, bursting from the spot where he'd just been, filling the air with dust.

Basil, now gliding above the mountainside, knew he'd been saved. By what? Another hungry predator who didn't want a tasty little meal to go to waste? Expecting to find a fierce dactylbird, or a vulture perhaps, he bent his body to see what held him by the tail.

A hand! The small but sturdy hand of a round-bodied sprite grasped Basil firmly. Seeing the mass of silver threads that billowed above them, forming a parachute, he remembered hearing crows chatter about pinnacle sprites, solitary little people who lived in the highest peaks of Stoneroot, floating casually from ridge to ridge on parachutes they could produce from their backs at will. Looking into the smooth, beardless face of this particular sprite—which, like the rest of his body, was an angry shade of purple— Basil surmised that he was very young. And very grumpy.

"Hmmmpff," grumbled the sprite as he glanced down at his catch. "I save your life and all you can do is stare? Rude little beast! Didn't they ever teach you any manners in lizard school?"

"I'm not a lizard," answered Basil, feeling a bit grumpy himself.

"Well then, bat school."

"I'm not a bat."

The sprite, whose long hair fluttered as they sailed above the boulders, peered closely at Basil. "Hmmmpff, what in Dagda's name *are* you, then?"

Seconds passed, while an updraft filled the parachute, carrying them higher. At last, Basil shook his head and said, "I'm—I—I'm . . ."

"A stutterer, I see," growled the sprite. Although his voice sounded as gruff as ever, his skin color changed a little, softening to lavender with a few swirls of gray.

Finally, Basil completed his sentence, whispering just loud enough to be heard above the wind that ruffled the parachute: "I really don't know what I am."

"Hmmmpff. Maybe you're telling the truth, maybe not. Or maybe you're just plain stupid as well as rude."

Even though he was dangling by his tail, Basil arched his body so that his face drew near to the sprite's. Glowering, he said, "Rude, maybe. But stupid? No, that word belongs to somebody who's easily fooled."

"Right," sneered the sprite, turning an amused shade of orange. "Somebody like y—"

He broke off suddenly, catching the pungent odor of a goblin vulture, whose talons often smelled of rotting carrion. The sprite's color instantly went white. He whirled around in midair, tangling his own leg in the strings of his parachute. As he tried to pull his leg free, the chute collapsed. He started plunging toward the rock-strewn slope, taking Basil with him.

For seconds that seemed like hours, they dropped downward. Basil tried to free himself from the sprite's grip, but to no avail; in his panic, the sprite only squeezed harder. Locked together, they fell toward the boulders, faster and faster.

At last, the sprite managed to free his leg. With a desperate lurch, he threw his weight sideways. A loud *whomp!* announced the chute had filled again with air. A fresh updraft from the mountainside carried them higher once more.

Having stopped their free fall, the sprite still didn't relax. He cast his head anxiously from side to side, staring into the sky around them. His liquid purple eyes seemed about to pop out of his head.

"Looking for something?" asked Basil nonchalantly.

"Yes, you idiot! You really are dimmer than an ogre's eyeball! There's a goblin vulture up here somewhere."

"No," declared Basil. "There's not."

"But I smelled . . ." The sprite's voice trailed off. As he stared at his small passenger, his skin color melted from frosty white to wrathful red. "You did that! You! Why, you demented, idiotic smell-maker . . . you could have killed us. Murdered us. Destroyed us. Or worse!"

Basil waited patiently until the sprite's ranting stopped. Then, ears cocked innocently, he asked, "Can I help it if you're so easily fooled?"

The sprite opened his mouth to speak, found absolutely no words, and shut his mouth abruptly. Then, as his color changed to muddy orange, he did something new, something highly unusual for a pinnacle sprite. He grinned. Well, almost. The corner of his mouth lifted ever so slightly, though it could have been just a twitch.

"Not bad, you little mystery beast. That foolish prank of yours was insanely risky . . . but effective. And pinnacle sprites appreciate a good prank."

With a tilt of his head, he added, "My name is Nuic. I may be a young sprite—not even a hundred years old—but I am an excellent judge of character. And I can spot someone with the true heart of a prankster."

"And I can spot someone with the true personality of a goblin vulture," said Basil wryly.

"Ah, you mean my happy disposition?" Nuic's almost-grin vanished. "Hmmmpff. Sweetness is much overrated, if you ask me. Except in a honeycomb." His voice lowered. "You still haven't thanked me for saving your life."

"Manners are much overrated. Except in a sprite."

Nuic's skin, like his mood, darkened.

"I can tell you this, though, Master Nuic. Whatever kind of creature I am, my name is Basil. And I'm pleased to meet you."

"Hmmmpff. Not at *all* pleased to meet you."

"And now, if you don't mind, how about letting me go? I can fly on my own, you know."

Nuic's eyes widened. "No, you're trying to fool me again. Those dried, crumpled leaves there on your back are certainly not wings?"

"Yes indeed," answered Basil, ignoring the insult. "Let go of my tail and I'll show you."

The wind strengthened, lifting them both higher. Below them stretched the high peaks of Olanabram, ridge upon ridge of mountains that wore massive glaciers like fluffy white shawls upon their shoulders.

The sprite released his grip. Basil opened his bony wings and coasted freely, then caught a swell and spun a trio of backward loops in quick succession. Gliding back to Nuic's side—while keeping a safe distance from the parachute strings—the little fellow's green eyes glowed with satisfaction.

"One more thing I'd like to say," Basil announced.

"Hmmmpff. Just because you can fly, it doesn't make you any less rude and sassy."

"True," agreed Basil, banking a turn and sailing over to Nuic's other side. "But there is still one more thing I'd like to say."

The sprite's color darkened to muddy brown. "Get it over with, then."

"I just wanted to say . . . thanks. For saving my life down there."

Although Nuic's grimace remained, a few subtle traces of pink appeared in his chest and at his temples. Gruffly, he said, "You're *still* rude and sassy, you ogre-brained bumpkin."

"And you're still easily fooled." Basil chuckled, flattening his ears against his head.

"Just be glad—keep that cursed wing away from my parachute, you oaf!—that I just happened to come along when you were about to get spattered on a stone." Frowning, Nuic added, "Knowing what I know now, I wish I'd come to the wedding a day early. But we all make mistakes."

Tilting his leathery wings, Basil glided closer. "Wedding? Whose wedding?"

"You really are as daft as a doltbug! Why, the wizard's, of course. Don't you know anything? Anything at *all*?"

Caught off guard, Basil muttered, "No, actually. And it feels like I know less every day."

"Hmmmpff," said the sprite, his colors lightening a bit, "some people would call that a mark of wisdom. Although personally, I'd call it utter f—"

"Wait!" interrupted Basil. "Did you say it's a *wizard's* wedding? The wizard Merlin?"

"Who else, bubble brain? Wizards don't come along every day, you know! That's why half of Avalon is gathering down there right now." Proudly, he added, "The *invited* half, that is."

The pinnacle sprite tugged on a parachute thread, making them float toward the highest peak in the area, a square-shaped mountain topped with snow. Hundreds of people of all descriptions had gathered there, forming a circle on the summit. Though Basil recognized some of them, from the tales he'd heard over the years, many bore no resemblance to any creature he'd ever heard about. Yet there was one he knew instantly. As immense as a rocky ridge, the giant Shim sat just outside the circle.

"Merlin's wedding," said Basil in wonder. "So he's really come back to Avalon?"

"No, you dithering dunderhead! He decided to miss the whole thing! Right now he's sitting on a shore, somewhere on Earth, counting grains of sand. When he gets to a trillion trillion—"

"All right, all right," said Basil, annoyed at his own ignorance. He floated awhile beside the sprite, watching more guests of all kinds climb the mountain to witness the wedding. "Looks like every sort of creature you could imagine will be there."

"Yes, and some you couldn't *possibly* imagine. Why, there will be people from every corner of all seven root-realms. Practically every race in Avalon."

"Has Merlin arrived yet?"

"Over there, by the edge of the circle. See his black hair and white tunic?"

Basil gasped at the sight—and not just because it reminded him of his terrible dream. Having heard so many stories about the wizard—whose true name, Olo Eopia, meant *great man of many worlds, many times*—he couldn't believe that Merlin was right down there. Right now.

His ebony mane blowing in a mountain breeze, Merlin stepped into the center of the circle of spectators. The sleeves of his tunic, whiter than the snow, fluttered as he beckoned to someone in the crowd. A woman emerged, stepping gracefully to his side. Equally tall as her companion, she wore a long braid that glinted with the tans and auburns of marsh grasses. The braid reached down the back of her robe of azure blue, a color as rich as the summer sky.

"Who is she?" asked Basil. "Standing next to Merlin?"

Nuic shook himself, scowling. "Have I ever told you that you're a pin-brained jabberjaw?"

"Not recently. But who is she?"

"Hallia, of course! They've been planning this for decades, ever since Merlin lost his senses and went to Earth for a while. But he finally saw his folly and returned."

The sprite's liquid eyes rolled toward the mountaintop. "Poor fellow never had a chance, really. Once she taught him how to change into a deer, so they could run together in the meadows, he was thoroughly besotted."

Struggling to understand, Basil sputtered, "She's . . . a deer?"

"No, you cabbage-brained, addleheaded know-nothing! She's a *deer woman*, one of the ancient Mellwyn-bri-Meath clan from the Smoking Cliffs, the same place where Dagda used magical sea mist to weave the famous Carpet Caerlochlann."

More confused than ever, Basil pressed, "A deer woman, you say? So she can change from one form to the other?"

"Right, you moronic, piddle-mouthed puddinghead. And whatever form she takes, Merlin's totally infatuated with her. Why, he even named that mountain down there Hallia's Peak."

Enthralled with all these discoveries, Basil ignored the insults. *Travel really can enlighten you*, he thought. Then he glanced down at the site of the recent landslide, and at the flicker of green flames still visible there, and added, *If it doesn't kill you first.*

"Well," declared Nuic, "I can't say it's been a pleasure. But good luck to you anyway. Now I must be going."

"Wait." Basil glided closer. "Did you say people from every part of Avalon will be there? Some from every race?"

"Not every race, you empty-headed hinkletooth! No gobsken or ogres were invited, and no mer people could make it, for some reason." The sprite chortled. "But you are nearly right. Almost every race will be there."

"Which means," said Basil with a shake of his wings, "that if I were ever going to find someone from *my* race, whatever that is, someone who actually looks like me—"

"Stop right there." Nuic's color darkened. "Don't even think about it! Do you have any idea how *rude* it would be to barge into somebody's wedding uninvited?"

"Well . . ."

"Or how *dangerous* it would be?"

"Well . . ."

"I'll take that as a no, you blister brain. For a start, the great white spider called the Grand Elusa—famous for her skill at splitting open living stones and swallowing them in seconds—has promised to eat any intruders. And if that's not bad enough, the hapless jester Bumbelwy, whose voice is so grating that whenever he sings, birds drop dead right out of the sky, has offered to serenade uninvited guests."

Basil gulped. "But I need to know what—who—I really am! This could be my only chance."

"Hmmmpff. You'll have many more chances to die, I assure you. And I haven't even mentioned what Merlin *himself* would do if he caught you."

"But—"

"Don't do it, Basil." The sprite's entire body pulsed scarlet. "Do you hear me?"

"Sure," he replied, with a somber flap of his wings. "I hear you."

"Good. Then you'll live to see another day."

Basil said nothing.

The sprite started to lean into his parachute, then glanced back at him. "If you ever do figure out what kind of creature you are, I'd like to know. Otherwise, I'm glad to say we'll probably never meet again."

Despite his disappointment, Basil couldn't feel offended. Nuic was almost amusing, in a tortured sort of way. Despondently, he watched the grouchy little fellow depart, floating down toward the summit, shifting color to vibrant green.

Abruptly, Basil jolted, as if a sudden gust of wind had blown against his wings. But the jolt didn't come from something he'd felt. Rather, it came from something he'd *seen*. From out of the clouds, a family of creatures appeared— one fully grown mother and seven or eight children. They soared out of the sky with mythic strength and grace, their jagged wings cutting through the air so powerfully that the very sight made Basil's heart quake with fear and wonder.

Dragons. They are dragons.

Basil watched the powerful beasts fly down to the summit, joining the rest of the invited guests. His gaze then turned to Merlin, the greatest wizard his world had ever known. And then, once more, he scanned the assembled creatures who had gathered—creatures of all kinds, from every realm.

In that instant, Basil knew what he must do. Banking his own minuscule wings, he swooped down to join them. Whatever the risks, he was going to watch a wedding.

11: STRANGE COMPANY

Never, until that day, had I realized that I could feel two opposite emotions at once. To belong to the immense, bizarre, riotous diversity of life—and still stand utterly alone. To feel wholly connected, and yet completely apart.

Basil plunged downward, the cold mountain air buffeting his wings. As he swooped closer to the snow-draped summit, he studied the creatures gathered there, creatures who had traveled from all across Avalon to attend the wedding of Merlin and Hallia. There were even more of them than he'd guessed from on high. Quickly, he lost sight of Nuic's small green form in the throng.

He couldn't miss Shim, however. The giant sat at the far side of the summit, wearing a huge scarlet snake around his neck. Though knotted up like a fat red bow tie, the snake seemed resigned to its fate and didn't struggle. (It did, however, rouse itself to hiss at a cheeky gull who dared to land on its forehead.)

As Basil approached from above, Shim leaned forward to scratch one of his immense toes, knocking several branches

off his vest of woven hemlock trees. Though he didn't seem
to notice, the family of centaurs walking beneath him certainly did: When the broken branches crashed down on their
backs, they whinnied, cursed angrily, and galloped off to
the opposite side of the summit. Meanwhile, Shim watched
his old friends Merlin and Hallia step into the center of the
circle of admirers—who by now covered the entire mountaintop. The enormous fellow's eyes glowed pink, and he
chortled quietly, not much louder than an ordinary earth-
quake. Meanwhile, his long mane blew wildly in the mountain breeze, slapping unlucky birds out of the sky.

"Oh, I do muchily love a wedding party!" he bellowed.
And at that moment, Shim's eyes swung from the wedding
couple to the enormous vats of honey awaiting the guests.

Basil drifted downward, anxious to avoid attracting
anyone's attention. *Mustn't be seen*, he reminded himself.
Not by anyone who might care about an intruder. He kept
a wary eye, in particular, on the great white spider who had
just seated herself in the center of the throng. The crowd
quite courteously parted to give the huge spider room to
stretch her eight legs; a pair of living stones seemed especially eager to give her plenty of space, and rolled away
across the snow.

Fortunately, no one seemed to notice the approach of a
scrawny little lizard with batlike wings and oversize ears.
Most of the guests were focused exclusively on the wedding
couple in the middle of the ring. The only exception was
Shim, whose gaze remained fixed on the vats of honey.

As Basil descended, he scanned the wedding guests who
stood, sat, or crawled upon the snow—and, in a few cases,
hovered or glided above the crowd. *People of all kinds are
here!* he thought excitedly. *Every size, shape, and color.
Every possible description.*

He paused, swallowing. *But is there someone—anyone—who looks like me?*

Floating nearer, he suddenly spied a lone creature bounding up the snowy ridge—and the sight made him gasp. The Sapphire Unicorn! She seemed to flow up the ridge, moving as effortlessly as the breeze itself. Her powerful muscles flexed as she loped to the summit, kicking up clouds of snow with her hooves. The unicorn's spiraling horn, like her coat and mane, radiated blue even deeper than the color of Hallia's dress. For this blue sparkled as if alive. One by one, each of the wedding guests turned to watch her arrival. For they, like Basil, knew that she was the only one of her kind in all of Avalon—the creature bards called *the most elusive beauty in all the lands*.

Drawing closer, Basil saw a pair of women approach the wedding couple. One, an older woman whose flowing blond hair shone like the stars, wore a silvery gown that shimmered as she moved. *That's Elen, mother of Merlin*, he realized. Though he'd heard about her High Priestess gown, woven entirely from spider's silk, it was even more beautiful than he'd imagined. As Elen moved, the gown seemed more rays of light than thread, more air than substance.

The other woman Basil also recognized: Rhia, Merlin's sister, clad in her famous suit of woven vines. What had he heard? That she'd grown up living in a great oak tree. And she moved, indeed, like windblown boughs; her feet left hardly any marks upon the snow. Her curly brown hair, decorated with blossoms, bounced with every step. Around her head and shoulders flew dozens of light flyers, their little wings glowing so bright they looked like floating candle flames. And upon her back lay beautiful, translucent wings—a gift, it was said, from the great spirit Dagda himself. As he drifted lower, Basil gazed in awe at Rhia—her garb, her wings, and most of all, her radiant face, which glowed even brighter than the light flyers.

I can't believe I'm here, he thought. *Seeing these people . . . this place . . . this gathering. It can't be real!*

But Rhia's bell-like laugh, released when she embraced her brother, removed any doubt. No imaginary laughter could radiate such joy.

Then another sound caught Basil's ear. From right below him came the deep, echoing hoot of an ancient owl. Though missing many feathers, the old owl could still hoot loud enough to frighten the silver stallion on whose back he was sitting, as well as the family of eiderdown geese nearby. The horse neighed and swished his tail, while the geese honked and fluttered with annoyance.

By contrast, a golden-feathered phoenix, seated on a jagged stone beside them, didn't even seem to notice. She continued to stare at Merlin and Hallia, never blinking. Even when she was almost stepped on by the splayed roots of a huge, branching figure—a tree spirit, Basil guessed— the phoenix didn't bat an eye.

Basil circled the summit, looking for someplace he could land and remain inconspicuous. Meanwhile, he also searched for anyone below who resembled himself, who might help explain the mystery of his origins. As he listened to the crowd's swelling din—all the neighing, bellowing, growling, singing, chattering, hissing, and buzzing—he could only wonder whether he would hear, sometime today, a voice that sounded like his own.

He watched the last guests arrive. A pair of ragged-winged vultures gave him a start—they strongly resembled dactylbirds—but he was relieved to see them perch peacefully on an elephaunt's back. A group of gnomes straggled up the ridge of bright snow, very different terrain than their dark underground tunnels, then reluctantly obeyed a centaur's command to leave their weapons in a pile away from other guests. Nowhere, though, did Basil see the family of dragons who had arrived earlier. That puzzled him, but not enough to be concerned. After all, the mountaintop was teeming with Avalon's diversity of life. Even in the final few seconds before he landed, he saw many creatures he hadn't noticed before.

Elves from Woodroot, clad in woven barkcloth, stood as tall and graceful as the trees of their homeland. Deer people of Hallia's clan, all with slender chins and rich brown eyes, stayed near each other, often glancing over their shoulders to check for any signs of danger. And human men and women, many with children, were scattered throughout the ring of guests. One of them, a jester wearing a floppy hat rimmed with tiny bells, caught Basil's eye. Could that be Bumbelwy, the one Nuic had warned about?

A few guests Basil recognized from the tales of Merlin's youth. There, wasn't that the queen of the dwarves, Urnalda? Her earrings of gnomes' teeth clinked ominously whenever she moved. And over there—Cwen, last survivor of the treelings, who lost an arm, along with Rhia's trust, in a fight with warrior gobsken. Upon a large yellow snail sat Lleu of the One Ear, scribbling madly on a tattered piece of parchment. It had to be him: the lad who fought so bravely alongside Merlin at the final battle of Fincayra, and who later became one of Elen's first disciples in the new order.

There! Basil spied an excellent place to land, the moss-draped boughs of a grove of pine tree spirits. Hidden amidst all that greenery, he could remain safely undetected, yet have a superb view of the crowd. He banked, gliding toward the nearest branch.

Suddenly he saw, just beyond the trees, the mother dragon and her brood. Abruptly, he veered aside. *Much too close! I don't want to be near any dragons.*

Flapping vigorously, he flew off. As he passed over the dragons, he watched the mother, whose orange eyes glowed like molten lava, entertain her seven children by swatting them with the tips of her wings. Then, to the dismay of the tree spirits, she started spitting small bursts of flame at their bellies. From the way her children squealed and shrieked with delight, they seemed to enjoy this game. The tree spirits, though, backed away.

Looking more closely, Basil noticed that the mother dragon had two long blue ears—one of which stuck straight out sideways, as if it were a misplaced horn. Peering at her iridescent purple scales flecked with scarlet, he suddenly felt a surprising—and inexplicable—urge to come closer. Was it some sort of evil magic? Some way dragons lured their prey to come near, much as the portal's green flames had drawn him into danger? His heart beat harder . . . yet he slowed his escape.

What was it about this beast that tugged at his curiosity? Surely he knew enough about dragons already! Especially the most important thing of all: *Stay away.* Yet somehow, this dragon seemed interesting. Alluring. Almost . . . *familiar.* As if he'd met her before this day.

No, he hadn't. Impossible. He'd never met any fire-breathing dragons. Fortunately!

Must be those wild stories from the crows, he assured himself. *Yes, that's it.*

He started to beat his wings faster. Air, warmed by the dragon's breath, rushed past his face. Below, the sounds of her children squealing, and of snow sizzling from the bursts of flame, began to fade away. Even so, he couldn't keep from looking back at the mother dragon. Wait. Could it be? Was it possible she was the famous Gwynnia, the only surviving child of Wings of Fire, the most dreaded dragon in history? That dragon had been the scourge of Fincayra—until he'd joined forces with Merlin.

Basil, in mid-flight, shook himself sternly. *Forget your curiosity! Land as far away as possible from those beasts. And don't go back.*

And so he did, setting down on a snow-streaked boulder across the circle from the dragons. From this removed perch, he could still watch them, but at a safe distance. As he folded his leathery wings against his back, he noticed that he had landed in the middle of an especially bizarre group of onlookers.

Just to his left stood a group of four stern-faced people, three men and one woman, whose eyes smoldered like hot coals. Flamelons, that's who they were. From the scorched realm of Fireroot. He wondered whether they truly worshipped Rhita Gawr. Ignoring the warlord's urge to conquer, they supposedly viewed him as something good—a force for renewal.

Suddenly he started. There, behind the flamelons, stood a man who was actually on fire! His entire muscular body, including the broad wings that sprouted from his back, burned bright orange, sizzling and crackling—as if he were made more of flames than flesh. Though he couldn't take his eyes off the man, Basil backed away to the other side of the boulder. Unlike the flamelons, whose expressions were so grim, this man looked utterly peaceful. *He seems*, Basil thought, *like an angel. An angel of fire.*

Not far away, a pair of long-limbed hoolahs wrestled in the snow. They punched, kicked, hurled clumps of snow, stabbed fiercely with icicles, and ripped at each other's baggy tunics—laughing hysterically all the while. *Hool-ahs*, thought Basil glumly. Having run into them a few times in Woodroot, he knew that they had no sense of dignity, no sense of honor—basically, no sense at all.

Turning to the other side of the boulder, Basil caught his breath. More winged people! Though no flames danced on their bodies, they looked just as majestic as the fire angel. And more like mortal men and women.

Eaglefolk! Basil recognized them from all he'd heard. Six of them stood together, rustling their powerful wings. Their yellow-rimmed eyes flashed with fierce pride; their powerful talons clutched the snow. Row upon row of feathers, entirely silver except for their red tips, shimmered in the light from Avalon's daytime stars. Feeling suddenly inadequate, he pulled his crumpled little wings tighter against his back.

What's the point of looking for relatives? he thought glumly. *Nobody who looks like me would have been invited! This wedding is for mighty folk like angels and eagles, giants and unicorns.*

Then, crawling by his side on the boulder, he saw a pair of rust-colored beetles. One carried a broken wing, hanging loosely from its back; the other seemed so old and frail it could barely move its legs. Yet here they were, scaling a small tuft of snow on the boulder, doing their best to get a better view.

With a nudge from his tail, Basil helped them climb their little mountain. The older beetle waved a wing in thanks, and Basil replied with a courteous nod. Just then his attention was caught not by another creature, but by a fluffy cloud of mist that was sailing just over the heads of the deer people. It moved in a focused, almost deliberate, way. As the cloud turned sharply and passed right above him, he clacked his teeth in surprise.

It's moving against the wind. Amazed, he dug his tiny claws into the snow on the boulder.

As Basil watched in wonder, the mass of mist sailed straight into the gusty breeze that flowed across the mountaintop. Completely unaffected, it flew into the center of the ring and approached Merlin and Hallia from behind.

Somehow sensing the cloud, Merlin spun around. And then the wizard did something unexpected: He waved his hand in greeting. At that, the cloud did something even more unexpected. Rippling like a windblown sail, it rose into a vertical position. Then, slowly, its upper portion bent forward in a stately bow.

It's alive! Basil realized. *A creature of mist!* A sylph from Airroot, that's what it was. Ever since he first heard of them, he'd wanted to see one. Wise as well as mysterious, they rarely left their realm, preferring to float silently through the Harplands, where the clouds themselves made music, or to roam across the skies, moving with the wind.

All at once he remembered another creature of wind! One whose touch he hadn't felt since the day he was born. At the instant his egg fell into Woodroot and cracked open on a bed of moss, a warm breeze had swept around him—full of the smell of cinnamon and the gift of friendship. Could she, perhaps, be here? Could she find him once more?

Basil scampered over to the boulder's highest edge. Stretching his neck upward, he lifted his small head toward the sky. Then, remembering the danger of being caught as an intruder, he hesitated—for an instant. With a hearty shake, he banished the worry. His first friend might be here! And so he cried:

"Aylah, are you anywhere near? Come find me, wind sister! Come find me again."

The chill breeze scurried across the mountaintop. But it carried no answer.

"Call as you wish," whispered a voice right behind him. "Yet expect a reply you should not."

12: MYSTERY BEAST

Here's the hard truth, straight from me:
  To know who you are, it is less important to find who you were than to decide who you will become.

Whirling around, Basil saw an immense creature who towered over the boulder. Never had he seen anything like this before! The creature, whose whispered voice sounded distinctly feminine, stood more than twice as tall as Merlin. As she bent her rounded head lower, her deep-set eyes, as brown as the rest of her body, examined Basil closely. All the while, her four slender arms, each with three long fingers, stirred the air as if plucking invisible strings, making some sort of silent music.

"Who—who are you?" he demanded, spreading his wings to take flight.

"Aelonnia of Isenwy am I, a mudmaker of Malóch." Her resonant whisper somehow seemed to calm Basil's nerves. He felt himself relaxing as she spoke. Just to be safe, though, he kept his wings wide open, ready to fly in an instant.

Her deep brown eyes peered at him, so intensely that

he wondered if she were reading his mind. Nervously, he slapped his tail on the boulder, sending up a puff of snow. Her gaze never wavered, making him feel more anxious by the second. The tension grew and grew—until, at last, she spoke again.

"Your name I know not, little one." With each word, her delicate fingers wove flowing patterns in the air. "Yet you a riddle could be called. Truly I speak! Many creatures have I seen, in many realms. Yet none like you have I ever found. Even possible, it is, that no one else like you exists."

Basil caught his breath. A deep chill, colder than the snow, spread through his body. How could she say that? How could she be so sure? With a shiver, he declared, "I don't believe you."

"Perhaps not. But wonder you do, I can tell." Her resonant whisper softened. "Tell me, little one, why do they matter so much, my words?"

"Because they do!" he blurted. "Wouldn't it matter to you if you had no family? No race? No identity?"

"An identity you have," she declared, bending her rounded head lower. "But unlike any other it is. True that must be—whether or not any more of your kind exist."

Basil's cupped ears trembled. "What *am* I, though? If there are no others like me . . ."

"Then," finished the mudmaker, "you are a mystery beast."

"That much I already knew." He gave a halfhearted chuckle and tucked his wings against his back. "Now, tell me. Do you always talk with people about—well, about what they . . . um, well, what they—"

"Truly are?" Her fingers stroked the air ever so gently.

Hesitantly, he nodded.

"No, little one. But with you . . ." She paused, tilting her massive brown head. "Strange magic do I see in your eyes. Yes, strange magic indeed."

Uncomfortable with this whole conversation—and not at all sure what to make of this tall, sinewy creature—he decided to change the subject. Right now.

"Never mind about that," he snapped, drumming his tail on the boulder for emphasis. "Why did you say what you said before? About Aylah—that I shouldn't expect her to answer me. What did you mean?"

The mudmaker sighed. "Only that a wishlahaylagon she is, a wind sister of the sky. Always moving, never at rest." Her delicate fingers swept through the air like swirling wind. "Answer the call of other creatures they do only quite rarely."

Feeling the truth of her words, Basil blinked his green eyes. Quietly, he asked, "So I shouldn't hope . . . to meet her again?"

"Hope you may, little one," Aelonnia whispered. "But only because, here in Avalon, anything is possible. How else to explain the magical mud of my realm? Power it holds, thanks to Merlin—power to make new creatures."

"Creatures? From mud?" In a flash, he remembered what the gossiping crows had said. "So it's really true?"

Aelonnia's deep-set eyes seemed to smile. "Like you, little one, the mud of my realm is more than it seems. For all the elements of élano it contains—including the magic of Mystery."

"Mystery?"

"Yes, little one. A gift from the gods that is, a gift to Avalon."

Before Basil could respond, a loud, heartrending wail erupted from the snow by Aelonnia's feet.

"Oh, terribulous painodeath! My endalife, tragicmost,

all too soonswift. Such a dastardous fate, horribulous end!"

Peering over the edge of the boulder, Basil looked for who was dying—for surely nothing less could cause such mournful keening. What he saw, rolling in misery in the snow, was a creature unlike any he'd ever imagined. Dark, rounded, and sleek, the creature resembled a seal—except that he had three claws on each fin, plus a row of several tails, each one coiled into a spiral. Suddenly the creature wailed again, his long whiskers quivering.

"Mepoorme, to shriveldie so soon! And I still so young-sweet, almost a barebaby."

With a groan, the mudmaker stooped down and picked him up. "There now, little ballymag. Stop your whining, you must."

"Is he going to die?" asked Basil, his eyes wide with concern.

"Yes!" shrieked the ballymag. "Oh, such agonywoe, such painodeath."

"No," declared Aelonnia, sounding rather annoyed. "Perfectly fine, he is. Misses the mud of our realm, he does. When home to Malóch he returns, all well will he be."

Puzzled, Basil scrunched his lizardlike nose. "You mean he's just homesick? Making so much fuss?" Seeing Aelonnia nod, he asked, "Why didn't he just stay in Mudroot?"

Aelonnia's round shoulders shrugged. "A friend of Merlin and Hallia he is, from long ago."

"Tried to cookpot and swalloweat me, Merlin did!" wailed the ballymag. "But I somehow survivedstill." His head drooped, and tears welled in his eyes. "Only to die here today, in this dreadulous, mudforsaken place."

"Here," declared Aelonnia, fixing her eyes on his. "Give

you something magical to help, I will. But only if *quiet* you stay."

The ballymag instantly fell silent, though his body still shuddered with sobs. He lay like a baby in her arms, waiting for help.

With one of her delicate fingers, she rubbed the side of her head, scraping off a single flake of dirt. Whispering a soft, lilting chant, she pressed the dirt against the ballymag's round belly. At once, the dirt began to expand into a clump of dark, gooey mud. Sliding across his skin, the clump grew and grew until it covered all his belly, his back, and most of his tails. It continued to swell, covering him like a thick, luxurious blanket. Soon his entire body was coated in mud, right up to his eyes.

Seeing all this, the ballymag shivered with delight and hugged himself joyously. As he squeezed, sticky mud oozed everywhere, flowing across his body like thick molasses. A dreamy look came to his face—the look of someone who, after long suffering, had found paradise at last. Licking some of the mud that dripped from his whiskers, he sighed contentedly. And then he said the happiest word that Basil had ever heard.

"Mooshlovely. Ah, mooshlovely."

At that moment, the boulder where Basil sat began to vibrate. The shaking grew stronger by the second, until the entire stone seemed about to explode.

13: THE MUSIC OF LIGHT

Little troubles me now, after everything that's happened. Very little. Yet still, to this day, I wonder how he could have seen so clearly into the murky depths of my mind . . . and made me consider the weight of a single grain of sand. Or a single life.

The boulder quaked violently. Suddenly a jagged crack opened right under Basil! He leaped into the air and flapped over to the tall mudmaker's shoulder. Landing there, he perched among the folds of her soft brown skin.

Meanwhile, the crack expanded and deepened. Finally, with a resounding *crraaaaack*, it split the rock like a deep crevasse. Or, perhaps, like a gaping mouth.

"Warned you, I should have," whispered Aelonnia. "A living stone that is. Always hungry, they are, especially when food touches them."

Aghast, Basil watched from his perch as the living stone's bumpy gray tongue emerged. Slowly, dripping pebbles of hardened saliva, it probed, spending several seconds caressing the spot where Basil had sat so comfortably.

At last, the tongue withdrew, the boulder shook again, and the crack closed completely.

Basil stared down at the creature who looked, once again, like a snow-frosted boulder. And heaved a sigh of relief.

"Basil, you ogre's eyeball! What are you doing here?"

Recognizing that gruff voice, the little lizard cringed. Slowly, he turned his head. Sure enough, he found himself face-to-face with Nuic. The grumpy sprite was seated high in the branches of a tree spirit—a willow, judging from the long, swaying tresses of hair. Nuic scowled at him, all the while shifting colors from outraged purple to angry red.

Drawing a deep breath, Basil said casually, "Just thought I'd, well, take a closer look."

"After all my pleadings? All my warnings? You crumple-brained cockleshell! The wedding is about to begin! Leave now before you get caught. Or are you as stupid as you are ugly?"

The mudmaker swiveled her head, turning her deep brown eyes on the pinnacle sprite. "Greetings, Nuic," she said in a resonant whisper that bore an unmistakable hint of sarcasm. "Your flattering tones would I recognize anywhere."

"Hmmmppf. Can I help it if I'm surrounded by idiots and vagabonds?" His colors darkened to a wrathful shade of crimson. "Did you know your little friend there just barged in, uninvited?"

Basil winced at the words. Furtively, he glanced around to see if anyone else had heard—especially anyone who resembled a gargantuan spider. Fortunately, with the constant din of the crowd, no one seemed to have noticed. And the mudmaker seemed unperturbed.

Then, as he turned back to Nuic, Basil's heart froze. The sprite looked as if he were just about to shout something at the top of his lungs. And Basil felt sure he knew what that something would be. He braced himself to hear the word *intruder.*

Nuic inhaled all the air he could hold and shouted: "Hear me, everyone! There is someone here—"

"Say no more," urged the mudmaker.

But Nuic kept going. "Who is—"

"Please," Basil pleaded, fluttering his wings anxiously. "Don't say it. Don't."

"An int—"

Nuic paused, drawing out the word. Heads on all sides turned toward him. Tree spirits clacked their branches angrily; eaglefolk raked the snow with their claws; flames of outrage sprang into the deer people's eyes. And over in the center of the ring, the wizard Merlin suddenly turned— and traded glances with the spider Grand Elusa.

"An int—" repeated Nuic, obviously pleased with himself for garnering so much attention. His skin, now radiant yellow, shone brightly. Meanwhile, the commotion swelled around him as more and more heads turned his way. As he readied himself to finish the word, he gave one final glance at Basil.

The little lizard said nothing. He merely met Nuic's gaze. *Please,* he thought, with such urgency that his ears trembled. *Please don't.*

Nuic turned away and looked straight at Merlin. Then he finished his sentence by declaring for all to hear: "An int . . . eresting person!"

Cries of puzzlement and confusion filled the air—and from the Grand Elusa, a loud grumble of dismay. More than a few onlookers (including Merlin) remarked on poor Nuic's lost sanity. But the sprite didn't seem to mind. His color, now golden yellow, showed deep satisfaction.

When he looked again at Basil, he saw only relief in the lizard's green eyes. But if Nuic felt any compassion, he didn't reveal it. He merely said, in his gruffest voice, "That'll teach you not to be so annoyingly sassy! And not to play pranks on me ever again."

Basil held back a grin. Seemingly calm, as if nothing at all had happened, he raised his nose and sniffed the air. "Say, do you smell something rotten? Goblin vulture, maybe?"

Nuic's skin color instantly darkened to beet red. "Why, you cheeky little slackbrained scalawag! I'd skin you and turn you into a handkerchief, but you're not good enough to wipe my nose."

Before Basil could reply, a sudden new sound cut across the mountaintop. It caused everyone to fall silent; even Nuic seemed unwilling to speak. Within seconds, the noises of all the wedding guests faded away. The summit was utterly quiet—except for the new sound.

Louder it grew, and louder. It was a rolling, layered hum that sounded, at once, star high and ocean deep. It vibrated in Basil's ears, his bones, and somewhere beyond his body. Like most of the wedding guests, he turned, looking for the source of this wondrous music. And when he found it, he could only gape.

That great river of sound was coming from a single creature not much bigger than himself! Shaped like a teardrop, with turquoise eyes and copper skin, it wore a translucent robe that rippled in the breeze. It sat atop an equally strange but much larger being—an immense, hunchbacked figure with woolly fur, one great leg, and dexterous fingers that could have belonged to a craftsman. Yet what was most striking about this small creature was not its colorful appearance, or its unusual companion, but its overwhelmingly beautiful music.

As the figure's humming grew ever more richly layered, Basil realized that he was hearing more than sound. This was truly magic, in the form of song. It was hope, wisdom, love, and dreams—all made into music.

"A museo," whispered Aelonnia, waving her slender arms in rhythm. As the layered humming grew ever more rich, she declared, "Announcing the wedding, it is! Arrived now has the time."

The museo's voice swelled, inspiring thoughts and feelings too numerous to name. Basil swayed a bit, feeling almost giddy, as if he'd been drinking some musical mead. Then, as abruptly as the song had started, it ceased.

A deeper kind of hush—expectant, uncertain—fell over the wedding guests. Even Merlin looked around the summit anxiously. Suddenly the silence was broken by the powerful screech of a canyon eagle, perched on Shim's enormous shoulder. The screech ripped the air, echoing back and forth across the mountain ridges, until the whole world seemed to be answering the eagle's call.

The canyon eagle, with her sharp eyes, had been the first to see a small but regal band walking up the mountainside. Four in number, they were the very last guests to arrive. For they had come all the way from the Otherworld of the spirits.

In the lead, a powerful stag and a pure white doe stepped with impossible lightness over the snow. The stag, bronze in hue, carried a great rack of antlers with seven points on each side. The doe, whose coat gleamed whiter than the snow, had eyes that were bottomless brown pools. Behind them came a silver-haired man, and, upon his shoulder, a small hawk with fierce golden eyes.

At the sight of them approaching, the crowd stirred with murmurs, gasps, and whispers, like the leaves of a tree shaken suddenly by wind. Then, all at once, they fell silent again. This was not the quiet of listening, as before, but the quiet of awe. Even the scuffling hoolahs halted their wrestling match and sat still.

"Dagda!" exclaimed the fire angel, his voice crackling like flames. "The stag is Dagda, great god of wisdom."

"And the doe," rumbled a brown bear nearby, "is Lorilanda, goddess of birth and renewal."

"Dagda and Lorilanda?" asked Basil, looking up at Aelonnia. "Really here?"

"Not the gods themselves, but their mortal forms. Come here, they have, to honor Merlin and Hallia."

Even before the group reached the ring of guests, the hawk screeched loudly and leaped into the air. Instinctively, Basil cringed, fearing the predator's sharp talons. But the hawk flew straight over to the center of the ring, where the wizard and his bride stood waiting. With a rush of air, he landed on Merlin's shoulder.

"Trouble!" The wizard reached up and gently stroked the bird's wing. Then he wrapped one finger around a talon, as two old friends might shake hands. "Trouble, it's good to see you again."

The hawk's golden eyes peered at him. And then, lifting his perilous beak toward the sky, Trouble released a triumphant whistle.

Just then, as if by silent command, the ring of onlookers parted. Together, the stag and doe, along with the man, approached the bride and groom.

Elen gasped, recognizing the tall, silver-haired man. Amazed, she put her hand over her heart. For she had never loved another person the way she loved him: the poet Cairpré.

He took both her hands in his own. "My love," he whispered. "I have ached for you—yes, constantly. But today, for this moment at least, we are together again."

She watched him, her sapphire eyes radiant. "And some-day, when the moment comes, we shall be together for all time."

He squeezed her hands, but said nothing.

Basil watched intently from his perch on Aelonnia's shoulder. *Even a bard*, he realized, *can be at a loss for words.*

A breeze gusted, scattering flakes of snow onto the wedding guests. But no one seemed to notice. All eyes were on the great spirit Dagda, who stepped to Merlin's side, coming as near as his rack of antlers would allow. "You have come far, Olo Eopia, through many worlds and many times. Far indeed."

As he spoke Merlin's true name in his deep, mellifluous voice, Dagda nodded. At the same time, shreds of mist formed in the air around his antlers. Glowing mysteriously, these shreds started to weave in and out, sometimes wrapping themselves around the points, sometimes shooting upward in luminous arcs.

"Much time has passed, and no time at all, since I last saw you," Dagda continued, as the incandescent mist danced around his antlers. "On that day, you brought Fincayra's many races together, a true community at last, after centuries of suffering. And for that feat I gave your people wings."

The spirit lord paused to glance over at Rhia. With a grateful bow, she opened her translucent wings—part feathers, part air, and part starlight.

"You showed us all on that day," Dagda went on, "that one life, no matter how small, can make a difference. Just as the smallest grain of sand can tilt a scale, the weight of one person's will can lift an entire world."

His words, though said to Merlin, reached the entire gathering. Yet they echoed strangely in Basil's mind; it almost felt as if they were being whispered to him. He shook himself, sure that the feeling came from snowflakes that had lodged in his ears.

"You have been serving those same ideals," Dagda told the wizard, "on that world of mortals called Earth. Yet you have not forgotten," he added with a tilt of his antlers toward Hallia, "where your heart truly lies."

Once more, the words echoed in Basil's mind. Even as he shook himself, he heard again and again the phrase *where your heart truly lies*.

Merlin, meanwhile, drew a deep breath. "As many hopes as I have for Camelot and its young king on Earth, my highest hope has long been to stand here on this mountaintop." He reached a hand toward Hallia. "With you."

Taking his hand, she stepped to his side. "Your hope," she said softly, "and my prayer."

"A prayer now answered," declared Lorilanda. She pranced closer with the grace of a deer. And to Basil's amazement, wherever her hooves touched the snow, tiny flowers—sweet woodruff, crocuses, and lilies of the valley—instantly blossomed.

The doe's rich voice, while not as deep as Dagda's, carried equal power. As she approached, her bottomless brown eyes gazed at Hallia. "We came here today in the form of deer, young one, in honor of you and your people."

Hallia gazed back, the breeze toying with the loose hairs of her auburn braid. "Really, you know, it's the other way around. My people long ago took the form of deer so we could share in all the grace and beauty of your creation—to run through your fields, stand in your glades, browse on your flowers."

Lorilanda nodded, then turned to Merlin. "You are well matched in wisdom, I would say."

Grinning mischievously, he replied, "And also in stubbornness."

Hallia gave him a wink. "My stubbornness is a virtue, but yours is a flaw."

"Too true," agreed Merlin, his eyes gleaming. "But at least I haven't forgotten the first rule of marriage."

Hallia cocked her head, curious. "Which is?"

"The bride is always right."

Hard as she tried to keep herself from grinning, she couldn't.

Dagda nodded approvingly. "That, my good lad, is why you are a wizard."

Trouble released a jovial whistle. He paced across Merlin's shoulder, ruffling his wings and piping with amusement.

Merlin himself broke into laughter. So did Hallia—along with Rhia, Cairpré, Elen, and many of the guests. But no one laughed harder than Basil.

In fact, he laughed so hard that he lost his balance, slipped on the mudmaker's smooth brown skin, and tumbled down to the snow. But before he could open his wings to fly back up to his perch, something snarled and attacked.

Something with hundreds of tiny, knife-sharp teeth.

14: PERIL AND PETALS

Answers come and go, I've found. But the questions?
Those remain forever.

A baby dragon!

Even before Basil touched the snow, the terrible beast pounced. Though still only an infant, he utterly dwarfed his prey, looking like a monster by comparison. Just one of his dragon ears was bigger than Basil's whole body.

Grabbing the lizard's tail in his sturdy young jaws, he squeezed with brutal ferocity. Before Basil could even begin struggling to break free, the baby dragon started shaking his new toy wildly, trying to break its spirit—or its back.

Despite this thrashing, Basil managed to curl his body backward over his tail. With all his strength, he slashed his wing down on the dragon's nose. The sharp, bony wing tip sliced into the scarlet-colored skin that hadn't yet hardened into scales.

"Yeeeeee!" shrieked the young dragon, as a few drops

of silver blood trickled down his snout. He let go, thoroughly confused: None of his playthings had ever fought back before. Then his confusion turned to rage. His orange eyes seemed to kindle into roaring flames.

Basil, too, seethed with rage. The tiny club at the tip of his tail throbbed painfully, and several of his scales had been torn. The whole tail now resembled a bent and twisted twig.

Without an instant's hesitation, he leaped into the air, flapped his wings, and flew straight at the dragon's face. "You may be a hundred times my size, you big moron, but you'll regret that attack!"

Wings whirring, he dived at his assailant, green eyes aglow. *Slam!* Something very hard—and very powerful—knocked him completely out of the air. He thudded into the side of the living stone and fell to the snow.

Dazed, he looked up, then weakly shook the snow off his wings and snout. Shapes and colors, all disconnected, spun before him. Suddenly, his brain put enough of them together to recognize the creature who had struck him so savagely. The mother dragon!

Gwynnia, daughter of the terrible Wings of Fire, stood before him. Her enormous body, from the tip of her sideways-jutting ear down to her perilous claws, quaked with wrath at the little green beast who had dared to harm her child. Peering down at her baby's bloody nose, her triangular eyes glowed like superheated lava. Her massive, barbed tail, which had swatted Basil to the ground, lifted to strike once again.

Most ominous of all, though, was the terrible rumble gathering in her chest. Although Basil had never seen a wrathful dragon breathe fire, he instantly guessed the meaning of that sound. He was about to be blasted by flames! And these flames, unlike the magical green fire of the portal, would incinerate him completely.

He tried to focus on flying away. But with his head still spinning, he could barely stand, let alone fly. Gwynnia's massive jaws, studded with rows upon rows of daggerlike teeth, opened wide. Basil stared down the dragon's throat, unable to move, unable to save himself. He would never survive this day—and never find out who he really was.

She breathed a dreadful blast. Directed right at Basil, the fire exploded on top of the spot where he'd been standing. Sizzling hot flames licked the snow, instantly melting it down to the bare rock of the summit. Burning the very air, the fire crackled angrily. As the last flames trembled on the wet rocks, then vanished, the dragon snorted in triumph.

Abruptly, she started, making her horizontal blue ear slap against her jaw. For Basil had completely disappeared. Not a single charred bone, nor even a smoking heap of ashes, remained.

Suspicious, she stretched her long neck, which glistened with purple and scarlet scales, toward the spot. All at once she saw him—not on the ground, but resting in one of the slender arms of the mudmaker. For Aelonnia, seeing his danger, had snatched him up just in time.

Gwynnia faced the mudmaker, another rumble swelling in her armored chest. But the tall, gracious being stood fast. Cradling Basil, she spoke firmly to the wrathful dragon.

"Revenge seek you not," she declared. "A wedding this is, not a battlefield."

Gwynnia hesitated, and her orange eyes narrowed a bit. Then her baby whimpered, pressing his sore nose against her leg. Instantly, her anger flared again. The threatening rumble grew stronger.

"Stop!" shouted a commanding voice.

Gwynnia, along with Basil and Aelonnia, turned to see Merlin striding toward them. Trouble, the silver-plumed hawk, gripped his shoulder tightly. Hands raised, Merlin surveyed the group, then looked squarely at the irascible mother dragon.

"No one gets eaten today," he declared.

Gwynnia bared her terrible teeth at this outlandish idea, but Merlin continued, "Just as no one gets scorched. Or pounded. Or torn to shreds. So put aside your grudge against that—" He halted, waving toward Basil. "That . . . well, *whatever* it is."

Basil cringed. *So even a powerful wizard has no idea what I am.*

Merlin, sensing the dragon might disobey his command, leaned toward her gargantuan head. Trails of black smoke curled from her nostrils. Quietly, he said, "I'm asking you not for me, Gwynnia, but for Hallia. Your old friend who took care of you when you were no bigger than your child."

The dragon's eyes flicked toward Hallia. She was still standing between the great doe and stag, a plaintive look upon her face. Reluctantly, Gwynnia sighed, exhaling a blast of hot air that melted all the remaining snow around the living stone. Gathering her infant in the cupped edge of her wing, she turned to go and rejoin her other offspring— but not before she cast a withering glance at the little lizard who had caused so much trouble.

As their eyes met, something strange occurred. While they started out glaring at each other, both creatures suddenly tilted their heads. For both of them had sensed something unexpected. A new look transformed Basil's expression, a look that Gwynnia shared.

It was a look of surprise, mixed with confusion. As if . . . their destinies, so utterly different, were actually somehow connected.

Gwynnia snorted loudly, sending up a cloud of smoke, as she banished such an impossible, insulting notion. She turned to depart without giving Basil another glance. Even her child, wrapped in her wing, pointedly looked away.

The object of Gwynnia's ire, though, continued to stare after her. *What was that about?* Basil wondered. *Probably just that knock on my head, that's all.*

Merlin himself started to go, but paused to give a respectful bow of his head to Aelonnia the mudmaker. As she did the same in return, the wizard's gaze fell again on the peculiar little creature she now held. A look of puzzlement creased his brow, and he asked, "Do I know you, little fellow?"

"N-no," stammered Basil, thumping his tail nervously against the mudmaker's arm.

The wizard's bushy eyebrows lifted. More sternly this time, he asked, "Did Hallia or I invite you to this wedding?" His voice lowered. "Or are you . . . an intruder?"

Basil's heart pounded wildly within his chest. Yet he was less aware of his own rising panic than of the harsh scrutiny by the wizard—and by others. Above, on the branch of a willow spirit, Nuic clucked his tongue knowingly. Off to one side, the jester with the floppy hat lined with bells started clearing his throat to sing. And nearby, the Grand Elusa perked up, gnashing her immense jaws—so vigorously that the shredded remains of a living stone, caught between her teeth, flew off and hit one of the hoolahs, who howled in pain.

"Answer me," commanded Merlin.

Basil gulped. His wings shook uncontrollably. Finally, he admitted, "No one . . . invited . . . me."

For a timeless moment, Merlin peered at him. At last, with a decisive nod, the wizard declared: "Then, little fellow, I will invite you myself. Consider yourself my guest."

Stunned, Basil could barely open his mouth. But he did manage, somehow, to whisper, "Thanks."

Although his voice was barely audible over the surprised murmuring of the guests—and the loud snarling of the great white spider—Basil's response caught the wizard's attention. Merlin leaned closer and gave him a wink. "I'd do anything, anything at all, to keep that fellow over there"—he waved at the jester—"from singing! Why, a few notes from him would make most of our wedding guests leave. Or fall down dead."

Merlin grinned. Yet Basil's mind had locked on the wizard's final phrase. *Fall down dead.* In a flash, he remembered the horrible dream from long ago—a dream in which Merlin did, in fact, fall down dead.

A new spasm of panic seized him. Should he tell Merlin? Warn him? But what, exactly, was the warning? He could tell Merlin to avoid any creatures with jagged, bony wings. But wouldn't that include Basil himself?

However crazy it may sound, he decided, *I must tell him. Must warn him!*

But by now the wizard had turned to go. He was already several steps away when Basil cried out, "Merlin! Wait."

Too late. His words were drowned in the rising chorus of cheers, neighs, growls, and whistles that accompanied Merlin's return to the center of the crowd. For everyone sensed the ceremony was about to begin. When the wizard reached for Hallia's hand, the chorus rose to its peak.

Alone among the crowd, Basil watched glumly. He had missed his chance!

As soon as Merlin and Hallia joined hands, the powerful stag beside them stamped his hoof on the snow-covered ground. The entire summit fell silent once more. "It is time," Dagda proclaimed.

Raising his head with its massive rack of antlers, the great spirit declared: "Many are the wonders, great and small, that fill the wide universe. And many are the mysteries to be found in the stars and the spaces between them. You stand here now in a world profoundly rich in both wonder and mystery—the Great Tree of Avalon. It is a world of unfathomable beauty, a place where all creatures may learn to live in harmony, a place that has never been touched by the wickedness of Rhita Gawr."

At this, Merlin nodded. "Long may Avalon stay free of that evil spirit! We have no place here for Rhita Gawr."

Supportive murmurs, growls, hoots, and cries arose from the crowd. The hawk on Merlin's shoulder released a sharp whistle, and Rhia applauded vigorously. Virtually everyone in the ring of guests, save the flamelons and a few of the gnomes, made clear their approval.

Dagda waited for silence to return before continuing. "And yet," he said, glancing at Merlin and Hallia, "there is no greater wonder, and no deeper mystery, than the bond of true love between two people."

His words echoed a long moment, as if carried aloft on the breeze. Then, with a graceful bow to Lorilanda, the god of wisdom stepped aside. As he did so, the goddess of birth and renewal came forward.

With a flick of one hoof, she kicked at a snowdrift. As the icy flakes flew into the air, they transformed magically into rose petals. Hundreds of bright red petals, carrying the scent of spring, showered the young couple.

"May this gift remind you," the goddess said kindly, "that you share in all the powers of nature. You hold in yourselves the miracle of a seed . . . and the light of a star. You can find new morning light after long darkness. You can move from violent thunderclouds to the sweet serenity after a storm. And you can, like the spring, transform crystals of snow into petals of flowers."

Nodding, Merlin faced Hallia. "So where," he asked, "does the source of music lie?"

She smiled, remembering the riddle of the harp they had learned so long ago. Softly, she spoke the second part: "Is it in the strings themselves, or in the hands that plucked them?"

"The answer lies in both, my love," he offered. "Just as the answers to our deepest questions lie somewhere in both of us."

"Yes, young hawk. And whatever those answers might be, we will look for them together."

"Indeed you shall," declared Dagda. Glowing shreds of mist twined themselves about his antlers. "For now you enter this world as husband and wife. And wherever you may go in your mortal lives, you shall go with our everlasting blessings."

At those words, Merlin and Hallia kissed. The crowd erupted. Rhia raised her arms and cheered; Elen cried. Trouble, still perched on Merlin's shoulder, whistled triumphantly.

Shim pounded his giant fist happily on the mountainside, so hard that the tremors from his blows caused a stampede among the deer people and nearly knocked over the wedding couple. As his enthusiasm swelled, he unwrapped the scarlet snake from his neck and started to swing it in the air above his head—all the while continuing to pound his fist harder than ever. Landslides crashed down the mountain's lower slopes, sending clouds of dirt and crushed rock into the air. Birds and beasts for leagues around tried to find someplace safe to hide, hoping to survive the quake.

But Shim remained unfazed. Grinning broadly as he swung the huge snake, he bellowed, "Today is a happily day! One of the bestest ever. And now . . . time for some honey! Certainly, definitely, absolutely."

Meanwhile, the sturdier guests at the wedding continued to celebrate. A trio of canyon eagles leaped skyward and screeched loudly, raking the air with their talons. By contrast, the misty sylph floated silently, spinning graceful circles above the summit. Tree spirits raised their ethereal voices in a song that, when joined by the museo, made every listener feel both the joy of spring's beauty and the sorrow of its brevity.

The fire angel flamed bright, blazing like a great winged torch. (A dramatic way to celebrate, to be sure, but not so pleasant for the guests who happened to be standing next to him when he lit up.) Aelonnia's tall brown form swayed happily to the tree spirits' song. Urnalda, the dwarf queen, danced with her murderous battle-ax. Nuic, losing all his grumpiness for a moment, turned a celebratory shade of rouge. Gwynnia's baby dragons cavorted happily. And somewhere in the snow, two hoolahs continued to wrestle as if nothing unusual had happened.

Among all the guests, however, one in particular summed up the whole affair. From deep within the crowd came a quiet, cooing voice, barely audible over all the sounds of celebration (not to mention the sound of Shim slurping down an entire vat of honey). That voice uttered just a single word:

"Mooshlovely."

15: DARK DREAMS

*When your feet are most firm, when your winds are most
steady, when your plans are most assured—that's when
everything changes. Believe me, I know.*

Following the wedding, the guests departed straightaway
for their homes. And Merlin and Hallia journeyed to
some secret location for their honeymoon. Basil, however,
decided to stay for a few days. Why not explore Stoneroot's
high peaks a little, since he was here?

Catching chilly updrafts on the mountain slopes, he
floated over the ridges, snowfields, and boulder-strewn
basins. While food wasn't nearly as plentiful as in his
home realm of Woodroot—being limited to rock lichen,
alpine herbs, and the occasional beetle or fly that landed on
the boulders—he enjoyed the absence of dactylbirds and
other airborne hunters. Aside from a pair of wide-winged
eaglemen who soared past him one morning, and a jabber-
ing flock of crows, he saw no other creatures who could be
called predators.

Only once did he spy a pinnacle sprite's parachute.

Gleaming silver in the bright starlight of midday, it rode an air current over the western flank of Hallia's Peak. *Nuic?* he wondered, tilting his wings to swoop closer. But before he could get near enough to tell, the parachute disappeared behind a distant ridge.

Finally, Basil decided to return to the portal. Despite its dangers, which Aelonnia had kindly explained to him before she departed, it clearly offered the best way to travel between realms. No wonder so many creatures—including the mudmaker—preferred to move around by using portals. Whenever Basil was ready to go home, the portal would take him there in just a few seconds. By contrast, even if his small, leaf-thin wings could have carried him all the way to Woodroot, the trip would have taken him many years to complete.

"The question isn't *whether* to ride through that portal again," he mused aloud as he flew back to the boulder slope where he'd arrived in this realm. "No, the question is *where*."

Should he go right back to his treasured forestland? Where majestic trees, far higher than the stunted spruces of these ridges, covered leagues and leagues with their web of interwoven branches? Or should he venture farther? Explore the mists of Airroot or the molten lands of Fireroot? Or even . . . the endless darkness of Shadowroot?

Spotting a blue-winged fly zipping past, Basil suddenly remembered he hadn't eaten since the day before. Instantly, he veered and flicked his tail with expert precision. The knob at the end of his tail clubbed the fly straight into his open mouth. Tiny as his teeth were, they crunched down hard. Chewing contentedly, he banked to one side, resuming his flight to the portal.

As he leaned into the turn, he saw his wing at an unusual

angle. Backlit by Avalon's bright sky, it seemed to glow; it loomed large before his eyes, although it was really no bigger than an oak leaf. What struck him most, though, were its bony, jagged edges, as sharply etched as dagger points.

Instantly, he remembered his dream. The wicked beast with batlike wings. The vicious attack on Merlin. The screams of anguish. The horror of it all—and the regret he felt for failing to share the dream with Merlin. To warn the wizard in whatever way possible, even if it turned out to be not a vision after all, but merely one creature's nightmare.

He shuddered, making his wings flutter in the wind. Either way, the dream remained as vivid as ever, after all this time. *Why can't I forget it? Why can't I just move on?*

Eyeing the boulder slopes below, he recognized the one with the portal. Though he couldn't yet see the telltale flicker of green fire, he knew that slope—just as he knew its dangers. Yet even though he'd almost died there in a rock slide, he didn't dread returning. Why was that sight so much less frightening than the memory of a dream?

Because that rock slide was part of my past, he told himself grimly. *And the dream—the dream is part of my future. I don't know why I feel that way . . . but I do.*

He gazed at the rocky ridges below, rising like waves in an endless sea of stone. But at the edges of his mind lurked other shapes—darker, more jagged, more deadly. *Did those wings belong to me? Or someone else?*

From deep in his slender throat came a growl. *The only way I'll ever find out is to discover who I really am. What I'm meant to be.* The growl deepened. *And the first step to doing that is to find out if there is someone—anyone—who belongs to my kind. Whatever kind that may be.*

Sure, he couldn't find anyone else at Merlin's wedding who looked like himself. But what did that prove? Nothing!

Even Aelonnia, who had been so struck by his unusual nature, wasn't entirely sure that he was the only member of his kind. She had said, in her lilting whisper, *Possible, it is, that no one else like you exists.* Yes—*possible.* But by no means certain.

Somewhere out there, he told himself, *is someone who looks like me! Who acts like me. Who maybe even dreams like me.*

A new resolve crystallized in his mind. *And I'm going to find that someone. Whatever it takes.*

He banked, gliding toward the slope with the portal. *And so I will travel—yes, far and wide! I'll go to all seven realms if I can. And somewhere out there . . . I'll find what I need to know.*

The power of this decision surged through Basil, overflowing, as if a swollen river had suddenly filled an empty channel. His eyes glowed brightly as he declared, speaking to the sky and the stone and everything in between: "I will go where I choose. Seek what I want. And find what I need!"

Even as he nodded, emphasizing his resolve, he saw a thin plume of dust rise up from the steepest part of the slope. As the plume thickened, spreading across the boulders, a grinding, roaring noise filled the air. It swelled into a rolling explosion, a gargantuan thunder.

Rock slide!

He watched, aghast, as the entire mountain seemed to tumble over itself. For a brief instant, he glimpsed a flash of green amidst the dust and blur of motion. Then it disappeared.

Bending his wings, Basil sped downward. Straight toward the spot where he'd seen the portal's flames he flew, whizzing through the air like a hawk plunging toward its prey.

By the time he neared the slope, the boulders had mostly settled again. The thunder had diminished. And the clouds of dust had started to clear. Yet despite the improved visibility, he stared harder than ever before.

The portal had vanished!

Basil swooped lower, circling the area. Again and again he flew across the cluttered slope, peering into crevasses and between boulders, searching for any sign at all of those magical flames. But he found none.

His snout furrowed. The portal . . . gone! It had disappeared under a mountain of rock—and with it, his best chance to travel to other realms. His best hope to find his own identity.

Tiny though his claws were, he squeezed them tight. *I'll find it*, he promised himself. *I'll search every crack, every shadow, every mote of dust. For as long as it takes.*

Flames of a different kind sparked within his eyes. *Forever, if I must.*

16: BRIGHT DREAMS

Magic is merely a tool. A strange, mysterious, powerful tool . . . but a tool nonetheless. Like a carpenter's hammer, it can be used to build a house—or to smash a skull. For peace or war. For delight or torment. The most important quality of any magic is not the power it provides, but the person who wields it.

YEAR OF AVALON 30

Relentlessly, Basil searched. Scouring the slope with his gaze, he flew above it every day, heedless of rain or hail or snow. Between flights, he explored the mass of boulders, crawling between them and wriggling under them. Not a single stone on that slope escaped his scrutiny.

Yet he found nothing. No sign whatsoever of the magical green fire that could transport him off this mountainside . . . and into the future. A future that would reveal, at last, who he really was—and what he could become.

Even so, he persisted. Often, he started each day before the morning's first light, when the stars of Avalon were still dim, probing the darkened gaps between boulders. Just as often, he ended the day in the same fashion, searching among the evening shadows.

And so . . . three years passed in Stoneroot.

One chilly autumn morning, Basil crept slowly through the brittle fringe of moss that lined the bottom of a gulley. In the spring, this path would hold a splashing rivulet, a vein of melted snow from the ridges above. Now, though, it held nothing but moss and bronze-colored stones that had been rounded by centuries of wind and water. And one thing more: a chubby little gnat who had caught Basil's eye. Or really, his stomach, since he hadn't eaten for three days.

Slowly, stealthily, he wriggled through the moss. His prey, seated on a bronze-colored stone, was too busy caressing its own feet to notice. Just to make sure, though, Basil sent into the air a whiff of mountain sage—a fragrance so sweet that it overpowered other smells, including his own.

Closer he crawled, hidden from both sight and smell. Finally, he crept up to the edge of the stone. The gnat stirred, buzzed nervously for a few seconds, then went back to cleaning its feet. Meanwhile, Basil readied himself to pounce. Holding his breath, he braced his feet and judged the exact distance.

Now.

Just as he was about to leap, a thunderous *boom* shook the slope. Though it came from somewhere distant, it rattled the mountain's bones from foothills to summit. Pebbles shifted and scattered; boulders wobbled, threatening to slide. The gnat, startled, took flight. Basil jumped into the air in pursuit, but even as he started to fly, the bronze stone rolled and struck his outstretched wing. The blow flipped him over, and he slammed into the ground.

As he lay in the gulley, head spinning, the booming

sound came again. And again. And again. Each time it grew louder—and, Basil suddenly realized, closer.

Boom. Boom. Boom.

All at once, he knew what it was. Footsteps! The footsteps of a giant.

Sure enough, over the ridge came a huge, hulking figure. All Basil could see, at first, was a great silhouette, rising above the ridge like a shadowy mountain and growing bigger by the second. Then, as the silhouette turned, he saw a wild mane of hair, a big bulbous nose, and a lopsided grin he knew all too well.

Shim! Strangely, the giant wore several cart wheels, tied together with ropes, from one of his gargantuan ears. With every explosive step, the lone earring jangled loudly, making a sound about as melodious as toppled trees snapping off and thwacking the ground.

Stranger still was what sat on Shim's other ear, instead of an earring. Nestled comfortably above his earlobe were passengers. And not just any passengers.

Basil scurried up to the edge of the gulley for a closer look. "Ogres' eyeballs!" he exclaimed, astonished. "That's Merlin!"

He squinted, peering closely. *No doubt about it. And in Merlin's arms—why, it's his son! The boy I've been hearing about from the crows for months.* Still not quite believing his eyes, he watched as the giant carried them closer. *I knew that Merlin wanders all over Avalon. But for him to come right here—to this very slope—I'd never have thought that could happen. And with his son, too!*

Evidently out for an autumn stroll with his father and his favorite giant, the young boy seemed to be enjoying himself greatly. Squeals of high-pitched laughter came between each of the giant's pounding strides. Basil had heard that young Krystallus, as his parents had named him, liked nothing better than to travel. And what better way to travel than on the ear of a giant?

Topping the ridge just a stone's throw from Basil, Shim finally paused. He wiped his immense brow, then exhaled so forcefully that a flock of geese soaring over the peak were blown all the way to the Dun Tara snowfields. Amidst the drifting feathers, he wearily declared, "I is all puffily, Master Krystallus. Time for a sitly rest."

"No, no, Unky Shim," protested the child. "No rest! More stomping an' bomping."

But Shim ignored his pleas. Exhausted, he lay down on the slope, gently enough not to crush his passengers—but heavily enough to rearrange the ridge's contours by flattening a cliff with his weight and knocking over several pinnacles with his arms and legs. In truth, Shim seemed to become a new ridge himself. For by the time he'd stretched out fully, placing his head on the summit and resting his feet far below, he looked like another mass of craggy cliffs. With hair that blew wildly in the mountain breeze. Only that blowing mane and the rhythmic movement of his chest as he breathed—and, very soon, snored—made it clear that this particular ridge was alive.

As the giant's snores echoed across the mountainside, an idea dawned in Basil's mind. *This is my chance! To speak to Merlin—to warn him about my dream. When will I ever be so near to him again?*

Excitedly, the lizard's tail thumped on the edge of the gulley, causing a few pebbles to dislodge and tumble down the small slope. At once, a second idea came to him. *Maybe Merlin could help me find the buried portal!* With his powers—which were practically unlimited, as everyone knew—the wizard could surely restore the portal to working order. And Basil, at last, could embark on his search—wherever it might lead.

I'll just wait for the right moment, then ask. His slender body, from the tip of his snout to the knob of his tail, quaked with anticipation. He rustled his wings. Suddenly, unbidden, an image flashed across his mind: wings, dark and dangerous. Wrapping around the wizard. Smothering him to death.

No! he told himself, now quaking from something other than excitement. *It won't happen. Can't happen. I'll make sure of it.* The image faded from his mind, though its shadow lingered—a shadow he could feel rather than see.

Slowly, he crept along the gulley's edge, wriggling like a tiny green snake across the stones and pebbles. All the while, he kept his eyes on the wizard, who had started to climb down from Shim's ear. Holding young Krystallus in the crook of his arm, Merlin grabbed hold of one of the giant's hairs that dangled by the enormous ear. Carefully, he slid down the makeshift rope, until his boots hit the rocks of the ridge. Then he released the hair, pulled the staff from his belt, and gently set down his son.

"Go play awhile, Krystallus. See if you can climb any of these rocks."

The little boy, standing unsteadily, peered up at his father. His pure white hair contrasted starkly with Merlin's black locks. "Sure, Da, but then we ride Unky Shim again?"

Merlin smiled. "Yes," he promised, even as he glanced up and saw a large glob of drool about to drop on them from Shim's mouth. Calmly, he aimed the top of his staff at the unsavory glob. A bolt of white light shot out of the staff, striking the liquid missile just as it fell. The air sizzled, and then with a flash, the drool completely evaporated.

The boy, who had already started to climb a lichen-dappled rock, abruptly stopped. "Da," he asked enthusiastically, "when you teach me magic stick?"

The joy drained out of Merlin's face. He stared absently down at his boots for several seconds. "I don't know, Krystallus. It depends on whether or not . . ." He kneeled down to face his son. "Whether or not you, well . . ."

"What, Da?"

"Show any magic of your own."

What? thought Basil, lifting his round ears in surprise. Had he heard correctly? How could the son of a wizard not have any magic of his own?

He crawled a bit closer, careful not to knock even a pebble into the gully. For he didn't want to make any sound. He didn't want to miss a single word of this.

"You see, Son . . ." began Merlin, pausing to swallow. "Wizards' powers often skip generations. It's possible— I'm not saying it will happen, just that it's possible—you might not develop your own magic. And without that, you can't . . . well, control a staff."

The wizard halted, looking much older than his years. Solemnly, he peered at the boy's brown eyes, which shone as brightly as his mother's. "Do you understand what I'm saying?"

Krystallus nodded. Then, in a gleeful voice, he asked, "So when you teach me? Magic stick fun!"

Pushing some stray locks off his brow, Merlin merely mumbled, "I don't know, Son." He stood slowly. With a sigh, he leaned heavily against his staff, which crunched on the ground. "Just find something safe to climb on while Shim naps."

The boy frowned. While he didn't comprehend his father's words, he clearly knew that his question hadn't been answered. And it seemed to Basil that he also sensed, somehow, that he'd been judged inadequate. Whether to impress his father or simply to prove him wrong, he started to climb the highest thing around. Not a rock, or even a boulder—but Shim.

"Look now, Da!" he cried, as he started to scale the folds of Shim's gigantic vest made from woven willow trunks.

But Merlin, lost in thought, hardly heard him. Without turning around, he began to walk slowly away. From his moss-filled gully, Basil watched him with concern. For a man who had defeated the powerful spirit warlord Rhita Gawr—more than once, if the tales of Lost Fincayra were really true—he now looked thoroughly beaten.

Basil knew this was his chance. He scurried ahead, racing along the gully, barely avoiding a rock sporting dozens of needle-sharp quartz crystals. Then, abruptly, he stopped. His tail swayed indecisively. Merlin seemed so troubled right now. Was this really the best time to talk with him?

No, he told himself. *But it might be the* only *time.*

Raising himself up on his hind legs, he called in his thin voice, "Ah, hello. Master Merlin?"

Instantly, the wizard spun around. Seeing this unusual creature, as green as mountain moss, he straightened in surprise. "You?" he asked. "Aren't you the little fellow I saw at my wedding?"

Basil's snout turned pink at the tip. "*Saved* at your wedding is more like it." He nodded, which made his ears flap against his cheeks. "I have something important—very important—to tell you."

"Really?" The wizard's brows lifted in curiosity. He stepped closer, as a breeze fluttered the sleeves of his tunic. "What could that be?"

"I, well, I . . ."

"Yes?"

Basil took a deep breath, even as he steadied his wavering body by bracing his tail against a rock. "I had . . . well, a dream."

"A dream?" Merlin pursed his lips, disappointed. "My friend, I am not a fortune-teller. I don't interpret people's dreams."

"No, no," protested the lizard. "This isn't like most dreams! It's different. And it involves—"

A sharp, terrified shriek ripped the mountain air.

The shriek of a child.

Merlin whirled around. "Krystallus!"

Shim, in his sleep, had lifted his enormous hand and placed it on his chest—right on top of the tiny boy. From somewhere beneath the hand, buried under an immense slab of flesh, came a muffled cry: "Help, Da, help!"

Instantly, Merlin turned to a jagged boulder, as big as himself, that lay by the giant's elbow. Shouting an incantation, he pointed his staff at the boulder. With a grinding lurch, the big stone lifted slowly into the air. It hung there, quivering slightly. All at once, Merlin swung his staff with tremendous force. The boulder flew straight into Shim's hand, smashing into an oversize knuckle. The stone exploded into shards.

Basil watched, certain that such a stinging blow would cause the giant to awaken, howling with pain. And, most important, to move his hand.

Shim, however, did none of those things. He merely lifted his little finger, as if shooing away a pesky fly. Still fast asleep, he went right on snoring, a lopsided grin on his face.

"Curse you, Shim!" shouted Merlin furiously. "Wake up, fool!"

"Da," came the muffled cry again, from deep under the giant's palm. Yet the boy's voice seemed much weaker. "Da . . ."

Frightened for the boy's life, Basil crawled as fast as he could, feet slapping on the rocks, to get closer. He leaped onto a flat stone—and what he saw made him all the more agitated. Shim's hand, larger and heavier than an ancient oak tree, was starting to press down against his chest. In a matter of seconds, the boy would be completely crushed.

Seeing this, Merlin swung his staff toward the giant's head. *"Anzalay luminari!"* he commanded.

A sizzling bolt of white-hot lightning flew out of the staff and exploded on Shim's forehead. Fiery sparks lit the air, raining down on the slope.

But Shim didn't wake up. He only stirred slightly, grinding his shoulder into what remained of the cliff beneath him. His silly grin widened, as if he'd just had an especially luminous dream. Meanwhile, his snores continued unabated.

Now, from beneath the giant's hand, came a very different sound: a weak, smothered whimper. It lasted only briefly. Then, with ominous finality, it ceased.

Merlin, wild-eyed under his bushy brows, dashed over to the giant and tried to climb onto his massive chest. But he slipped, lost his balance, and toppled to the ground. Springing to his feet, he lifted his arms to the sky and called out desperately: "What do I do? Dear Dagda, what do I do?"

No answer came from above. No help at all.

Then, all at once, a different sort of answer appeared. It came in a most unlikely form, from a most unlikely source.

Honey. The sweet, drippingly delicious smell of honey.

The aroma wafted over the mountainside, making the air seem as thick as syrup and as sweet as summer clover.

Immediately, Shim woke up. Eyes wide open, he looked around eagerly. "Honey?" he rumbled, sniffing vigorously. "Me smells some sweetly honey."

Seeking the source of his favorite smell, he sat up. As he did so, his hand fell to the side and landed, palm up, on the ridge. In its center lay a small, squirming boy with pure white hair.

"Krystallus!" In a flash, Merlin sprinted to his son. He vaulted over Shim's thumb and leaped into the giant's open hand. Rolling across the palm, he eagerly scooped up the boy.

Kneeling in the center of Shim's hand, Merlin held his son tightly and tousled the mop of white hair. "Krystallus," he cried. "Are you unhurt? Are you all right?"

The little boy responded by throwing his arms around his father's neck. Swaying unsteadily on the fleshy hand, Merlin held him close.

Meanwhile, Shim's eyes scanned the slope. His gargantuan nose quivered as he sniffed avidly. For some strange reason, though, the wondrous smell had vanished. And there was no honey to be seen anywhere.

"Trolls' tongues," roared the disappointed giant, his grin vanishing. "Me surely smelled honey! Sweetly, definitely, absolutely."

Hearing those words, Merlin suddenly understood what had happened. Someone had magically projected the smell of honey into the air. Someone with considerable power. But who? There was nobody else here on the mountainside. Nobody, at least, with that kind of magic. He caught his breath. Unless . . .

He turned toward the bizarre little beast—some sort of

winged lizard with glowing green eyes—who was watching from a stone nearby. The same little beast who had wanted to talk about a dream. As Merlin stared, the lizard simply met his gaze, swishing a slender tail on the stone.

"Not . . . *you*," the wizard said doubtfully. "That couldn't have been you, could it?"

Basil shrugged bashfully. "Just a small thing, Master Merlin." He cleared his throat. "Now, about that dr—"

Shim smashed his heel down on the mountain, causing dozens of boulders to roll and crash down the slope. Passionately, the giant declared, "I *knows* me smelled honey! Maybily I can still finds it." He glanced down at the people he held in his hand. "Time to wakes up, you two. No more restily lounging around! We have some sweetly honey to finds."

"Wait, Shim!" called Merlin.

"Wait, please!" echoed Basil.

But the giant ignored them. With a thunderous grunt, he stood up, knocking over a tower of rocks the size of a hillside. Eagerly, he sniffed the air again, then took his first gargantuan stride.

"Wait!" both Merlin and Basil cried again, but to no avail. It took only two more steps for Shim, along with the passengers in his hand, to vanish behind the ridge.

In the last instant before they disappeared, the wizard called out: "Thank you, little fellow, whoever you are! May we meet again before—"

The voice ended in the tumultuous *boom* of a giant's footstep.

17: DISTORTION

What you see isn't always real, and what is real is only rarely what you see.
That, I can tell you, is the first rule of magic.

Basil grew older—but alas, no bigger—with the passing of seasons. Reluctantly, he'd come to accept that his body—as unusual as it was—would always stay small. But he absolutely refused to accept the idea that his *life* would also stay small.

There's all of Avalon to discover, he promised himself each morning as he continued to search the slope, rock by rock, for the missing portal. *And all of me to discover, as well.*

At times, as he crawled into crevasses, squeezed between boulders, and followed the dank passageways of streams that tunneled under the stony slope, he'd try to imagine the faraway places he wanted to explore. What did Fireroot look like? Were all the creatures of Airroot as misty as sylphs? Who could survive for long in Shadowroot?

Yet no realm filled his thoughts more often, or more sensuously, than the one he had long called home. Woodroot. The land the elves called El Urien bloomed like a recurrent springtime in his mind. Sometimes, while he probed for the elusive green fire, his thoughts would drift to the forest realm's sights and sounds—and, most of all, its scents. Although he was surrounded by a mountain of rock, he could almost smell the sweet resins of pine and hemlock, the rich aroma of woodland mushrooms, the musty odor of deer prints in a marsh, the snappy scent—almost as strong as ginger—of a newly woven spider's web, and the freshness of rain-washed leaves.

One day, Basil sat on a cliff atop the slope. As he scanned the boulders below, looking for any hint of the portal, he tried—for the thousandth time—to produce that smell of deer prints in a marsh. Sure enough, the smell appeared, hanging over his head like a devoted cloud. But as always, the imitation couldn't compare to reality.

"You're really just a half-witted trickster," he grumbled to himself. The aroma dissipated, carried away by the breeze that constantly swept across the cliff. "What was it that old field mouse in Woodroot used to say? *Smells aren't real. Give me something to swallow.*"

He kicked at the lichen, shredding its edge. A tiny flake of yellow broke off, spun in the air, and drifted away. He watched it go, thinking, *Is that all I am? A tiny little shred . . . carried by forces I can't steer?*

Clamping his tiny teeth around a leaf of lichen, he tore off a bite. It tasted sour, but that fit his mood. Thoughtfully, he chewed.

In the time since he'd seen Merlin on this mountain, he'd often thought about that day. That missed opportunity! Why in Avalon's name had he delayed? Why didn't he explain that his vision of dark wings was much more than a dream? That Merlin's future, as well as his own, was at risk?

Whenever he recalled that encounter, he also wondered about the wizard and his son. About their shared friendship . . . and their shared magic. From what he'd heard from the crows (and one slightly tipsy owl who had sipped some farmer's home-brewed ale), young Krystallus wasn't showing any signs of magical powers. Maybe it was the fact that wizards' powers often skipped generations. Or maybe it was the pressure of an entire world watching and waiting for him to be like his famous father. Either way, it couldn't be easy for the little fellow.

And what of Merlin himself? Basil chewed, recalling the most recent news. The wizard's mother, Elen, who labored for decades to create the faith she called the Society of the Whole, had recently died. A few weeks earlier, Merlin had given her something she dearly treasured: a book of her beloved Cairpré's poems. And this particular book, thanks to an added dose of magic, could read aloud to her, in Cairpré's voice, anytime she opened its cover. So she had spent most of her final days listening to her favorite bard—often joined by Merlin, and also by Rhia, who now wore the spider's silk gown of the High Priestess.

Well done, Merlin, thought Basil. From what he'd seen of her at the wedding, he felt sure that Elen must have been quite ready, after so many years, to join the spirit of her loved one. Nothing would have eased the pain of her last days more than to hear Cairpré's resonant voice—a voice she would soon hear again at last.

Then, remembering what he'd heard about the achingly long journey to the Otherworld, he frowned. "How long will it take her to go all the way to the spirit realm?" he asked aloud.

"Not as long as you might think," declared a profoundly deep voice behind him.

Basil spun around. There, striding toward him on the cliff, was a great stag with a mighty rack of antlers, seven points on each side. The stag's eyes gleamed with extraordinary wisdom, at once radiant and shadowed, brighter than light and deeper than dark.

"Dagda!" he exclaimed, his eyes bulging with surprise. "You're here? You've returned to Avalon?"

"Yes," replied the stag.

"But why?"

"To escort someone to the Otherworld."

The lizard's round ears trembled with awe. "You would really do that?"

"I would indeed," answered the stag. "But only for a mortal of the highest grace and deepest wisdom."

"Elen."

"Yes, little fellow. I have come to take her home." He flicked his tail at a curl of mist that hovered behind him, causing it to separate into three distinct circles. At a glance from the stag, they spun silently away. Each circle of mist floated in a different direction: One flew over the ridge of the mountain; one soared upward to melt into the wispy clouds above; and one, to Basil's astonishment, sailed straight down into the rocks of the cliff where he sat.

At once, Basil realized this could be his chance—maybe his last chance—to find the lost portal! Dagda was, after all, a god. And not only that, he was the leader of the gods— except, of course, for those who followed Rhita Gawr. Surely even now, in mortal form, he retained great magic. Enough, at least, to assist.

"Dagda," he asked anxiously. "I—I need something. Some help."

The rich brown eyes peered at him. And, it seemed, right through him. "What kind of help?"

Basil's tail thumped nervously on the stone beneath him. "I need your—"

Abruptly, he caught himself. For he'd just noticed, beside the stag's head, a strange vibration in the air. All around one antler point, the air quivered, making everything nearby look slightly distorted. Worse, the spot seemed to throb, oozing colors—as if it were an open wound, bleeding something more precious than blood.

"You were saying?" asked the stag, an edge of impatience in his voice. "I must go soon. Time does not dally, even for me."

"It's—um, well . . ." He started to tell Dagda what he was seeing, but doubts suddenly bloomed in his mind. *How could anything be wrong with him? He's immortal, beyond harm.*

The stag stamped his hoof on the rocks; several stones cracked with the force. The message was unmistakable.

Still, Basil couldn't bring himself to say anything. More doubts buzzed in his head, crowding out other thoughts. Wasn't he wasting the great spirit's time? Who did he think he was, anyway, offering advice to a god?

Dagda bobbed his head. "Changed your mind, then? Well, I must go."

The stag turned and began to trot away. Basil watched, his unease swelling rapidly. He watched the air around the antler, pulsing and oozing. *Something's wrong. I know it.*

Forcing himself to speak, he barely managed to croak a single word: "Wait."

Though his voice sounded weak and scratchy, like that of a newborn frog, it carried across the crumbling stones. The stag stopped and slowly turned his head. Impatience showed in the brown eyes, along with something else, unfathomably deep.

"Yes?"

With great effort, Basil forced out some words. "Your . . . antler," he said in a hoarse, strained whisper. "Sick. Wrong. Maybe . . . ev—"

But before he could finish saying *evil*, his whole throat constricted. He gagged, gasping for air. Desperately, he swished his tail, sending broken bits of rock over the cliff's edge. Finally, using all his will, he took a ragged breath. But even then he felt as if an invisible hand was wrapped around his throat, choking him.

Dagda cocked his head. "My antler?"

The invisible hand squeezed tighter. Basil collapsed on the stone. He rolled on the lichen, unable to speak, unable to breathe. His throat felt closed down completely; his tongue seemed as lifeless as a shard of rock.

He struggled, rolling back and forth, kicking his legs in the air. *I've . . . got to breathe! Speak. Warn him.*

Meanwhile, Dagda asked, "What is wrong, little fellow?" But Basil, head buzzing, could barely hear the words, let alone answer them.

The terrible hand squeezed even more. His neck seemed about to break. As he rolled helplessly on the stone, pain surged through him, convulsing his body, twisting his wings. Dark shadows filled his mind, clouding his vision. His lungs felt ready to burst.

That . . . thing. Bad for Dagda! Bad . . . for Avalon.

At that final, disjointed thought, something new bubbled up inside him. It was simple, yet strong, flowing more from his heart than from his mind.

Love. For Avalon, this enchanted world. For Dagda, who had already done so much to protect its many lands and peoples. And for a simple notion, what Merlin famously called *the Avalon idea*: that all creatures of all kinds could live together in harmony, with themselves and with their world.

Deeper than pain, stronger than fear, this love flooded through him. And with it came another feeling: *I have more living to do! Much more.* This new feeling deepened the first, gave it power as well as direction. *I want to live—to do what I can for myself . . . and my world.*

Slowly, very slowly, the grip around his throat began to subside. The anguish relented. He drew a thin, quaking breath. Then a deeper one, and a still deeper one.

Weakly, he rolled back onto his feet. As the dark clouds evaporated before his eyes, he blinked—and found himself gazing straight into the face of Dagda.

The stag nudged him gently with his nose. "You, my little friend, are more than you appear."

With that, the great spirit breathed upon Basil. All at once, the remaining ache in his throat vanished, his chest swelled, and he breathed freely. But Basil didn't pause to celebrate.

"Your antler!" he exclaimed. "The air around it is shaking. And dripping—almost bleeding."

The stag's eyes narrowed. He shook his enormous rack. "Where exactly?"

"The lowest point on the right," he replied, amazed to be talking with ease again.

The stag snorted with fury. "How could I have missed . . ." He halted, then spoke again to Basil, a new urgency in his voice. "A dangerous spell is upon me! There's only one way to break it."

"A spell? Who cast it?"

"Later!" commanded Dagda. "Right now you must help me break it. I cannot do it alone. I need all your great strength—what you used to break that evil grip just now."

Basil shook himself in disbelief, flapping his little wings. "Me? Great strength? You—you must be mistaken."

The stag stamped again, smashing stones with his fury. Gusts of wind whistled across the cliff, raising spirals of dust. "Do not doubt me, little one. Now, will you help?"

"Why yes, of course. What should I do?"

"There is something—or someone—on my antler," the stag declared, his eyes blazing. "He has stolen a ride on me from the Otherworld. And he has blinded me to his presence with a powerful cloaking spell."

Basil gave a brisk nod. "And to remove him?"

"He must first be seen! Only when that happens, shattering his cloak, can he be removed. And then punished."

"How do we see him?"

"It won't be easy. Only someone other than me can do it, since I am the object of the spell. And very few others can succeed. But since you saw the vibrations of his wicked magic—and found the strength to tell me—I believe you can do it."

The stag snorted angrily before continuing. "Just try to pierce through the veil of his magic, to see his mortal form.

The instant you do, his spell will collapse." He nodded, bobbing his great rack, as his voice lowered to a rumble. "I will deal with the rest."

He paused, gazing at Basil. "I must warn you, though. He won't like this. He might attack you again, worse than before."

"Let him try," growled Basil. He thumped his slender tail on the stone for emphasis.

Folding his wings tight against his back, he drew a deep breath. Then, clenching his little jaw, he peered straight at the antler, turning all his strength toward one goal: to see beyond the veil. Carefully, he noted all the shifts in light and color, sensing the most subtle vibrations. He opened his green eyes wide, trying to see through the distortions that shielded this assailant.

Who is it? he wondered. But he couldn't guess. He knew only that this was someone vile enough to attack not just him, but the greatest god of the spirit world.

Layer by layer, he felt his gaze go deeper, plunging into the magic, all the way to its source. A sharp pain exploded in his head, splitting his tiny skull like a bolt of lightning. But he hung on to his goal. Through the searing pain, he continued to look deeper. He would not stop.

All at once, the vibrations ceased. His vision snapped into clarity. And he could see, buried in the fur at the base of the antler, a small but repulsive beast.

"A leech!" he exclaimed. "An ugly, bloodsucking leech."

The instant he said those words, three things happened at once. The leech—a black worm with twisted folds of skin, a circular mouth, and a single bloodshot eye— suddenly straightened. Dagda bellowed in rage, pounding his hooves on the rocks. And, as the leech's eye fixed on Basil and flashed like a ruby, the lizard felt a powerful wave of malevolence.

Basil shuddered, fighting off the urge to retch as his stomach twisted with nausea. Knifepoints jabbed at his scales, his wings, his rounded ears. His head buzzed; his eyes throbbed, swelling inside his head. The pain returned to his skull, making him want to shriek.

Yet throughout all this, he continued to glare at the leech. "How dare you?" he groaned, refusing to turn away. "How dare you . . . attack Dagda?"

"I see you now," boomed the stag, "beneath your wretched disguise! You will regret this treachery, I promise."

Without warning, the leech released his hold with a shrill cry of rage, then sprang into the air. Tumbling on the breeze like a broken twig, the assailant fell behind a jumble of boulders. Almost as quickly, Dagda bounded over to the spot—but by then the leech had completely disappeared.

Basil, whose nausea and pain had ceased instantly when the bloodshot eye looked elsewhere, still felt dizzy and drained. Yet despite his shakiness, he opened his wings and flew over. Landing atop the largest of the boulders, a chunk of gray rock dotted with white quartz crystals, he surveyed the area. No sign of the leech! Watching the stag kick over rocks with his hooves, searching for the attacker, he asked dismally, "Gone?"

"Alas, yes." From the base of the stag's antler, a thin stream of blood trickled. But he seemed otherwise unharmed. His sturdy leg muscles flexed, as if he wanted to race after his enemy and run him into the ground. "At least, thanks to you, I am rid of him."

Discouraged, Basil shook his small head. "I have failed you. What good did all that accomplish if he escaped?"

"A great deal of good," replied the stag. His eyes darkened, like the sky before a storm. "For now I know his name."

18: MAGICAL SIGHT

If you've lived as long as I have, you realize that it's wise never—absolutely never—to answer a tricky question or accept a surprise gift. Unless, of course, you simply can't resist.

W ho is it?" demanded Basil.

With a flap of his batlike wings, he moved across the boulder to be closer to the great stag. As a fresh gust of wind raced across the cliff, whistling ghostly notes, he stretched his face toward Dagda and said: "Tell me."

"That I will," the stag declared with a bob of his antlered head. "First, though, I must tell you something else. Something very important."

Basil blinked his eyes, feeling a strange mixture of uncertainty and amazement. How could it be that this powerful creature, the mortal form of the god of wisdom, was speaking to him—and speaking about matters of importance? Surely there were plenty of wiser, stronger creatures in Avalon who better deserved to occupy Dagda's time.

Yet the great spirit didn't seem to harbor any such

doubts. Gracefully, he bent his muscular neck, lowering his rack, until the tip of his nose was almost touching Basil's. Solemnly, he said, "You, my son, have the Sight."

Basil blinked again. "The what?"

"The Sight. That rare ability to sense magic—even when it is cloaked by spells—that wizards call the Sight." The stag's warm breath poured over Basil's small, scaly body, wrapping him like a protective blanket. "But it is more than a way of seeing. Truly, my little friend, it is a way of living."

Still uncertain, Basil cocked his cupped ears forward. "And I have it?"

"You do, indeed. I can see that this is surprising news for you. And even more surprising, I suspect, is the fact that the Sight is found only in Avalon's most powerful creatures. Wizards have it. Unicorns have it. Some, though not all, dragons have it. But no others—until now."

Nervously, Basil shifted his weight on the boulder. He tapped the tiny knot at the end of his tail against the rock, sending up a thin trail of dust. "You must be mistaken."

Dagda's deep brown eyes observed him. "No, I am not. Just as I am not mistaken about the true identity of that wretched leech."

Reminded of the ugly, bloodsucking beast whose ruby red eye had burned with such vengeance, Basil scowled. "Who?"

"Someone who rode very far upon me, hoping to elude my notice. Someone whose overwhelming desire is to conquer and control. Someone who knows how much I despise his ultimate goals: to invade Avalon, make it his own, and use it as a stepping-stone to conquer mortal Earth."

Basil's throat released a spluttering hiss—his version of a growl. "So that leech is really—"

"Rhita Gawr! Not the warrior god himself, of course,

who is even now raising an army against me and Lorilanda in the Otherworld. No, this is merely his latest mortal incarnation. And much like the god, who so enjoys the taste of blood . . . he chose the form of a bloodsucking leech."

Shaking his snout in disbelief, Basil asked, "Rhita Gawr? Here in Avalon?"

The stag snorted with disdain. "No one else would have acted so wickedly. First he tried to hide from you. Then to strangle you. And when at last you shattered his cloaking spell, to harm you."

Basil cringed, remembering the waves of nausea that had surged through him. The agonizing blast of pain that seared his skull. The sheer malevolence that came from the bloodshot eye.

"I am afraid," Dagda observed, "that you have now made a lasting enemy of Rhita Gawr."

Shaking off the nauseous memory, Basil lifted his small head and said resolutely, "There is no one whose enemy I would rather be."

Though it might have seemed comical, to some, to hear a puny creature with crumpled wings declare himself the foe of an immortal warlord, Dagda didn't laugh. Instead, he declared, "Avalon is fortunate to have your brave heart."

The stag kicked over several more rocks, as if he still hoped to catch a glimpse of the leech. Seeing nothing but lichen-spotted stones, he turned back to Basil. With a sigh, he added, "All too soon, I predict, your brave heart will be needed. And the brave hearts of others, as well. For Rhita Gawr brings only evil to this land."

"I still can't believe he's here in Avalon! Remember what you said at Merlin's wedding? That Avalon was one place that Rhita Gawr had never touched."

The stag shook his head, making his antlers swish through the air. "No more. He is here—and for only one purpose. To conquer this world."

"Can't you stay here? Help us defeat him?"

Somberly, the stag shook his head. "No, my son. That is not my way. Unlike our enemy, I have promised never to break the law of free will—to interfere in the choices made by mortal beings, choices that shape their world."

"But . . ." protested Basil. "Rhita Gawr—"

"Has now been discovered. Your world has been warned." Seeing the doubt written on Basil's face, Dagda went on: "If Avalon is to be saved, if it is to become all it could become—that will require free will. If peace is to prevail over war, if arrogance and greed are to end—that, too, will require free will. For all those worthy goals are built on choices, important choices, that can be made only by mortals such as you."

"Me?" asked the lizard despondently. "What do my choices matter? I'm just a little beast, smaller than a spruce cone, who doesn't even know what he really is."

Dagda watched him for a moment, thinking. Then he said, in a gentle voice, "Your weight may be very small, my friend—but it is yours to use. And even a small weight could be enough to tip the balance of destiny."

Basil looked up at the stag, unsure whether he could really believe such an outlandish idea. Then, as if hearing a dim echo, he remembered what Dagda had said at Merlin's wedding: *Just as the smallest grain of sand can tilt a scale, the weight of one person's will can lift an entire world.*

All at once, Basil's thoughts turned to a different question. Cautiously, he asked, "When you said dragons sometimes have the Sight . . . did you, er—was that a way of saying, ummm . . . that I, crazy as it sounds, am really some sort of—"

"Dragon?" The stag shook his massive rack from side to side and answered decisively. "No. Definitely not."

Though he wasn't at all surprised, Basil couldn't help but feel a slight pang of disappointment. *Any* answer to the question of what he really was, no matter how far-fetched, would have been welcome. And for just an instant, despite everything he knew, he'd almost allowed himself to hope that he might one day be something as big and powerful as a dragon.

"What then," he asked plaintively, "am I? Can you tell me that?"

Dagda studied him with eyes unfathomably deep. "I really cannot say what you really are, or what you might become." His bass voice reverberating on the rocks, he added, "But I am sure of this much: Whatever you may be, you are not a mere dragon."

Basil coughed in surprise. "A mere dragon? They're the most powerful creatures alive! They can—"

"Nevertheless," interrupted Dagda, "you are *something else.*"

Rustling his scrawny wings, Basil demanded, "What?"

Instead of replying, the stag turned and started to trot slowly around the boulder where Basil sat. As he circled, his hooves clacked on the rocks, sending a few of them skittering down the cliff. He seemed to be sizing up the lizard, measuring him in some way that had nothing whatsoever to do with body length. When, at last, he stopped and spoke again, he asked a question—the last question Basil expected.

"What are your dreams, my son?"

Basil started. Surely Dagda didn't want to know about

that terrible dream from long ago! Furrowing his snout, he replied, "You mean my wishes? My longings? I want to know what I am—not just what kind of creature, but what makes me . . . *me*. What makes me, well . . . special."

The stag nodded. "That much I already guessed. No, I meant your dreams that come at night, in your unguarded moments. Call them visions—whether they are beautiful or disturbing." He peered at Basil. "Do you have any dreams of that kind?"

The lizard swallowed. Should he tell? Dagda might be shocked, might lose whatever goodwill he had toward Basil. Too great a risk! Clearing his throat, he answered firmly: "No."

Dagda merely watched him, waiting.

Anxiously, Basil drummed his tail. Though he wasn't sure why, he felt an urge to confide, to trust, in this wise being. "Well . . . yes," he confessed. "I did have one—a truly dreadful one. And it's come back many times over the years."

Dagda continued to wait in silence.

"Merlin was there with me. And—something horrible. A creature with wings. Jagged, bony wings. Like mine, only bigger, darker. It attacked him! It tried to—to . . ." He paused, gathering himself, but when he spoke again his voice was barely a whisper. "To *kill* him."

Basil gazed at the great stag, afraid he had revealed too much. Yet, seeing those rich brown eyes, he decided to say one thing more. "I've always feared," he whispered, "that the creature . . . was really me."

Gusts of wind blew across the cliff, carrying flakes of snow from distant peaks. A timeless moment passed before Dagda responded to what Basil had told him. And when he did respond, it was by saying a single word:

"Beware."

"What?" Basil asked, his voice as shrill as the wailing wind. "Myself? My fears?"

No answer.

"What should I beware?"

"Whatever might diminish you, my son," the stag declared. "Whether it lives within you or without."

The lizard shook his head. "That's not very helpful."

The stag stepped closer. "Perhaps not. But I would, in fact, like to help you—just as you helped me. Without your uncanny Sight, I might have carried that leech much farther, grown weak from loss of blood, or even taken ill from Rhita Gawr's evil toxins."

Coming still closer, he announced, "And so . . . I would like to grant you a boon."

Basil's heart leaped. Instantly, he knew what to ask for. "The portal! It was here, on this slope, then buried by a rock slide. Could you find it for me? And fix it so I can use it to travel?"

"I could," answered the stag. "First, though, tell me where you want to go."

"Everywhere!" Basil jumped into the air as he shouted, landing with a smack of his tail on the boulder. "I want to see all seven realms—and I have five more to go. I want to explore new places, find someone else like me, and on the way, maybe even find . . ."

Dagda tilted his head, waiting to hear how he finished the sentence.

"Myself."

The stag nodded, bobbing his enormous rack. "A worthy destination."

He paused, contemplating. "If I grant you this boon, I will make two requests."

"Name them," said Basil eagerly.

"First, in every realm you visit, I want you to find something."

"A treasure?"

"Of a kind, yes." Dagda's lips curled in a slight grin. "I want you to find . . ."

Basil braced himself, expecting the worst. Whatever the spirit lord wanted him to find, it would not be easy.

"A grain of sand."

Basil blinked, unsure he'd heard correctly. "A . . . what?"

"A single grain of sand, or soil, or rock. A piece of that magical place."

Relieved, the lizard sighed. "Well, that won't be too hard."

"And then," Dagda continued, "I want you to swallow it."

"To *what*?"

"Swallow it, my son. Take into yourself that grain of sand—and whatever secrets it holds." The stag's round eyes gleamed. "You see, I want you to do more than just travel through your world. I want you to *become* your world. Make it yours! Taste it, swallow it whole. Its wonders. Its mysteries. Its secrets."

"Like this?" Basil whipped his tail against one of the boulder's quartz crystals, whose facets had endured so many brutal mountain storms that they had started to splinter and crack. A small sliver of the crystal broke off, sparkling as it flew through the air. With the ease of a practiced hunter of insects, he spun around and snapped his jaws closed. Then he swallowed his prize—a tiny piece of Stoneroot.

Instantly, the light of crystals flashed inside his mind. *I am stone*, declared a deep, rumbling voice, rich and wise with years.

I have burned in the belly of a star, the voice continued, *flowed in a river of lava, inhaled bolts of lightning, and exhaled precious gems. Time has ripped me apart, melted me down, blended me together, compressed me flat, then stretched me tall. Yet I have endured. For I am stone—the body of mountains, the basin of oceans, the birthplace of crystals.*

Basil sat on the stone, blinking with astonishment. He could still hear the faint echoes of the rumbling voice.

Catching his eye, Dagda said approvingly, "Yes. Like that."

"But how—"

"Just consider it part of my gift to you, my son." The stag's head lifted high. The wound at the base of his antler had stopped bleeding, though it remained swollen and discolored.

"You said," prompted Basil, "there were *two* requests?"

"Yes," answered the stag, his expression suddenly grave. "Here is the second."

He glanced around the area again, then stepped so close that his nose nearly touched the lizard's snout. Basil could feel Dagda's warm breath upon his face. When, at last, the spirit lord spoke, it was in the quietest of whispers—and Basil understood immediately that Dagda didn't want to risk the possibility that Rhita Gawr, if he was still nearby, might hear his words.

"Find Merlin," the stag said urgently. "You *must* find Merlin."

Basil looked up at him, puzzled. "To warn him about my dream?"

"That—and more." Dagda's eyes narrowed grimly. "He must be warned that Rhita Gawr has . . ." The stag coughed, as if the words hurt his throat. "Entered Avalon!

Merlin is the one person who can lead all of the peoples of this world—to find the evil spirit, and then to fight if necessary. And Merlin is *also* the one person Rhita Gawr will most want to destroy."

He paused, peering into Basil's green eyes. "So you see . . . all of Avalon is in danger now. But no one—no one—is in greater danger than Merlin."

The lizard gulped. "Do you know where Merlin is now? Which realm?"

Dagda shook his head, then whispered, "He could be anywhere in Avalon—any of the seven realms. But I do know this. He is, right now, searching for a terribly dangerous creature. A kreelix—the greatest mortal foe a wizard can face."

Hearing this, Basil scowled. As if things weren't bad enough already! Cocking his head, he asked, "Could you tell me more? I've never heard of a kreelix."

"That, my son, is because they disappeared long ago. No one had seen one since the last days of Fincayra, and everyone assumed that Avalon was free of them. Until recently! Now one has been sighted, and Merlin has set out to find it—and to stop it from wreaking terrible havoc."

Narrowing his eyes further, Dagda spoke in a half whisper, half growl. "What you need to know is that a kreelix possesses wings—huge, jagged, and bony. It uses them to crush, or even smother, its prey."

Basil shuddered. He moved away, stepping backward on the boulder. "So my dream . . ."

"Could be a vision of the future. Merlin's future."

Deep furrows lined Basil's brow. "I must find him. Must warn him!"

"Indeed you must." The stag hesitated, glancing around once more, then whispered urgently: "The gravest danger of all—the worst nightmare—is if that leech, Rhita Gawr, finds the kreelix before Merlin does! For then Rhita Gawr could give the kreelix greater strength, as well as greater intelligence—something Merlin would never suspect. He would encounter a kreelix more powerful than any wizard has ever known. And the result could be . . ."

"His death," finished Basil grimly.

"One advantage we have," said the stag, "is that the leech does not yet know about the kreelix. So you must move with haste as you search! Yes, even as you remember to swallow one grain of sand from every realm."

Not far from the stag's hooves, hiding in a tiny crack beneath a boulder, a dark creature stirred. Its bloodshot eye burned intensely. For it had learned much of importance. And now, if it succeeded in its plan . . . the fearsome kreelix would soon be joined by a powerful ally. One who feasted on blood.

Unaware of the leech, Basil declared, "I must go. Now."

"Wait," replied the stag, returning to his full, resonant voice. "Before you depart, I must ask you something."

Uncertain what it could be, the lizard asked, "Which is?"

"Your name. Tell me your name."

"Basil. I'm called Basil. But don't ask me why."

The stag's ears swiveled. "From the smell of basil leaves, I would guess. One of your first magical scents, perhaps. Am I right?"

"Y-yes . . . but how did you ever—"

"A lucky guess, my son." From deep in the stag's throat came a sound like a satisfied chuckle. "And now, my good Basil, it is time for us to part. I must go to Elen, to guide her to the Otherworld. And you must start your search . . . wherever it may lead."

Grimly, the lizard nodded. "Wherever it may lead."

"Farewell, good Basil." Flexing his powerful legs, the stag whirled around, stamping his hooves so hard that stones splintered beneath them. He started to pace away, his gait quickening to a gallop across the cliff.

"Wait!" cried Basil, suddenly alarmed. "What about the portal?"

Dagda stopped. Swishing his antlers through the air, he turned back around. "You won't be needing that," he declared, a strange gleam in his brown eyes.

"But how—" protested Basil, waving his little wings.

"There are other ways to travel," said Dagda. "Some of them are slow . . . and others are fast—as fast as the wind."

19: TIME TO FLY

Journeys take endlessly varied forms. They are the ultimate shape-shifters. Only one thing do all journeys have in common: Somewhere, perhaps when you least expect it, they begin.

Instantly, a warm breeze swept over Basil, filling his lungs and fluttering his wings. The smell of cinnamon tickled his nostrils. Fresh wind encircled him, whirling constantly: an airy embrace.

"Hello again, little hhhwanderer."

"Aylah!" shouted Basil, so delighted he jumped off the crystalline boulder and landed on a rock at the very edge of the cliff. Small shards broke off and tumbled down the steep walls, clattering noisily. "I'm so glad to see—er, *feel*—you again. I've missed you."

"And I have missed you, little hhhwanderer. Though I have traveled many places, even farahhhway hhhworlds, I have thought of you often."

"Faraway worlds?" asked Basil, amazed, as Aylah wrapped an invisible knot of air around his tail. "I shouldn't be surprised, I suppose. You did tell me, long ago, that you're a ceaseless traveler."

"As hhhwatchful as the stars, as restless as the hhh-wind," she whispered in his ear. "Now, though, I am here at your side. For Dagda summoned me, hhhwanting me to take you on a journey."

At the mention of the great spirit's name, Basil turned to the spot on the cliff where he'd been standing only a moment before. But Dagda, in the form of a mighty stag, had bounded off. No sign of him—or the evil leech who had clung to his antler—remained.

As much to himself as to the wind sister, Basil muttered, "I hope Avalon will be all right."

"As do I, little hhhwanderer." The cinnamon scent grew stronger as Aylah brushed past his face. "For this is the hhhworld between all hhhworlds, a bridge hhhwhere all magic meets."

"But Aylah . . . Rhita Gawr is here! In Avalon! I saw him—in a strange sort of way. Disguised as a bloodthirsty leech. Believe me, Aylah. He's *here*."

The swirling wind grew colder, frosting Basil's ears. "That is dreadful news, little hhhwanderer. Dreadful beyond hhhwords. Avalon is in grave danger."

"There's more," the lizard snarled. He drew a sharp breath. "Merlin's in danger, too. He's searching for a kree-lix, right now, in one of the realms."

"A kreelix?" The wind sister gusted doubtfully, shaking Basil's snout. "They are gone, little hhhwa—"

"No more!" His tail pounded the rock, making it tee-ter on the cliff's edge. "One has been seen. Dagda told me so! And Merlin's searching for it, looking everywhere. We need to find him before—"

"Rhita Gahhhwr finds the kreelix," finished Aylah,

blowing decisively against his back. "Or else that leech could join hhhwith the kreelix, making it more pohhhwerful than ever."

In the darkness beneath a nearby boulder, a wormlike creature twisted its circular mouth. Its body trembled in what might have been a silent, sneering laugh. But its lone bloodshot eye burned with unfathomable hatred.

Basil nodded at the wind sister's words. Then his ears turned with a question. "What exactly makes kreelixes so dangerous? Dagda called them *the greatest mortal foe a wizard can face.*"

"Indeed they are," said Aylah with a sudden rush of air. "I hhhwill tell you hhhwhy, but later. Right nohhhw hhhwe must go! I hhhwill carry you, lifting your hhhwings."

Basil nodded gratefully. He stretched out his wings to the fullest. They resembled two ragged leaves; as the wind blew faster, they started to rustle.

"Hhhwhere do hhhwe start to look? Hhhwhat place do hhhwe go?"

"Every place! Aylah, we can't stop until we find Merlin. Wherever he is." His green eyes flamed. "We'll look in every realm. We'll fly all the way around the Great Tree, searching the whole world, if we must."

The wind fluttered, breathing warmly all around him. "You are truly a hhhwanderer, my friend."

With a gentle gust, she tapped his nose. "But you underestimate the size of your hhhworld. Even if hhhwe took many years, hhhwe could never see the hhhwhole Tree. Never! There are realms deep hhhwithin the trunk, and countless branches reaching starhhhward, that no one has ever explored."

She paused, and the wind fell still. All at once, she blew again, more strongly than before.

"Our best hope to find him," she declared, "is to move fast, soaring high above the root realms. I can see far, very far, searching for any sign of the hhhwizard. So hhhwe can look—but only as hhhwe hhhwhoosh past, flying like the hhhwind, never stopping."

Basil shook his snout. "I *must* stop, though. Just briefly."

"Hhhwhy?"

"I promised Dagda." He hesitated, recalling the rumbling voice of Stoneroot. "Promised him I'd taste—actually swallow—a bit of every realm."

Aylah buffeted him. "To take some of Avalon's magic into yourself?"

He gave an uncertain nod. "I don't know why, exactly. Or what good it does me. But I did promise."

"Then do it you shall, little hhhwanderer. Although it hhhwill delay us a bit, Dagda must have his reasons."

"What reasons, though? He's asking me to slow our search. To endanger Merlin—and also Avalon. For what?"

A windy voice rushed past his ear. "For your future, perhaps."

Basil frowned. How could anyone, even Dagda, have an idea of his future?

"Shall hhhwe?" urged the wind sister.

In answer, he slapped his feet against the lichen-covered rock, unsure where—or when—he would touch the ground again. "All right," he proclaimed. "Time to fly!"

20: MUD

What you see is temporary. What you cannot see is eternal. That's why I always prefer to look with eyes closed . . . and heart open.

Suddenly, with a rush of wind, Basil's feet left the rock. Warm air encircled him, buoying him, ruffling the edges of his ears. Then, all at once, he was flying—without any effort, without even a beat of his outspread wings. The cliff where he'd met Dagda shrank beneath him, becoming a mere wrinkle on the mountain ridge; the boulders where he'd lived so long diminished swiftly, becoming just a mass of pebbles.

High into the sky Aylah carried him, supporting his bony wings with her vast, invisible form. At first, he felt unstable, as if he should be doing more to keep himself aloft by flapping his wings, steadying his tail against turbulence, or banking his every turn. Soon, though, he gained more confidence. He could still turn or even dive if he chose, but he simply trusted Aylah to carry him wherever she wanted.

All he had to do was keep his wings open—and ride the wind.

"Hhhwest to east hhhwe shall fly," breathed Aylah's voice. "Until hhhwe find him! Even if hhhwe must go all the hhhway around the Great Tree. Is that hhhwhat you hhhwant, little hhhwanderer?"

Basil only nodded. Yet his expression of stern resolve showed the slightest hint of a grin. Here he was, sailing on wings infinitely wider than his own, riding on the back of the breeze. *Yes, Aylah. This is what I want.*

Currents of snow-chilled air, rising from the mountains below, buffeted his wings. He looked down, studying the landscape. There, towering above the rest of Olanabram's high peaks, stood the immense, snowy summit where Merlin and Hallia had been married. Across his mind flashed memories of their wedding, and all the creatures he'd seen there—ranging from a tiny light flyer, as small as a wind-blown spark, to the giant Shim, as huge as a hillside. A sylph . . . a clan of deer people . . . a fire angel. And that dragon, Gwynnia, with her nasty little offspring.

Basil gazed down at the mountains, which gleamed as if they were made more of light than rock. And at the shining glaciers of the Dun Tara snowfields. Even the feathery backs of the eaglefolk, soaring along the ridges far below, radiated light.

This brightness didn't fade as Aylah's warm wind carried him higher. All of Stoneroot seemed to shine. The immense circle of stones that was the heart of Elen's sacred compound looked as luminous as a ring of fire. The neighboring fields, home to bell-ringing farmers and animals, glowed like large green lanterns.

"Light is really part of this realm," he mused, squinting

at the radiant landscape. Now he understood why he'd seen a brilliant flash at the very instant he swallowed that piece of crystal and heard the words *I am stone.*

"Stars shine the brightest on Stoneroot, more than any other root-realm," Aylah replied. "Many hhhwonder hhh-why, but only the hhhwind sisters can explain it."

"Can you tell me?" he asked eagerly.

"No, I cannot. My sisters and I have promised not to reveal that secret to anyone." Then she added, after nudging him with a gentle gust, "Perhaps you hhhwill be the first of your kind to go to the stars, great explorer. Then you, too, hhhwill knohhhw hhhwhy."

Basil, though, had stopped thinking about the stars. That phrase *of your kind* rang in his ears. Just what kind was that? He might never know. After his conversation with Dagda, he knew that he wasn't related to dragons. But to what species *was* he related? Would he never see someone like himself? Or find out who his parents were? Or, for that matter, whether he had any parents at all?

The sudden roar of a rockfall shook him out of his thoughts. Having spent so many years among loose stones that could crush anyone who happened to be in their way, he instantly turned to the source of the sound. Strangely, it hadn't come from down below, in the mountains—but from somewhere higher, right at his altitude. How could that possibly be? There weren't any rocks way up here!

Puzzled, he peered in the only direction that wasn't crystal clear sky, at a thick wall of mist rising upward from the northernmost peaks. Then, through some gaps in the mist, he glimpsed patches of brown. Rocky cliffs!

Gradually, the mist shredded, revealing more of the cliffs—impossibly tall, dreadfully steep. Rows of dark brown ridges climbed straight up, higher and higher, far above Basil's head. *The trunk,* he realized in awe. *I'm looking at the trunk of the Great Tree.* He craned his neck, gazing upward, but he couldn't even begin to see how high those cliffs ultimately rose. All he could tell was that, somewhere far above him, they faded into the swirling mist. He tried to imagine, much higher still, the Tree's enormous branches reaching toward the stars.

Turning his gaze back to the realm below, he tried to guess how fast he was flying. Much faster than he'd ever flown before, that was certain! Way down on the grasslands near the southern marshes, he spied a pair of trolls—not quite as big as giants, but easily recognized by their rounded backs and hunched posture—running after a band of smaller creatures that looked like gnomes. Within seconds, Basil had left them all behind. He then spotted a herd of black oryx galloping eastward with the speed of antelope, their long straight horns stabbing the air with every bound. Barely a heartbeat later, Basil had caught up to them and flown past. Only an enormous canyon eagle, who was also riding the wind, kept pace.

"Alas, little hhhwanderer," said Aylah. "I see no sign of Merlin, as far as I have looked across this realm. Hhhwe must look further, keep going."

Despite the seriousness of her point, Basil didn't feel dismayed. "Yes," he agreed, "we must keep going."

Before long, the rugged eastern edge of Stoneroot came into view. Beyond that lay a sea of shadowy mist, where strange shapes constantly arose, shifted, and vanished. Dragons' heads formed and then shrank down to nothingness; noble birds started to fly, but their wings suddenly warped into bent, crooked twigs. Soaring above the dark mist, Basil couldn't shake the feeling that those shapes were more than random images—that they were, in fact, mocking him.

One formation, shaped like a lizard's head, grew to enormous size, then opened its gargantuan jaws. Out of the gaping mouth poured a thin wisp of vapors that quickly coalesced into a tiny egg. The egg cracked open and started to suck into itself the lizard's ears, eyes, and snout. Before long, the entire head had disappeared. Then, all of a sudden, a long tongue of mist reached out and wrapped around the egg, squeezing tight. The tongue compressed, strangling the egg—until, at last, it exploded into thousands of vaporous teardrops.

"Look not for long into the mists, little hhhwanderer," whispered Aylah. Her cinnamon smell grew stronger, sharper. "They reveal no future but their ohhhwn."

With effort, Basil tore his gaze from the shifting images. Lifting his sights, he saw, beyond the mist, the first hint of a brown, rolling coastline. Mudroot! Somewhere down there lived Aelonnia, the tall, graceful, and deeply mysterious creature he'd met at Merlin and Hallia's wedding. Could she actually make living creatures out of the mud? It just didn't seem possible.

Maybe, he suddenly wondered, the mudmakers had also made *him*? But no—he'd been born in Woodroot, not Mudroot. And besides, Aelonnia would surely have said something if he'd been one of her people's creations.

As Basil, borne by the wind, flew over the coastline, what he saw erased any question that this was indeed the realm of Malóch. That name, in the language of Lost Fincayra used by bards and mapmakers, meant simply *land of mud*. And there could be no better name for this place. As far as he could see stretched brown plains, with no trees or rocks. And no sign of Aelonnia's people anywhere. Except for some scattered brown mounds, a few glittering springs, and some triangular holes that were surrounded by odd, intricate markings, this land consisted of nothing but mud. Unbroken expanses of mud.

"I need to go down there," he said without much enthusiasm. "To keep my promise."

"This realm does not hhhwelcome strangers easily," the wind sister warned, slowing their flight over the muddy expanses.

"Oh, come on," Basil replied. "It doesn't look at all dangerous. Just, well, muddy. Very muddy."

"You should knohhhw by nohhhw," she whispered, whooshing around him, "things are not alhhhways hhhwhat they seem. As far as the hhhwind may blow, it is not as far as the distance between hhhwhat appears and hhhwhat is real."

Basil, strangely touched by her words, didn't reply. Perhaps, he wondered, Aylah herself was really more than she seemed.

"Set me down anyway," he said at last. "Just for a moment."

"Are you sure, little hhhwanderer? Perhaps hhhwe should stop at some, but not all, the realms? To save time in searching for Merlin! Besides, the realm of Airroot, hhhwhere hhhwe go next, is much safer."

Basil ground his teeth. "No, I promised Dagda."

"Ahhh," the wind sister sighed. "Then there is no swaying you."

"Right. But I'll be quick, so we can get back to searching." He jabbed the air with his right wing. "Let's try over there, by that triangular hole. I want to see what those markings are."

Wavering with uncertainty, she carried him lower. As they neared the dark opening, she slowed, then stopped, so Basil could steer himself. With a few flaps of his wings, he swooped down to the ground, landing on a low brown mound near the hole. All around him, the strange markings curled across the mud, making twisted patterns that looked almost like writing. Some parts of the patterns were as wide as deer paths; others were as slim as the tracks of snakes.

Peering closely at the patterns, he noticed another kind of mark in the mud. Footprints! They dotted the ground, especially near the edges of the hole. Though many were only faintly visible, he could tell they were larger than bear prints, with three toes apiece. *Who made these? And what's the meaning of these patterns?* Glancing over at the hole, he realized it probably wasn't a good idea to wait around here to find out. Best to fulfill his promise and then leave.

Spreading his wings, he jumped off the mound and landed on the soil beside the opening. High above his head, the wind gusted, making a sound like a worried sigh. But Basil didn't pay any attention. His mind was focused on the unappetizing notion of swallowing some mud.

Gingerly, he sniffed the moist ground. Surprisingly, it didn't smell like the mud he remembered from the stream banks of Woodroot. While it held aromas of moisture and rich soil, it also smelled of . . . something else. Something fiercely wild, yet unmistakably familiar. Weighty with age, yet curiously young.

Cautiously reaching out his tongue, he touched its tip to the ground. He took a tiny fleck of soil. And then swallowed.

I am new as springtime and old as starlight, said a vibrant, female voice inside his head, as a veil of deep brown colored his vision. *The magic of life, the miracle of birth, the serenity of death . . . they all reside in me. Along with another kind of magic—oh yes! a gift from Merlin himself—that fills me with the seven sacred elements. The essence of breath. The power of creation.* The brown veil deepened, darkened. *For I am mud.*

Gradually, Basil's vision cleared. Everything seemed as before—the brown soil surrounding him, the twisted patterns on the ground. Yet now the mud seemed to sparkle with its own inner magic. And in the depths of his mind he heard that voice again: *the magic of life . . . the power of creation.*

With a flap of his wings, he flew back up to the mound to have a better look at the patterns. He caught his breath. The patterns, like the mud, looked different now. He could read them! Gazing down at the intricate scrawl, he read aloud, his scratchy voice adopting a strange new cadence.

"All now must praise him, Gabbledar king! Enter his Underlands, worship the darkness. Seek only service, protect all his Gnomes. Kill those who threaten, spare nothing at all."

Swallowing hard, he stopped. Gnomes! So it was they who dug this tunnel. Who marked the mud with this warning. Who built their society on a simple, cruel idea: *Kill those who threaten, spare nothing at all.*

So engrossed in thought was he that he didn't notice the hint of movement in the shadowy mouth of the tunnel. Nor the odor, vaguely salty, that entered the air. Nor the keening gusts of wind on high.

All at once, shrieks and howls erupted. Three squat gnomes, wearing armbands and loincloths, burst out of the tunnel. Their jaws, wide with rage, showed jagged, flesh-tearing teeth. Though only half the height of humans, their muscular bodies exuded strength. Burly arms held stone axes and deadly spears.

Screaming wildly, they leaped at Basil. He didn't even have time to open his wings before grimy, three-fingered hands grabbed his body. And squeezed hard.

At that instant the mound beneath him began to quake. Its smooth brown surface rippled and bubbled—then, all at once, expanded. From the size of a tree stump it shot upward, swiftly growing to the size of the gnomes, then double that height, then double again. Four arms sprouted from its sides, each with immensely long fingers. At the top, a head emerged from rounded shoulders. Deep-set eyes, dark brown, appeared above a curving mouth.

The mudmaker roared, scattering the gnomes. With all four arms waving, the enormous creature stepped toward the tunnel, feet squelching in the mud. Dropping Basil, the frightened gnomes plunged back into their hole, their screeches echoing from inside the tunnel.

Gratefully, Basil gazed up at the tall being who had appeared so suddenly. Still panting with fright, he exclaimed, "Aelonnia! It's you."

"Again we meet," she said in her rich, resonant voice. She gracefully bent lower, peering at him with her brown eyes. "No greater in size are you . . . but now, perhaps, greater in wisdom."

Basil shook himself, nose to tail, unable to banish the feeling of muddy hands clutching him. "Not much, I'm afraid." He blinked up at her. "Thank you, Aelonnia. Always a pleasure to see you. Especially since you seem to have a knack for saving my life."

"A life worth saving, I believe it is."

Remembering those words from long ago, he stiffened. "That's what Aylah told me."

"This time, perhaps, you hhhwill believe the hhh-words."

The mudmaker's eyes turned upward. "And here now she is, that same sister of the wind."

"Hohhhw good to be hhhwith you again, Aelonnia," her voice whispered.

"And with you, my restless friend." Turning back to Basil, the mudmaker warned, "Dally not, little one. The gnomes—come back soon they will, with more warriors and weapons. Leave now, you should, to avoid the danger."

Scowling, he shook his head. "They aren't the real danger. Rhita Gawr is here in Avalon! It's true, Aelonnia. I saw him, disguised as a leech, in Stoneroot."

The mudmaker's entire body stiffened. Only her slender fingers moved, weaving through the air. "Rhita Gawr? Here?"

Basil nodded grimly. "Dagda told me to warn everyone. Especially Merlin."

Her fingers froze. "Here he was, only three days ago."

"Three days!" Basil shivered, snout to tail, with excitement. Looking upward, he asked, "Aylah, can we catch him?"

"I am not sure, little hhhwanderer. A hhhwizard can move as fast as the hhhwind. But I hhhwill surely try."

"Searching, he was," said Aelonnia. Her long fingers moved again, making mysterious patterns, as if tying invisible threads together. "For a terrible—"

"Kreelix," finished the lizard. "I can't believe he was just here!"

The mudmaker's fingers pulled an invisible knot. "Missed him just barely, you did."

"Did he say where he was going?"

"No, speak of that he did not."

Basil growled from deep in his throat—a small sound, but full of intensity. "I will find him."

Swaying from side to side, Aelonnia promised, "Spread the word, I shall! From the plains of Isenwy to the jungles of Africqua. Know will the people of this realm that Rhita Gawr has arrived! All must beware."

Gazing down at him, she added in a gentle tone, "Seen many large things, have you, for someone so small. Wonder, I do, whether you are really—"

A chorus of wrathful shrieks came out from the tunnel, cutting her off. "Go now we must!" declared Aelonnia. Instantly, she strode off, her enormous feet squelching noisily.

"Wait!" Basil called. "Can't you finish . . ." But his words were lost in the powerful wind that swept across the ground, lifting him into the air.

21: STARLIGHT

*What is starlight, anyway? Its birthplace is the stars, to be
sure. But its home, its dwelling place, is far away—across
the great reaches of the sky, in the eyes of every person
who gazes, in wonder, at the stars.*

Basil rose into the sky, riding the wind once more.
His thoughts, though, remained in Mudroot. What
had Aelonnia started to say? Was he, like the mud of that
realm, harboring some secret down inside? How would he
ever find out?

He shook himself, so hard his wings slapped the wind.
Right now, you've got more pressing things to think about.
Merlin was near! Yet the wizard, pursuing his foe, was
completely unaware of the much greater foe who wanted to
destroy him—and conquer Avalon.

"Starset hhhwill come soon, little hhhwanderer."

Aylah's soothing voice brought him back to the present.
He turned his gaze skyward. Through the tracery of brown-
tinted clouds, he could almost make out the first few stars,
harbingers of night. Now he waited, as he'd done so many

evenings before on the rocky ridges of Stoneroot, to see the flash of golden light that would mark the day's end.

There! Golden light burst across the sky, illuminating thousands of stars—an explosion of radiance that made Basil feel as if his whole world lay within an enormous crystal cave. An instant later, all those stars grew suddenly dimmer—and instantly more visible. For in Avalon, where the stars illuminated the sky all day, it was only at night, after they had dimmed, that their individual positions became clear.

Why did the stars dim at the end of every day? And why did they grow bright once again every morning? These were questions that had, since the very birth of this world, filled many a stargazer's mind—and many a bard's ballad. But such questions really boiled down to one basic puzzle: What was the true nature of Avalon's stars?

Basil worked his slim jaw. "Aylah, I may never know much about the stars, but I do know this. They're beautiful—more beautiful than anything I've ever seen."

"Come, little hhhwanderer. I hhhwill shohhhw you more." She carried him higher, rising upward in a spiraling swell. He glanced down at Mudroot, far below. From this altitude, he could see the whole eastern coastline, all the way to the knife-edge ridge that bards called the Cliffs Perilous.

Gazing upward again, he traced the outlines of his favorite constellations. There was the straight row of seven exceptionally bright stars that people had started to call the Wizard's Staff. And there, the Twisted Tree, whose curling branches stretched halfway across the sky. Now he could see the perfect circle of stars that lay within a larger circle, the constellation that Elen herself had named the Mysteries.

The wind sister stopped spiraling upward and leveled out. With a whoosh of air that ruffled Basil's wings, she started to soar eastward again across the muddy plains. But her passenger barely noticed the change. He'd turned his full attention to a remarkable new sight, something he had never been high enough to see before.

"Look there, Aylah! A line of light that cuts across the sky."

"Hhhwell done," she breathed in his ear. "You have found something that very fehhhw mortals have seen. That is the River of Time."

"It's a river?" He studied the luminous line that sliced through dozens of constellations. "It looks more like . . . well, a kind of seam in the sky."

Aylah chuckled, bouncing him on bursts of wind. "The Talihhhwonn people, fabric hhhweavers who live high up in the branches, have thought the same. They call the River *the seam in the tent of the sky.*"

Incredulous, Basil asked, "There are people up there? On the branches?"

"Hhhwondrous people," she replied, flying faster than ever. "And the River of Time really is a sort of seam. For it divides the halves of time, past and future, hhhwhile alhhhways flohhhwing in the present."

Though Basil didn't understand her words, he could feel her awe at the wonders above. Awe that he shared. For the first time in his life, he realized that the stars weren't really objects outside of his world. They were *connected* to his world, and to everyone in it. Including himself.

Gazing up at the boundless blanket of stars, he realized something else. They made him feel small—not in the way he'd felt his whole life, from the moment he first crawled out of his egg, but in a more profound way. He felt small, not just in size, but in importance. Humbled. And yet, at the same time, he felt large. Bigger than he'd ever thought possible. For as tiny as he was, he was still connected to the stars, still touched by their light.

How could he feel both incredibly small and amazingly large—at once? He couldn't explain it. He could only . . . feel it.

So this is the gift of the stars, he thought. To feel humbled by the vastness of creation—and also enlarged by his living connection to it.

"The nehhhwest realm is near," announced Aylah. Her breathy voice called Basil out of his reverie. He turned to look at the strange new vista as she started to descend, carrying him downward like a falling star.

22: Aeolian Harps

Illusions, though completely unreal, can still be annoying. Maybe even a little troublesome. Especially when they try to kill, maim, or devour you.

Riding the wind, Basil flew downward. Air rushed past him, fluttering his ears, whistling a windblown chorus. Lightning itself, he felt, couldn't fly any faster.

He gazed at the strikingly different scene below. Mudroot had receded, now just a dark brown smudge on the western horizon. Another realm approached rapidly. Even in the dimmer light of this starlit evening, he could tell that he was about to encounter an entirely new landscape.

Truth is, he thought as the wind whistled past his face, *it's not a landscape at all. It's a cloudscape.*

Below him stretched Airroot, homeland of the sylphs, who were themselves essentially clouds that had come alive. He recalled again the one he'd seen floating above Merlin's wedding. And he remembered that the sylphs' name for this realm, Y Swylarna, meant *mist haven*.

What name could fit this place better? he mused.

Clouds of every size and shape drifted nearby or massed in the misty distance, forming broad plains, rumpled hills, or towering peaks that gleamed in the starlight. Crisscrossing the plains lay broad avenues, paved with pure white clouds that looked as solid as marble. Cloudcake! He'd heard about it years ago (without believing a word, since it seemed so unlikely) from a bard who explained that cloudcake came from the very bottom of the Air Falls of Silmannon, where centuries of pounding had smashed the clouds into something as hard as rock. And now . . . there it was, right before his eyes: a web of streets made entirely from clouds.

"Look!" he cried, suddenly noticing some thin, glistening strands that stretched between two clouds. He pointed his wing. "That looks like—like a bridge."

"And so it is, little hhhwanderer. Sylphs don't alhhhways fly upon the hhhwind, you knohhhw. Sometimes they prefer to roll across the clouds, hhhwrapping themselves in fresh, nehhhwly made mist. So they make bridges, hhhwoven from strands of cloudthread."

Basil watched the ethereal bridge pass beneath them. Then he spied a massive, undulating cloud whose misty slopes held thousands of spiky pinnacles that resembled trees. Each of them glittered with the light of stars, turning the whole cloud into a vast, vaporous constellation. "What's—"

"The great Forest Afloat," answered the wind sister, anticipating his question. "Those are eonia-lalo trees, hhhwhose hhhwood is lighter than air."

Shifting direction with a sudden gust, Aylah swung southward, so that Basil now faced an enormous, many-layered cloud that was streaked with bright colors. So many colors radiated from the cloud, with such intensity, that even at night it seemed to be wrapped in rainbows.

Eerie blues, incandescent yellows, amber oranges, vibrant greens, haunting purples—all these and more shone from this misty palette.

"The cloud gardens," explained Aylah with a sigh of admiration. "Tended by thousands of hhhwhite mist faeries, since the very first days of Avalon. Their hhhwings are alhhhways a blur, and their heads are alhhhways adorned hhhwith silver bells."

As Aylah slowly turned back to the east, Basil caught sight of a stormy maelstrom in the distance. Its dark, lumbering clouds crackled constantly with lightning. Then, down below, he spotted a group of small, translucent clouds sailing together above the gardens. *No*, he realized. Those weren't clouds at all, but sylphs—a whole flock of them, barely visible in the evening light. Like living shadows, they floated across the sky.

Abruptly, Basil caught his breath. For he'd just noticed, beyond the sylphs, a misty valley that held cloudlike creatures of a different kind. These creatures didn't fly; rather, they twirled. Thin, graceful spirals of vapor rose high into the air, spun slowly in the starlight, and then melted back down into the valley—only to rise once again, spinning together in a stately circle. Never pausing, these living spirals danced to music only they could hear.

He watched, feeling the wind rush over his face, which made his ears flap against his cheeks. And he grinned, for he knew without being told that he'd come across a place made famous by bards: the Dancing Grounds of the Mist Maidens.

All at once, he heard a faint lilting sound. It came from somewhere in the deep distance of the cloudscape. Like audible starlight, it brightened and defined its surroundings. Here was a sound just as beautiful as this realm.

"Harp strings," he said dreamily, listening to the long, sweeping notes. They rippled with overtones that seemed to make harmonies with the realm itself. "Where are they?"

"Far, far ahhhway," answered Aylah. She paused as the notes swelled louder, receded, then rose again with tender sweetness. "Those are aeolian harps, made by the sylphs to sing hhhwith every breeze. Hhhwondrous threads of hhhwoven vapors are their strings, stretched bethhhween clouds so tightly that the merest breath of a baby sylph hhh-will pluck them. And hhhwhen a strong hhhwind blohhhws through them, their notes hhhwill carry across the realm. Hhhwhat is more, those magical strings hhhwill sense the emotions of hhhwhoever hears them."

"Really?"

"On my hhhword," she replied, skirting the edge of a heavy cloud. "Hhhwhatever you are feeling—joy, fear, rage, love—the strings hhhwill echo those emotions."

As if on cue, the harp strings swelled louder. A new wave of surprise and delight washed over Basil, while the harps sang exuberantly. The very air vibrated with gladness.

"Such music," he said with a sigh.

"Yes," agreed Aylah. "Those harps are the essence of magic."

Suddenly reminded of Merlin, Basil's worries abruptly returned. "Any sign of the wizard? Any sign at all?"

"No, little hhhwanderer. As far as I can see, no trace of him. I do hope he has not met some hhhwickedness."

Just at that instant, Basil glimpsed a huge, shadowy head rising out of a dark bank of clouds on the horizon. Higher the fearsome head lifted, showing immense, teeth-studded jaws. The creature's eyes, glowing red, turned toward him—and flashed angrily.

"A dragon!" he cried.

At that instant, the distant harp strings shifted to harsh, jangling tones that swelled louder by the second. Yet Aylah said nothing. She continued to fly toward the dark, brooding cloud bank—and the terrible beast rising from it. The dragon's eyes pulsed like fiery wounds, while its tongue slithered, caressing the terrible teeth.

"Aylah, can't you see?" Basil thrust both his wings to the fore, fighting to hold them against the wind. "Look where I'm pointing!" he shouted. "There!"

Ahead, the dragon's head gleamed darkly in the evening light. Now its whole neck, studded with bloodred scales, reached toward them. The gruesome jaws opened wide.

Still she said nothing.

"Aylah, look! Ahead of us!"

"I see no dragon, little hhhwanderer."

Agitated, heart pounding, Basil tried to beat his wings against the rushing wind. "How can you say that? It's—"

"Not there," she declared.

He froze. "Not . . . there? But I see it!"

"Hhhwhat you see is not a dragon, not at all. That dark bank of clouds is the Veil of Illusion, one of the strangest parts of this realm."

"But it looks . . ." he began, as harp strings twanged uncertainly in the background.

"So real," finished the wind sister, gliding heedlessly toward the cloud bank. "That is hhhwhat the Veil does. It takes the form of hhhwhatever you most fear."

Basil swallowed. "My fears *made* that?"

"Yes, my hhhwanderer. Fears, like dreams, can take lives of their ohhhwn."

Don't I know, he thought, recalling his dreadful dream about Merlin's death—a dream he still couldn't understand, let alone shake from his mind.

Glancing nervously at the dragon, he told himself sternly, *Worry about something real, will you? Like what Rhita Gawr is doing in Avalon. Or his plans for Merlin.*

Remarkably, the dragon's image started to soften. It seemed less substantial by degrees. Even its fiery red eyes now looked more like rosy mist.

Basil tried to believe it had been just an illusion. Still not completely convinced, he demanded, "All right then, tell me. What do *you* see up ahead?"

"Hhhwhy, I see exactly hhhwhat I always see hhh-when I fly over the Veil—the long, bony clutches of a hhhwindtaker."

"Windtaker?"

"The only creature in Avalon hhhwho can harm a hhh-wind sister." She sighed, and the harp strings plucked some somber notes. "I lost a lifelong friend to those clutches. That hhhwas ages ago, but it still aches like yesterday."

Air rushed over Basil as he nodded sympathetically. Peering at the cloud bank, he concluded she'd been right. The dragon, so frightening only seconds before, was fast melting away.

As Aylah spoke again, the harp music brightened a little. "Hhhwe have no need to fear illusions, my friend."

Sure enough, the dragon was almost entirely gone. All that remained were a few pearly white fingers of mist that seemed to grope toward the sky.

Remembering his promise to Dagda, Basil furrowed his snout. "How am I supposed to taste the soil of this realm? Eat a chunk of cloudcake?"

"Not necessary," answered the wind sister. "Here, the soil in hhhwhich everything grohhhws is the mist itself. Just open your mouth hhhwide, and drink in its magic."

With a nod, he opened his jaws. Moisture quickly gathered on his tongue. He swallowed—and a strange inner wind blew deep inside his mind.

I move, I change, I always grow. For mine is the soul of becoming. The voice, as soft as a faraway whisper, filled his head fully—just as air fills a cavern. *I shift, I blossom, I move without bounds. My breath is your breath, my body your blanket, my season your song.*

The whispering voice paused—and then returned with three final gusts. *I . . . am . . . air.*

For some time, Basil said nothing, and Aylah didn't disturb him. Without paying much attention, he glanced again at the long fingers of mist below them. For some reason, they didn't seem to be fading away. Even now, they were reaching slowly toward them, stretching across the wind-blown clouds. He shrugged, knowing it was merely the image Aylah had described.

"Well now," he asked, "what realm is next?"

"Fireroot hhhwill soon—" She caught herself, rising higher to get a better view. "Merlin! I see him!"

"Where?" shouted Basil, straining to catch a glimpse. His heart pounded with excitement.

The wind sister accelerated, whooshing past the clouds. "To the east, very far ahhhway. Yes! I am certain it's him."

The lizard's eyes, opened to their widest, watered from the rush of air. Yet still he couldn't see anything but clouds and more clouds.

Aylah shuddered, jostling him on the currents. "He is chasing something! Yes—something dark."

Instinctively, Basil glanced back at the dark bank where he'd seen the dragon. But his attention was drawn to another cloud formation, one that suddenly puzzled him.

"Aylah," he called, "did you say a cloud illusion can only be seen by the person who fears it?"

"Yes, but nohhhw hhhwe have more urgent—"

"Then why," he interrupted, his voice rising in fright, "do I see those bony fingers down there?"

All at once, the fingers leaped toward them. Distant harps jangled. Aylah gasped and shot forward even faster—just as a beast shaped like a monstrous hand snapped closed on the spot where they'd been an instant before. The wind sister raced ahead, battering Basil with gale-force winds.

Right behind them flew the twisted, skeletal hand. Its long white fingers opened and closed incessantly, as if they were some sort of jaws eager to crush their victims. As fast as Aylah flew, the giant, grasping hand drew closer.

Veering sharply, Aylah skimmed the edge of the cloud bank and plunged downward. But the windtaker pursued her closely. She streaked toward a pair of delicate bridges spanning the space between two clouds. Seeing the web of cloudthread ropes fast approaching, Basil guessed her plan: She would pass right through, while the huge hand would be utterly entangled.

With a resounding rush of air, Aylah swept through the bridges. They quivered, swaying between the clouds, but didn't slow her down at all. One of the ropes almost smashed into Basil, but he ducked just in time so that it merely grazed the top of his head. As soon as they had left the bridges behind, he turned around, expecting to see the windtaker's ruin.

But the monster, too, had guessed Aylah's plan. At the last possible instant it angled upward. Most of its skeletal form skimmed over the bridges, barely missing them—but one of its thin fingers caught on a single strand. The entire force of the windtaker's momentum yanked at the rope, snapping it loose. The whole bridge exploded, whipping lines in all directions.

The windtaker, tugged off balance, flipped over and careened through the air. Ropes whipped against its sides with brutal force, causing it to bellow with pain. The sound, like anguished thunder, echoed among the clouds.

Hopes rising, Basil watched their attacker spin out of control. Its bony mass slammed into one of the cloudcake pillars that had supported the bridge. The pillar collapsed, spraying shards that sparkled like miniature stars.

Then, to Basil's great dismay, the giant hand righted itself. Roaring with rage, it continued its pursuit, flying again with terrifying speed. At that moment, Basil discovered how the monster could see: At the extreme tip of each of the windtaker's six long fingers, a silver eye gleamed. Unblinking, the eyes glared angrily.

Although Aylah's maneuver had opened up some distance, the chase continued. She swerved to avoid a cloud forest, whose groves looked more like translucent spears than trees. Diving through a gauzy fabric of shredding fog, she surprised a flock of sylphs. Releasing eerie, high-pitched shrieks, the vaporous beings scattered—just as the wind sister, pursued by the groping hand, whooshed past. Magnifying the sylphs' frightened wails, the strings of the Harplands swelled in the distance.

Anxiously, Basil glanced behind. "It's gaining!" he shouted. "Gaining fast!"

Aylah veered sharply, sweeping past a long, flat cloud dotted with hundreds of sparkling blue pools. The powerful wind slapped at these cloud lakes, sending up fountains of spray. Thousands of birds—cormorants, drakes, pelicans, puffins, geese, and terns—all took flight, filling the air with their squawks and honks and chattering cries.

Straight through them plowed the windtaker. Feathers ripped from wings; birds spun wildly. Rushing past like an immense, bony cloud, the monster bellowed again, drowning out the birds' shrill cries as well as the piercing notes of the harp strings.

Basil looked back again. The beast was almost upon them! "Aylah, do—"

He swallowed his words as the wind sister suddenly veered downward. Hurtling through the air, she plunged into a thick, frothy cloud that spread across a vast expanse of sky. Half a second later, vaporous curls surrounded them. In another half second, the cloud covered them completely, its dense vapors blocking out the starlight. Then Aylah did what Basil least expected.

She stopped. Her only movement was a slight vibration, enough to hold Basil aloft.

Hovering there in the darkness, Basil understood at once. *Hiding! We're buried deep in this cloud, so deep that thing will never find us.*

For what must have been hours, they waited. At times they heard the monster's angry bellowing; once they felt its body sweep past them as it tunneled through the cloud. Still Aylah did not flee.

Basil grew colder from the vapors, but that didn't bother him nearly as much as the prospect of being seized by that horrible hand. And so he said nothing, desperately hoping Aylah's plan would succeed. From outside the cloud, the bellowing grew less frequent, then finally ceased.

More hours passed, maybe even days. Basil frequently licked his thin lips, coating his tongue with moisture, so he never felt thirsty. Only cold, chilled to the marrow of his bones. And hungry. He felt the kind of hunger that gnawed steadily, chewing at his innards. But he didn't dare speak.

At last, Aylah whispered the words that he longed to hear. "Hhhwe are safe nohhhw, little hhhwanderer."

He beamed, though his teeth chattered.

The wind sister shot ahead, scattering the vapors with her breath. As they neared the surface of the cloud, starlight broke through, bright enough to assure them that night had passed into day. Droplets of water glowed all around, luminous little realms of mist. And in the warming air, Aylah's cinnamon smell expanded, wafting around her passenger.

Without warning, a wrathful roar erupted. From the swirling mist came enormous, fingerlike jaws. They slammed shut, trapping Aylah and Basil in utter darkness.

As loud as they shouted, no one could possibly hear them. Just as no one could possibly find them. For they had been swallowed by a beast whose belly could not be escaped. Not even by the wind.

23: WHATEVER THE WIND WOULD DO

People make such an unnecessary fuss about dying. It's really just part of life, as the final chapter is just part of a book. Still . . . we can always hope there might be a sequel.

No light.
No escape.
No way to find Merlin.

Those realities now defined the companions' days. And yet, as Basil realized the instant the bone-white jaws of the windtaker closed around them, they were negative realities. No longer was life woven from the threads of all his senses and experiences—and his overwhelming need to warn the wizard. Instead, the fabric of life was now woven from the *absence* of things. The missing threads.

No light. No escape. No Merlin.

The only sound he heard now, aside from Aylah's sorrowful sighs and the thumping of his own little heart, was the occasional *drip-drip* of slime in the windtaker's belly.

His surroundings he knew mainly by their feel: the slippery hard surface of the monster's enormous ribs, and the oozing rivers of slime that flowed between them.

Even his favorite sense—smell—had been squeezed down to nearly nothing. Try as he might, he could find only one scent—one horrible scent and the equally horrible taste that went with it. Slime. For his sole source of food—if you could call it that—was the putrid, decaying slime that dripped from the dank walls around him. So strong was its stench that Aylah's normal scent of cinnamon, and most of the smells that Basil knew how to cast, were completely overwhelmed by the odor of rotting flesh.

To eat the slime—which he did as rarely as possible, only when his hunger pangs swelled to throbbing aches he couldn't ignore any longer—Basil crawled along the monster's ribs until he found someplace moist but not too terribly gooey, since the stickiest slime would lodge in his throat for days. Trying his best to ignore the smell, he would take just enough rotting slime to coat the tip of his tongue. Then came the hardest part: swallowing. The only way he could tolerate it was to emit, just at that moment, a powerfully sweet smell, such as fresh mint or rain-washed raspberries—something strong enough to mask the putridness. For a few seconds, anyway.

Over and over again, in the darkness of their prison, he forced himself to crawl to a river of slime, take some on his tongue, and then swallow. For he needed at least some nourishment to survive. And Basil wanted desperately to survive.

That's what I must do, he told himself soon after their capture. *Not only for me . . . but for Avalon. Somebody's got to warn Merlin! To tell him about Rhita Gawr.*

He ground his teeth angrily. They had been close—so close—to warning the wizard. Then this monster appeared, swallowing them along with their plans.

We must get out. Must! His eyes smoldered. *I'll find Merlin somehow. And stop Rhita Gawr. Yes—before he can bring his evil into this world.*

He winced, hearing himself think. Who was he, really, to take on Rhita Gawr? To come to the aid of Avalon?

Sure, he'd felt surprisingly hopeful after meeting Dagda. Even if it had all been just happenstance, he did somehow manage to help the spirit lord—and earn his gratitude. Although Dagda had told him, quite definitely, *You are not a mere dragon . . .* the god had hinted that Basil might have some sort of special power. Something beyond just making odd little smells now and then. But to be honest, more and more that whole notion sounded unlikely—even outlandish. Especially for a bizarre little half-lizard, half-bat who didn't even know what kind of creature he was.

Yet he couldn't quite let go of the idea, outlandish as it was. He might not be a dragon. But he was *something.* Maybe even something that could help Avalon.

Besides, he had another reason to survive. As difficult as life was for him in this slime-encrusted tomb, it was worse for Aylah. Far worse. For she was a wind sister—and a wind sister needs freedom to move, no less than other creatures need air to breathe.

I must move as freely as the air itself, she had told him the very first time they met. *Never sleeping, never stopping, never staying anyhhhwhere for long. That is a hhh-wind sister's hhhway.*

Without that freedom, he knew, his friend would surely die. A wind sister who could not move around would wither away, until one day she would simply vanish.

"I am sorry, little hhhwanderer," Aylah whispered, her voice echoing eerily in their slimy cell. "So hhhwoefully sorry."

"We'll get out of here," Basil replied, sounding much more certain than he felt.

"But hohhhw?"

"I don't know, Aylah. Somehow."

The days passed, melting into weeks. And he still hadn't thought of any way to answer her question.

As their confinement continued, time wasn't marked by the normal rhythms of day and night, falling asleep and waking up, chasing or being chased. Now there were no golden flashes at starset, no changing colors on the trees or stones to mark the seasons, no visible evidence of growing older.

Yet time was clearly passing. Basil knew it from the ceaseless dripping of the slime. Just as he knew it from Aylah's sighs—less frequent now, and growing steadily weaker. He knew it, too, from his own decreasing strength. Even making the smell of mint, once as easy as saying his own name, now felt like pushing a stone up a steep hill.

And still he couldn't answer Aylah's question.

For a little while there, I thought that my life might have some purpose. Some meaning. And that in following that purpose, I could maybe find out who I am. He growled, making a sound like pebbles scraping against each other. *Is it all going to end in the belly of this beast?*

He listened to the relentless dripping of slime. Leaning against the moist wall, he could feel the windtaker's body tilting to one side as it turned in flight. *Is this all my life was meant to be about? Nothing more?*

Long stretches passed without either of the companions speaking. What more was there to say? Why make the effort to talk? She was dying; he was barely surviving. Those two simple facts summed up everything.

Yet a day finally came when Basil, to his own surprise, realized he had a question. While seated on a rib, chewing on a particularly rancid glob of slime and trying not to gag, he thought of something that had vaguely puzzled him ever since their capture. The question had never seemed important enough to ask. But now, like a frail stream of water that had long flowed unnoticed beneath a desert, it bubbled at last to the surface.

"Aylah," he said quietly, hesitant to disturb the silence that wrapped around them like a heavy cloak, "I have a—" He paused, forcing himself to swallow the gooey slime. "A question."

The wind sister didn't respond. Whether she was too weak to talk or too despairing to hear, he couldn't guess. But he decided he might as well continue.

"Most living creatures need to eat, right? Maybe not wind sisters, but most everyone else. Including this monster that swallowed us."

Aylah still didn't speak, though she did release a long, low sigh that sounded more like a moan.

Basil swallowed again, trying to rid his tongue of the wretched taste, then went on. "What I don't understand, though, is *why* this thing wanted to eat you. What value could it get from swallowing the wind? I mean . . . you're not exactly a big hunk of meat or some sort of fruit."

A long moment of quiet ensued, interrupted only by the sound of Basil's feet squelching in the slime as he moved up the rib to a slightly drier spot. At last, Aylah answered him.

"The hhhwindtaker hhhwants me not for meat or

fruit, nor anything you hhhwould call food. It hhhwants me . . . for my spirit."

Basil jerked his head upright. "Your what?"

"My spirit, little hhhwanderer. That is hhhwhat it hungers for. The energy of my soul. You see, hhhwhen I grohhhw too hhhweak, I hhhwill no longer be able to hold my spirit hhhwithin myself. So it hhhwaits until I can resist no longer . . . then it hhhwill take my spirit into itself! Only then hhhwill it be satisfied. And only then hhhwill it hunt again, searching for another hhhwind sister."

He cringed. Devouring someone else's spirit! Never, in all his days, had he heard of such a thing. Even when a dactylbird murdered another creature for pleasure, that creature's spirit would at least live on and make the journey to the Otherworld. This horrible notion hung in the air, as if it were a kind of odor, smelling even worse than slime.

Suddenly he had an idea—and with it, the hint of a bizarre, irrational scheme. "Aylah," he asked eagerly, "what happens when the monster takes a wind sister's spirit into itself? Does it merge with the monster's own spirit? Or does it stay whole somehow?"

"Hhhwhat does it matter?"

"Just tell me," he insisted.

"Hhhwhy?"

"Tell me, Aylah!"

There was a long pause before she spoke again. Finally, in a somber whisper, she said, "I really don't knohhhw hhhwhat happens."

In the darkness, Basil's small brow furrowed. "All right . . . but let's just assume the spirit stays intact somehow."

"Hhhwe don't knohhhw that."

"Just assume," he declared. "If that's true, then the spirits of every wind sister this thing has ever eaten, over all the years it's lived, are here inside it somewhere. And maybe . . . they could be reached."

"Speak hhhwith the spirits? Nobody knohhhws ho-hhhw."

Basil thumped his tiny tail excitedly. The echo swelled, drumming all around them. "But if we could reach them—find them—maybe they could help us."

"No, little hhhwanderer." She whispered so softly he could barely hear. "They could not help us. Nobody can help us."

"I don't believe that!" His squeaky voice deepened with urgency. "Please, Aylah. Try with me. Just try."

She released a dismal sigh. "All right. But don't expect your idea to hhhwork."

"I don't," he replied, still thumping his tail against the rib. Abruptly, he stopped, waiting until the echoes faded away before speaking again.

"And yet," he said into the silence, "there's something I can't forget. Something important."

Aylah said nothing. So quiet was the windtaker's belly that Basil might have been completely alone. But he continued talking.

"You know how even the tiniest little breeze, so small it barely exists, still has a force of its own?" Hearing no reply, Basil swallowed, then went on. "And how that little breeze can sometimes blow on a dying ember, all that remains of a fire that's burned down to nothing?"

Silence.

"Well . . . sometimes, Aylah, that tiny little breeze is strong enough to coax that ember to get hotter and hotter—until, finally, it just might burst into flame."

He raised his head, though it seemed heavier than ever. "Aylah . . . maybe, just maybe . . . *we can be that breeze.*"

Only silence met his words. Basil waited, hoping to hear some sort of reply. But Aylah didn't answer.

Slowly, he lowered his head. Just then, from somewhere near his face, came a whisper.

"Hhhwhat do you hhhwant me to do?"

"Just this. Send your thoughts out to your sisters! To any of their spirits that still survive in this miserable beast. Tell them we need their help—need them to be more than just spirits. They must fill themselves with air, and . . ."

He stopped, unsure what else to say.

"And do," finished Aylah, "hhhwhatever the hhhwind hhhwould do."

Basil nodded gratefully. "Whatever the wind would do."

He drew a breath, trying to clear his mind of everything else—the sticky ooze beneath his feet, the ghastly stench, the despair that hovered just beyond the edge of his thoughts. Slowly, all those grim realities faded—not a lot, but enough for him to think about something new.

Wind sisters, hear me! Wherever you are inside this beast. Awaken and remember who you were, long ago. Help your sister Aylah and me.

He paused, listening. For what, he didn't really know. But he heard nothing new, felt no change at all.

Wind sisters, please. Remember your lost lives. Your lost freedom. Come back, if you can!

Still no change.

Basil went deeper in his thoughts. He tried to imagine the life of a wind sister—the feeling of unending flight, unrestricted movement, unlimited shape. He tried to feel a wind sister's thrill of constant movement. Her need, in the depths of her being, to fly, to flow, to move. And her fear of confinement, a condition as different from her life as being is from nothingness.

"Fly again," he spoke into the darkness. "Fly like the wind."

"Yes," repeated Aylah. "Fly again." Her words, like his, echoed around the walls.

Subtly, on the edges of his ears, Basil felt the slightest hint of movement. Was it air?

Probably just Aylah, he thought. *She's stirring a little. Or maybe it's just the monster moving again. No, wait—*

The flow of air grew stronger. He felt the barest brush of wind across his back, the lightest touch upon his snout. One of the scales on his neck, loosened by a fall on the rocks long ago, started to quiver like a leaf in an approaching breeze.

Then, at the remotest edge of hearing, he heard a sound. A whisper of a whisper of a whisper. It didn't seem, somehow, like Aylah. And while it came from somewhere nearby, in the belly of the beast, it also seemed strangely far away—so far away, in fact, it seemed to come from beyond the windtaker, beyond the cloudscape of Airroot, beyond the very borders of the world.

The faint whisper grew, swelling louder. Then came another whispered voice, and another. The number of voices steadily increased, along with their volume. Slowly, a chorus of whispers filled the air—and with it, a movement, a bustling.

A rushing of winds. Many winds, suddenly come to life.

The windstorm gained strength, swelling into a gale. It surged within the beast's belly; in that confined space it blew fiercely in every direction. Globs of slime broke loose, scattering with the forceful gusts, pelting Basil's scales. His tiny nostrils flared, not from his own breath, but from the whirling winds around him.

Soon the whispers grew into wails, and the wails swelled into roars. Basil's whole body lifted off the slimy surface and hurtled through the air, slamming into a rib, only to roll down to a place where the wind picked him up again and tossed him somewhere else. Meanwhile, the gale's intensity continued to grow.

Now the windtaker began to roll and twist, clearly in anguish from this inner tempest. The more violent the winds in its belly, the more its body contorted. Basil could sense somehow that it was flying, soaring above its realm, even as it suffered from the swelling pressures down inside. Yet its mouth never opened in a roar. It kept the fingerlike jaws clamped tight, for if it opened merely a crack, its prey might escape.

The storm gained intensity. Suddenly, though, it shifted. Instead of whipping frantically around the confined space, the winds abruptly turned all their force outward. Basil was hurled face-first into a slimy wall, but instead of being instantly blown to another spot, he stayed there, legs splayed, unable to move a muscle. He couldn't budge his wings, lift his tail, or turn his ears with all the weight of the winds pressing down on him.

That weight kept growing. Soon he found it hard to breathe, with such force pushing against his back. While the slime underneath him provided some cushion, keeping him from being totally flattened, he felt swelling pain all through his body—his face, his eyes, his chest all ached. He wanted to cry out, but couldn't get enough air. The pressure grew. He couldn't breathe at all. His head started to spin; a silent scream filled his mind.

Something's gone wrong! But can't . . . do anything . . .

Darkness filled his mind. Except for the constant pain, he sensed less and less. He couldn't breathe, couldn't think, couldn't feel. Only vaguely did he sense the surface beneath him start to vibrate, shaking faster and faster. And then, just before he finally lost consciousness, he heard a distant *crack*.

It wasn't his ribs breaking. Nor any of his bones. No, it was the windtaker itself: Its body was beginning to buckle.

All at once, the beast—who had swallowed so many wind sisters during its life, who had considered Aylah and the tiny speck of a lizard she carried to be just another meal—burst apart. Exploding high above the clouds of Airroot, the windtaker shrieked in agony. Shards of bone and fetid slime from its ruptured belly rained down upon the clouds. Its dying shriek soon faded, carried away by the rushing winds.

Basil, alas, knew none of this. For his unconscious body had been hurled into the air by the explosion. Now he plummeted, spinning helplessly, toward whatever lay below.

24: FREE FALL

*Air is substance, the bearer of wings. Air is life, the
essence of breath. And air is freedom, the habitat of hope.*

Basil awoke to the sensation of breathing, a feeling he'd
thought would never come again. Air, cool and misty,
poured into his body and reawakened his mind. He sucked
in more of the vaporous elixir.

Have we somehow escaped? That hope swelled inside
him, filling his thoughts even as air filled his lungs.

Harp strings! In the distance, he heard a lilting, triumphant plucking. And yet . . . something was wrong.

He opened his eyes. Falling! He was spinning downward through shredded clouds. Wind rushed past his face,
flapping his round ears. But it wasn't Aylah's wind. She
was nowhere near, he could tell—both from the lack of any
cinnamon smell and the lack of something deeper, something he sensed not with his nose or ears or eyes, but with
his heart.

Instinctively, he started to open his wings, to turn his

free fall into a glide. But no! A sharp pain shot through his right shoulder. *My wing . . . broken.*

He continued to fall, dropping like a lifeless shard of bone. *I'm going to die, that's certain. But Aylah . . . she will—*

"Survive," said a breathy voice nearby. "Oh yes, little hhhwanderer, I hhhwill survive. And so hhhwill you."

"Aylah!" he shouted, as warmer air flowed around him, arresting his fall. The familiar scent of cinnamon tickled his nostrils. Soon he was hovering in the air, borne by the wind.

"My wing," he said with a wince. "Broken, I think. Can you still carry me?"

"I can carry you, my friend." The wind rushed around him, an airy embrace. "Hhhwherever you may hhhwant to go, I can carry you."

"The windtaker?" he asked.

"Dead, hhhwithout doubt."

"And your sisters?"

"Free, little hhhwanderer. Brought back to life. By a hhhwondrous miracle . . . in the form of a small green creature." Warm air encircled Basil. "You have given us all a gift—a gift as boundless as the hhhwind."

Despite the aching of his wing, he smiled. "I'm glad for your sisters. But I'm even more glad for you."

Even as the air buoyed him, tossing him gently, it bubbled with laughter. "You are a loyal friend, little hhhwanderer."

"It's good to have a friend like you," he replied.

"And something more," Aylah went on. "You are brave, as hhhwell—brave as a dragon."

The word surprised him so much he instinctively raised his wings—until a sharp pain made him stop. "Dragon?"

he asked. "You're not serious! I'm no dragon, and never will be."

"I didn't say—"

"Good," he interrupted, "because there's no doubt about it. Even Dagda made that clear, though it wasn't necessary."

The wind swept around him, ruffling his ears. "I didn't say you hhhwere a dragon in body, little hhhwanderer, but in *spirit*. You see . . . there is more than one hhhway to be a dragon! You have all a dragon's courage and ferocity—just not its size."

Basil shook his snout. "I'm not convinced, but it doesn't matter. We're free, Aylah, that's what counts." His mouth curled in a grin. "And now . . . could I ask you a favor?"

"Hhhwhy, yes. Hhhwhat hhhwould you like?"

"To eat!" he exclaimed. "Something—anything. As long as it doesn't taste like slime." He swished his tail. "Then we've got to find Merlin! He could be anywhere in Avalon by now. As could Rhita Gawr."

"True," she said with a sigh. "Hhhwe hhhwill find him somehohhhw." Suddenly, currents jostled him as she swept around to the east. "But first, your meal. And I knohhhw just hhhwhat you need, little hhhwanderer. From hhhwhat I have heard, it is healing for both body and soul."

His thin tongue licked his lips. "I like the sound of that. Is it far from here?"

"Not if you ride the hhhwind! It lies just across the sea of mist, in the realm of fire."

"All right, then," he declared. "Time to fly."

The wind sister's speed increased. Air whistled all around. She blew with the force of a gale—flying through the gauzy clouds like someone who, after a long imprisonment, was finally free.

25: ONE OF A KIND

Personally, I'd rather keep things simple, but the plain fact is that life is full of paradox: We are all alike, while at the same time, we are all unique. That's utterly crazy, I know—but also utterly sane.

Aylah swept across the sky, banking graceful turns around billowing clouds, clearly savoring her new-found freedom. Although the tiny green-scaled creature she carried could no longer fly, he felt the same delight in soaring freely. With every sweeping turn, Basil leaned into the coursing wind, his round ears fluttering. He loved to feel the air rushing past, just as he loved to hear its endless serenade of whistles.

As they flew beyond the edge of Airroot and into the dark sea of mist that rolled between the realms, cold currents of air jostled them. One gust hit so abruptly it flipped Basil onto his back. His wounded wing, which he'd been holding tight against his side, blew wide open.

"Aaaggh!" he shouted in pain. Rolling back over, he folded his wing again. But it throbbed intensely.

"Do not hhhworry, little hhhwanderer," said the wind sister, raising her breathy voice enough to be heard above the gusts. "The very best person to mend your hhhwing is the same person we are searching for."

"Merlin?"

"Yes, my friend. Hhhwe seek him for Avalon's sake . . . and nohhhw also for yours."

"I hope we'll find him soon," Basil muttered.

With that, Aylah flew lower, losing altitude steadily. Soon the dark swirls of mist began to shred. Warmer air blew over Basil, smelling like rotten eggs. Hot dust particles burned his eyes. All at once, the remaining mist evaporated, revealing a new landscape below.

Charred ridges of red and black stone, many of them crested with flames, stretched into the distance. Volcanoes rose out of the ridges like huge, fiery snouts, belching clouds of sulfurous smoke while their slopes glowed with molten lava. Between the ridges flowed rust-colored rivers whose banks swirled with smoke, as if their very waters were aflame.

So this is Fireroot. Gazing down on the blazing landscape, he shuddered. How could anything survive here? Yet he knew some creatures did—including the flamelons, known for their skillful metalwork . . . and also for their tempers that burned hotter than lava.

Aylah swept even lower. As they sailed across one wide valley, Basil saw a thick cluster of ironwood trees, whose fiber was so hard, he had heard, that it couldn't burn. Even so, he wasn't impressed. *Is that what passes for a forest here? Compared to Woodroot, it's just a bunch of dry grass.*

Swooping down into the valley, Aylah dropped him gently onto a fire-blackened boulder. "Hhhwait here," she commanded. "I hhhwill make a quick search for Merlin.

The fastest hhhway for me to do that is to spread myself to the absolute hhhwidest—hhhwhich hhhwill make me too thin to carry you."

Basil swished his tail across the boulder, scraping off flecks of charcoal. "You'll come back soon, right?"

"Ohhh yes, and I hhhwill bring nehhhws of hhhwhatever I find—hhhwhether of our hhhwizard or a meal you hhhwill hhhwelcome."

As she flew away, leaving him behind, a fire plant suddenly flickered at the base of the boulder. Reaching out of the charred ground like a ghoulish hand of flame, its fiery fingers stroked the side of the rock, stretching up toward his tail. Quickly, he crawled away to the other end of the boulder. But with a spurt of fiery gases, another flaming hand erupted at that end.

They sense I'm here, he realized. *Whatever they are! And they want to roast me for a meal.*

Instantly, he scurried back to the center of the boulder. Safely out of the fire plants' reach, he could now survey his surroundings. Fire-blasted rocks lay all around. Curls of smoke hung in the air, spiraling through the needled branches of the ironwood trees. Flecks of dust, smoldering like ashes from a campfire, stung his nostrils. Vents opened in the ground every few seconds, spewing hot lava.

Then he noticed a narrow crevasse that split the nearby ground. Waves of heat rose from it, making the air above quiver constantly. It wasn't this motion, though, that caught his attention. No, there was a different sort of motion down *inside* the crevasse. The fissures along the edges seemed to be moving, slithering as if they were alive.

Dozens, maybe hundreds, of tiny orange lizards were moving in and out of the heated fissures. Salamanders!

Basil had heard bards' tales of these little creatures, so well adapted to the extreme heat of Fireroot that they could actually sleep in molten lava and never get burned. Right now, as he watched, some of them were casually rolling around inside a fire plant at the rim of the crevasse. Though spurts of flame licked their bellies, the salamanders didn't even seem to notice.

A sudden, bizarre thought struck Basil. *Is there any possible way . . . ?* He squinted his eyes, irritated from the dust, while he peered at the salamanders. They were just about his same size. Their heads were the same shape, though not their ears. They had small clubs at the ends of their tails, just as he did.

He swallowed with difficulty, as if fire had scorched his throat. Just then a smoldering fleck of dust landed on his ear. "Eeeeyaaah!" he cried in pain, leaping into the air. As he landed back on the boulder, the hot particle fell away.

Glumly, he shook his head, wincing from the burn on his ear. *Foolish fungus-brain! Just because you look a bit like them, you're not related—any more than you're related to eaglefolk just because they have wings.*

Air gusted suddenly, whooshing so loud he could no longer hear the surrounding sputter and crackle of flames and lava vents. "I have returned, little hhhwanderer."

"Any sign of Merlin?"

"No," she said glumly. "He is nohhhwhere to be seen! Hhhwe must keep searching." Brightening a little, she added, "I did, hohhhwever, find your meal—not far from here."

Basil, still preoccupied, glanced again at the salamanders.

The wind sister spun closer, lifting him off the blackened boulder. So strong were the odors of sulfur and smoke, he could barely smell her cinnamon scent. "But I can tell that you are hhhworried. Hhhwhat troubles you?"

He drew a breath, shallow enough to avoid inhaling too much smoke. "Aylah, you've seen much of Avalon, haven't you?"

"Hhhwhy, yes. And other hhhworlds, as hhhwell."

"Can you tell me something, then? Have you ever seen someone else who is—" He paused to swallow. "Who is . . . like me?"

The wind sister whirled for a moment. Hovering in the air above the grove of ironwood trees, she replied, "No, little hhhwanderer. From all I have seen, in all the hhhworlds, there is no one else like you."

Grimly, he nodded. "Of course not. I should have guessed."

"That needn't hhhworry you, little hhhwanderer."

He gave a mirthless laugh, scoffing at her. "So it's good to be one of a kind?"

"Perhaps," she replied, whispering softly.

Flying lower, she carried him down to a lone flower that grew among the twisted roots of a tree. Its delicate orange petals quivered in the wind. "This flohhhwer, you could say, is one of a kind. Found only here in Rahnahhhwyn, it's called firebloom, and it looks unlike any other flohhhwer in any realm. Frail and small, it seems—yet it's surprisingly strong. After a fire, it's the very first living thing to grohhhw back. So in a hhhway, it's much like you: strange to look at, but more than it seems."

He shook his head. "But that's not the same, is it? There are lots of these flowers in this realm. Not just one."

Aylah heaved a sigh.

"And that isn't all," he went on. "The worst part isn't being one of a kind. It's not knowing what kind that is!

Aylah, so much has happened since that day you saw me hatch—but I still have *no idea* what I am."

The wind sister spun around him for a long moment. At last, she whispered, "You are my friend, little hhhwanderer."

Basil nodded—still feeling glum, but maybe not quite so much. "Yes," he said finally. "That's one thing I do know I am."

"And I knohhhw you are also something else."

"What?"

"Hungry."

"Right! You found—"

"A hhhwonderful meal." She flew into the grove of ironwoods, carrying him on a rapid zigzag through the maze of branches. He swooped under one branch and, the next instant, over another and then through the middle of a forked trunk. Diving beneath a precariously leaning tree, he shot straight through a drooping bunch of rust-colored needles. Then, as needles drifted to the ground, he veered to make a sharp turn past another tree—coming so close that its bark scratched against his tail. Never slowing, he zipped around, over, and under branches, more than he could count. When, at last, his flight came to a halt, he found himself hovering directly in front of a massive old tree with a hole in its trunk as big as a melon. And that hole was jammed with bees.

Bright red bees. Crawling over one another, they buzzed as they swarmed in the hole, moving in and out of the tree.

"Those, my hhhwanderer, are burning bees, whose stings burn worse than fire."

He frowned. "They must be delicious."

Currents of laughter bounced him. "They are not. But their honey is! And it is also rich in healing pohhhwer."

He scrunched his snout. "But to get anywhere near that honey, you have to—"

Without warning, she dropped him. He plunged into a thick bed of needles, deep enough to cushion his fall. Just as he lifted his head out of the needles, he witnessed an amazing event.

A mighty gale-force wind slammed suddenly into the tree. Twigs flew, clusters of needles exploded, and roots popped as the trunk bent backward under the weight of this screaming wind. The hole in the trunk burst apart, spraying honey-soaked shards of bark across the grove.

Then, as abruptly as it had arrived, the violent wind departed. As the trunk sprang back to its upright position, that whirling gust tore through the grove and blew down the valley, carrying along with it countless twigs, shards, needles—and bees. Basil stared in astonishment at the old tree, where golden honey now oozed from the gaping hole.

"Not a single bee left behind!" he crowed. "Aylah, you are incredible."

Knowing he had little time to lose, he waded through the bed of needles and climbed onto a knobby root of the old tree. Taking care not to bump his injured wing, he slid under a broken branch and continued crawling up the root until he reached the base of the trunk. For an instant, he thought back to his glimpse—back at the start of his journey—of the steep cliffs that were really the base of another, far greater Tree. Then, with no further delay, he lunged at the stream of honey dribbling down from the bees' overflowing cache.

Licking the sticky substance with his tongue, he drew back in surprise. This honey tasted very strange—not sweet, but roasted, like charred nectar. Yet it made him feel refreshed—as if he'd swallowed a whole field of zestflowers. It also renewed his strength, so that even his broken wing throbbed a bit less painfully. Best of all, it filled him with warmth, a slowly swelling heat that moved from the tip of his tongue down to the middle of his belly.

He took another lick. This time, his tongue swept up a big glob of honey—and also a tiny fleck of burned dirt that had blown into the bees' hideaway. That was why, when he swallowed, he tasted the soil of this realm.

I am flame! The voice in Basil's mind crackled and spat like burning coals. *Hot do I burn—ever hungry, ever alive. My body is bright light and dark smoke. And my essence is change: ashes to soil, soil to wood, wood to ashes. Transformation is my deepest longing, my greatest power. Nothing resists me forever. All things I can become.*

The voice crackled with delight. *For I am flame.*

By the time Aylah swept back into the grove to retrieve him, he felt revived by the honey . . . and renewed by the strange new warmth inside him. It felt, almost, as if a different kind of fire had been kindled in his heart: a fire of change. *All things I can become.* Those words echoed in his mind.

He wondered, as he'd done so often, what kind of creature he might really be. Yet this time, aware of the magic of change within him, the focus was different. This time, he wondered what he might someday *become.*

Whatever that turns out to be, he felt sure, *it will be unique. Like this journey—and like me.*

Still savoring the taste of honey on his tongue, he nodded. *One of a kind.*

26: ECHOES

The older I get, the stronger my hearing. Not because my ears are any better, mind you—but because I've learned how to listen. Hearing less talk; hearing more truth.

Basil caught one last view of Fireroot, as Aylah carried him up into the rust-tinted clouds: a pair of jagged volcanoes that spewed unending streams of smoke and lava. Between their summits yawned a massive crater, blackened by ash and soot. Dozens of rocky pinnacles poked up from the crater's rim; tilted in all directions, they looked like the crooked teeth of a huge, perilous mouth.

"Wouldn't want to land down there," he mused. "We might get swallowed."

Aylah jostled him as she chuckled.

"Are those—yes! I see people walking down there."

He pointed at three people walking along an open stretch of the rim between the pinnacles. Two men and one woman, they all had long, silvery hair. Despite the harshness of the landscape, they strode casually, seeming entirely at home.

All of a sudden, they started running straight at a sheer cliff that plunged into the crater. Rather than slow down as they neared the cliff's edge, they sped even faster. Their silvery hair streamed behind them, bouncing with every stride. When they reached the edge, all three leaped into the air.

Basil caught his breath, certain he was about to see them all die, smashed against the rocks below. Instead, though, all three of them suddenly sprouted enormous wings. Red-tipped feathers covered their backs, while fearsome talons grew from their feet. Leaning into the wind, they soared across the crater and over a flaming river of lava.

"Eaglefolk!" Basil's green eyes watched in wonder. "Look at those wings, so wide and strong."

Aylah swept around her passenger, lifting him higher. "You miss your ohhhwn hhhwings, don't you? Soon, little hhhwanderer, hhhwe hhhwill find Merlin, and he hhhwill heal you."

"Good," he replied, adjusting his broken wing against his back. The movement made the whole wing throb, sending shafts of pain through his ribs and down his spine. Even so, he declared, "But that's our least important goal. Much as I want to be healed, I want even more to warn him about Rhita Gawr. We've lost so much time!"

"Hhhwe hhhwill find him," she promised, yet her voice didn't sound quite certain.

Careful not to move his wing again, he tilted his head thoughtfully. "Maybe we should look in some realm besides the three we haven't checked—Shadowroot, Waterroot, and my old home, Woodroot? I mean . . . as much as I'd like to see all seven realms—is there someplace, other than those three, where we're more likely to find him?"

"No," answered the wind sister, ruffling his ears. "There is no realm more likely than any other. Hhhwe should try those three—and if hhhwe don't find him, hhhwe hhhwill return to the realms you have already seen."

"Again and again, if we must."

"Yes," she agreed. "And on the hhhway, you hhhwill keep your promise to Dagda."

"Only if it doesn't slow us down."

"Do not hhhworry! Hhhwe hhhwill travel very fast— hhhwith the speed of the hhhwind. And I hhhwill stretch myself out to the hhhwidest, everyhhhwhere we go, to see if Merlin is near."

The clouds thickened around them, weaving a red-tinted shroud. With each passing second, the darkness deepened. While Aylah kept flying, soon Basil couldn't see anything but blackness. Only the continual rush of air against his face, vibrating his ears, assured him that they were, in fact, still moving.

Many minutes passed as they continued to fly. But the darkness showed no sign of dissipating. Rather, it only deepened. It pressed against them, squeezing tighter, like a solid fist. *Never*, he thought, *have I seen a cloud as thick as this.*

"It is not a cloud," whispered Aylah, guessing his thoughts. "It is night. The eternal night of Shadohhhwroot."

He stiffened. "You're right! There aren't any clouds now. I don't feel their coolness, their moisture. All I feel is . . ."

"Night." The wind sister surged ahead, never slowing. "In this realm, little hhhwanderer, there is no light, no dahhhwn, no starlit sky. The lands hhhwe are flying over nohhhw have never seen a single ray of light."

He shivered, though not from cold. "How terrible.

Nothing but darkness! Every day, every year. Why was this realm so cursed?"

"Only the hhhwind sisters knohhhw hhhwhy it is alhhh-ways dark in Shadohhhwroot." She slowed slightly, so the air gusted less forcefully against him. "Yet it hhhwas not because of any curse, ohhh no. Hhhwhile this realm holds many terrors, it is true . . . it holds many hhhwonders, as hhhwell."

"Wonders? Not likely." He shuddered. "I've never much liked the dark, Aylah. For a little fellow like me, it can be more dangerous than a flock of dactylbirds."

"Ahhh, but even a dactylbird is not hhhwholly evil."

"You don't know them like I do! They can make a wrathful dragon seem like a songbird."

"But the dark, little hhhwanderer, can hold surprising virtues. That is hhhwhy the museos, hhhwhose songs are so very soulful, come from Shadohhhwroot. Hhhwhy some elves have chosen to live not in the forests of hhhWoodroot, but in the dark valleys below the Evernight Peaks. And hhhwhy this realm's true name is Lastrael, the elvish hhh-word for *hidden treasures*."

Unconvinced, he shook his head. "Sorry, Aylah. You'll never persuade me. Take me down there so I can taste the soil, but I don't want to stay long."

She blew upon his face, so hard his eyes watered. "For a brave hhhwarrior hhhwho destroyed a hhhwindtaker, you sound rather hhhworried."

"We're flying into a realm of total darkness! I'm just being sensible, that's all." He blew a breath back at her. "Now, take me down so I can keep my promise to Dagda—though I don't expect to find anything special about this place."

"All right, my hhhwanderer. And hhhwhile you are doing that, I hhhwill scour the landscape for Merlin."

"But how? You can't possibly see him."

"True. Even my sight cannot see in such dark. But the hhhwind can also feel and hear, and hhhwith those senses I hhhwill search."

Abruptly, she descended, carrying him down toward the dark landscape. His heart beat fretfully, but he tried to push back his fears. *Steady, now. What could be worse about Shadowroot than what we've already survived?*

As the wind swirled around him, fluttering the loose scale on his neck, he tried his best to calm himself. He knew that Aylah would never knowingly put him in danger. And he also knew that he had no choice but to go wherever she took him.

Her flight slowed. Into his ears, she whispered, "The place you hhhwill land is called the Vale of Echoes. Make no sounds, little hhhwanderer, no sounds at all. For in this valley a single sigh hhhwill be as loud as a hhhwindstorm."

He swallowed, unable to shake his sense of foreboding. "Aylah," he asked, "do you really need to . . . ah, leave me . . . down there?"

A sharp smell of cinnamon pricked his nostrils. "I hhhwill return for you soon. And besides, hhhwould you be a true hhhwanderer if you saw all the realms but one?"

"I guess not," he admitted. "Though there isn't much to see."

"In this realm," she replied, "you don't see hhhwith your eyes. You must see instead hhhwith your mind, as you do in a dream."

At the mention of that word, he started. Dark wings, bony and jagged, moved through his mind. And there was

Merlin—dying! By whose doing? His own? He heard, in his memory, the deep voice of Dagda: *Beware. Beware. Beware.*

"I am about to leave you, little friend. If I have aimed hhhwell, you hhhwill soon feel beneath you the soft leaves of ravenvine."

"*If* you've aimed well?"

Suddenly he felt a tangled mass of leaves brushing against his belly. He skidded across them, as the wind abruptly ceased. A few seconds later, he slid to a stop.

Yet even as his body's motion ended, a burgeoning sound began. Quietly at first, like a distant breeze, the rustling noise swelled. Except there was no breeze—only the sound. It grew and grew, getting steadily louder, shaking the ravenvine leaves with its vibrations.

Certain that a storm was fast approaching, sweeping toward them in the blackness, Basil braced himself. Judging from all the noise, it was going to be a furious gale. Anxiously, his feet grasped the vines beneath him.

In a flash, he remembered. *You idiot! This is the Vale of Echoes.* That approaching storm was really just the sound of his own landing! He was hearing the echoes of his body sliding across the leaves.

Almost as soon as he realized the truth, the sound started to fade. Rapidly it quieted, until it was less a gale than a rustle. Then a whisper. Seconds later, it had melted away into silence.

All right, he thought, knowing that the wind sister was now far away. *I'm here—alone.*

But in truth, he was not alone. At that very moment, he was being watched. Only a few paces away crouched three mangy bloodboars, among the most vicious beasts in the realm. Relying on their supreme sense of smell and their powerful eyesight, they could locate any prey in the dark. Then their terrible tusks and sword-sharp teeth would take care of the rest.

Without making even the slightest movement—which would, in this valley, cause more than enough noise to warn their prey—the bloodboars turned their attention to Basil. Tiny as he was, they could smell the meat upon his bones. Having found nothing to devour in days, the merest scent of this little morsel was enough to make them salivate. Already, frothy spittle formed at the corners of their mouths.

Unaware of any danger, Basil pressed his snout against the vine leaves. Sliding his tongue along the leaves, he was tickled by their delicate hairs. Then a tiny clump of dirt, lodged in the notch between two leaves, caught his attention. Drawing the clump back into his mouth, he swallowed.

We are the dark, said a host of hushed voices inside his mind. *Many secrets do we hold, many treasures do we keep. Subtly, we share our beauty—but only with those whose sight does not blind.*

Basil blinked, suddenly sure that he sensed real creatures somewhere nearby. Somewhere in the darkness. But no, he knew better. These were the voices of this realm's innermost magic—nothing more.

So, too, the hushed voices continued, *we hold fear and longing, rage and grief, as well as yearnings so deep they cannot be named. Yet in those places of shadow, sightless seers may also find truth and love and yes—a dark kind of light.*

Even as the voices said, once again, *We are the dark*, the bloodboars tensed their powerful leg muscles, preparing to spring. In another second, they would pounce—and tear their unlucky prey apart.

At the same time, on the other side of Basil, *another* creature stirred in the darkness. Its eyes were fixed on him—and unlike the wide, hungry eyes of the boars, these eyes shone with a hint of green. They looked, in fact, very much like Basil's eyes. For the creature itself resembled him—so much that it could have been his twin.

His identical twin.

Unnoticed by anyone, this creature was slowly, silently lifting himself out of a deep hole in the vine-covered ground. First came his small, triangular snout. Then his eyes, below a pair of rounded, batlike ears. Next came his scaly green neck, belly, and back, upon which rested two crumpled wings. Although neither wing was broken, they mirrored Basil's, right down to the veins that lined the leathery skin. Behind, dangling down the hole, hung a thin tail that ended in a bony knob.

Now, Basil couldn't see at all in this pervasive blackness. But if he *could* have seen, and looked to his left, he'd have been instantly terrified—for he would have discovered three deadly boars about to rip him to pieces. And yet . . . if he could have looked to his right, he'd have been instantly enthralled. For he would have found the first creature in all of Avalon who truly resembled himself. The first creature who might be able to help him, at last, solve the mystery of his own identity.

The boars' leg muscles tensed. Their powerful bodies quivered, ready to attack and kill. Meanwhile, Basil—the lizard they intended to devour—sat perfectly still, blithely unaware. And not so far away . . . the identical lizard quietly emerged from hiding.

As the twin lizard came out of his hole, one of his ears

brushed against a leaf of ravenvine. On that leaf sat a louse, an insect so small that it would have been very difficult to see even with any light. As the lizard's ear touched the leaf, the louse instantly sensed a good chance for a meal, and latched on. Feeling the tender skin, it opened its minuscule jaws—and took a bite.

The twin lizard, feeling the nip, instinctively flicked his ear. When its edge hit the scales on the back of his head, it made a soft little tap—the sort of sound that almost nobody would have heard. Unless, of course, it happened in the Vale of Echoes.

That tiny tap reverberated, quickly swelling in volume. It grew into a drumroll, then loud pounding, then unrelenting thunder. Soon the echoing sound filled the air, moving from one end of the Vale to the other and back again.

That very instant, something else moved through the air. Returning from her search, having found no sign of Merlin, Aylah drew near. Sensing trouble, she plunged downward. Wind suddenly gusted all around Basil and swept him up into the darkened sky.

At the same time, the three bloodboars pounced. Although one of their tusks grazed Basil's tail, they hadn't moved fast enough to catch him. As the wind sister carried him out of reach, their heavy bodies slammed onto the vine-covered ground. That impact, together with their angry snarls, raised the echoes to a deafening roar.

Meanwhile, Basil rose higher. Though he couldn't see what was happening below, he knew that Aylah's quick reaction had saved him from danger. And maybe death. What he didn't know—and would never have guessed— was that he had also missed, by a fraction of a second, meeting an identical twin.

Below, in the darkness, the boars snapped and butted heads ferociously. Having lost their meal, they were hungrier, and also angrier, than ever. Fur flew as they pounced on one another, rolling on the vines. Suddenly, one of them caught the scent of another tasty lizard on the ground nearby—and instantly stopped fighting. The other boars, also smelling new prey, did the same. All three instantly crouched in the attack position.

The twin lizard, sensing danger, froze. Should he try to dive back down into his hole, or hope to avoid being detected by three such powerful adversaries? He chose, instead, to do something else entirely.

Even as the boars leaped, snarling viciously, the tiny lizard suddenly transformed into his true shape. A changeling! The form he had temporarily assumed just a moment before—a mirror image of his intended victim, Basil—disappeared. In its place stood a tall, murderous beast with powerful limbs, deadly claws, and hundreds of terrible teeth. Enraged, the changeling plunged into battle. Before the boars even hit the ground, one of their necks was torn by his terrible jaws.

Flesh, fur, and blood splattered across the ground. Screeches and snarls erupted, gathering into an onslaught of echoes that ripped through the air. No more than ten seconds later, the battle ended. With a grunt of satisfaction, the changeling tore into the meaty bodies of his three latest victims.

Soon, nothing remained of the bloodboars but a tangle of sinew and bones. The changeling, assuming for now the shape of a black snake, slid his bloated body underneath the vines. There he would wait, digesting, until his next unwary meal appeared.

While Aylah and Basil flew swiftly eastward, with no notion of what they had missed, the echoes of battle faded away. In time, the last sounds vanished. An eerie quiet fell upon the realm of eternal night.

27: A DEEPER DARKNESS

What shows above isn't nearly as interesting as what lies beneath.

As they sailed over the outer reaches of Shadowroot, shrouded by darkness, Basil searched the sky for something he longed for, something he ached to see. At last, through a gap in the dark clouds, he found it.

"Light," he said gladly. "Light again."

He watched as the first glowing rays shot through the gap, illuminating the wispy edges of the clouds and then radiating through the mist. Steadily, as they flew eastward, the clouds around them brightened. Light permeated the very air, making the sky glow like a celestial candle.

Less than a day had passed since their escape from the belly of the windtaker. Yet so much had happened, it seemed more like a week. He had seen the realms of fire and darkness—every bit as strange, beautiful, and dangerous as the realms of stone, mud, and air. And he had tasted their mysterious magic, magic he could still feel inside him. *I don't feel any wiser*, he thought, *but I do feel a little . . . larger.*

Starlight streamed over the clouds as he said to Aylah, "Whatever happens . . . I'm glad we've taken this journey! You know, the world is bigger than I ever thought."

"And so, little hhhwanderer, are you."

"Maybe so," he replied, the hint of a grin on his face. Then the grin abruptly vanished. "But Rhita Gawr could ruin everything. Everything! We've seen so much of the world but no sign of Merlin since our escape. We've got to find him!"

Aylah's breath blew colder on his face. "Hhhwe must get to the last realms: hhhWaterroot and hhhWoodroot. But hhhwe are a very long hhhway from those places, little hhhwanderer. To reach them hhhwe must fly all the hhhway around the tree, and that hhhwill take time—more time, I fear, than hhhwe have left."

His snout furrowed. "Is there any faster way?"

She banked to the left, swooping around a spiraling tower of mist. "Yes, there is. But I must hhhwarn you, it hhhwould take us back into darkness. Not the darkness of Shadohhhwroot, mind you . . . but a deeper kind."

"Impossible! What darkness do you mean?"

"The darkness at the edge of the Otherhhhworld."

"The world of the spirits?" Basil shifted uneasily on the wind sister's airy cushion. "But that's so far away! How could that way be quicker?"

"Instead of taking you all the hhhway around the Great Tree, I hhhwould carry you *under* the Tree—beneath the roots. That hhhwill bring us through the mists that divide the hhhworlds—mists that are very deep, and very dark."

Basil gulped. "I don't care how dark they are. If that way is faster, let's do it."

Abruptly, Aylah plunged downward. Slicing through the starlit clouds, so fast that whistling winds screamed all around, she seemed to be racing the beams of light. Basil, ears blown flat against his head, imagined he was a great bird of prey, diving out of the sky.

Clouds darkened, as light grew scarcer. To the right, he saw the rugged outline of a long black ridge, so completely shadowed that it made the dusky clouds seem bright by comparison. Could that be the outer edge of Shadowroot?

The light around them dimmed swiftly. As they continued diving downward, rare spots of light illuminated the crest of a misty wave over here, the shredding vapors of a cloud over there. Then, all at once, everything went black. Darkness swallowed them whole.

Are we back in Shadowroot? he wondered anxiously. *Or is this really . . . the edge of the Otherworld?*

Still grateful for the brief interlude of light they'd experienced earlier, he peered all around to see if he could find any remaining beams. But no, he saw only darkness, unbroken in every direction. In the uniform blackness, he couldn't even begin to judge their speed or direction. In fact, it was only by the constant rush of air on his face, and the shrill whistle of wind, that he could be sure they were moving at all.

Yet after a few moments of gazing into the darkness, he began to notice something odd. *It isn't all black out there*, he realized with amazement. He stared harder, making sure he was really seeing correctly. *Or at least, not all black in the same way.*

Indeed, he was starting to see subtle differentiations. The darkness seemed, in places, not lighter—but *thinner* somehow. In some areas, thin and thick darkness formed layers, like the sand and mud along a streambed. In other areas, the darkened vista rippled with veins of even richer, deeper blackness.

"Hhhwelcome to the Otherhhhworld," said Aylah's voice directly in his ear, loud enough to be heard above the wailing wind. "Nohhhw hhhwe are under the roots of the Great Tree. Hhhwatch hhhwell, my little friend . . . and you shall see some things that no mortal but Merlin has ever hhhwitnessed."

"No one but Merlin? I don't deserve such special treatment." He chortled, swaying his slender tail. "But that won't stop me from enjoying it."

"Good," she replied. "Nohhhw hhhwatch."

As winds whistled around them, they swept deeper into this new, subtly varied darkness. Soon, Basil began to see not only layers, but shapes within the layers: some as boldly defined as a huge, castlelike cloud; others as fleeting as a flash of black lightning. He gasped, seeing a flock of shadowy, sylphlike forms fly out of one dark spot that could have been the entrance to a cave, turn in unison, then fly straight into another.

Beyond, he glimpsed another amazing shape—what looked like a gigantic upside-down tree. Mighty black roots anchored in the mists above, the tree's twisted branches stretched downward, far past what he could clearly see. The top of the tree lay hidden in the swirling mists below, yet for an instant he caught a hint of its shape—the merest shadow of a shadow.

Then, in the distance, he saw something that made him catch his breath. A landscape! An entire darkened landscape with billowing hills and wispy waterways, black mountain ridges and shaded hollows.

Even more remarkable, this landscape constantly shifted its shape. Turning endlessly into itself, the dark vista swelled and diminished and renewed. Hills spiraled upward to become mountain peaks, valleys receded into cavernous pits, and rolling contours flattened into limitless plains.

Suddenly, a strong current of wind blew across their path, jostling both Aylah and her passenger. The wind carried a group of ghostly shadows, dark figures astride even darker steeds, whose great hooves glinted like obsidian. The riders galloped right over them—and, Basil felt by the intense chill in his bones, right *through* them.

"Owww!" he cried in pain, as the jolt of turbulence twisted his broken wing.

Whoever they were, the shadow-riders passed in an instant, disappearing into a swelling black hole in the mist. But something they'd caused didn't disappear. The pain in Basil's wing continued to throb.

"Are you all right, little hhhwanderer?"

"No, not really," he grumbled. "This wing—ahhggh!—is worse . . . than ever."

"Merlin can heal you, and hhhwe hhhwill find him soon." In an airy whisper, she added, "I hope."

Trying to find a new position so that wind didn't blow against his injured wing, he sighed in anguish. "I . . . hope so, too. For more than my wing."

New visions, landscapes, and—occasionally—creatures appeared as they continued to fly through the dark mists. Basil didn't notice many of them, though. His wing kept throbbing, as if a heavy hammer were beating on the anvil of his shoulder.

Abruptly, Aylah angled upward. "Get ready nohhhw," she whispered in his ear.

"Ready? For what?"

Before she could answer, the mist grew heavier and

much wetter, like a sodden blanket. More rain than mist, it weighed upon them, soaking them with moisture. The wind sister kept flying, but more slowly now. She moaned rather than whistled; the rush of air felt more like a wave of water. She sputtered, laboring hard, forcing her way through the thick wet wall.

Light! All at once, brightness surrounded them. Basil blinked, hoping his eyes—utterly accustomed to the deep darkness of the Otherworld—would quickly adjust to normal light. All he could see now, though, were wet, blurry beams.

With a sudden splash and a spray of droplets, they broke through the watery wall. Mist, shot through with light from the stars, glowed all around. Before them stretched a rolling sea of blue, spanned by endless rows of rainbows.

"Hhhwe have reached," breathed Aylah heavily, "the realm of hhhWaterroot."

"And, let's hope, the realm where we find Merlin."

28: EVER FLOWING

People are like oceans: sometimes deep, sometimes shallow. One moment calm, the next moment stormy. And they are always mysterious.

Carried by Aylah's invisible arms, Basil coasted just above the surface of the ocean. Foaming waves licked at his underside, splattering his tail. Looking down, he saw a school of golden-scaled fish, as well as a subtle glint of sparkles within the water. Nearby, a turtle lazily surfaced, its barnacle-crusted back as white as the waves.

Basil's slim chest expanded as he drew a breath of air. Instantly, his nose tingled with a rich array of smells. Some of them he couldn't recognize, though he knew others from his encounters with the seabirds he'd met as a youth in Woodroot. For thousands of migrating seabirds had gathered there every winter in noisy flocks that filled the branches from the highest spruce tree to the lowest alder bush.

He smelled sea salt, pungent and yet always alluring. Kelp, floating on the waves. Driftwood, along with a hint of algae. Fish, fish, and more fish. Plus the feathers of gulls—

whose smell had long annoyed him, since seagulls made a habit of dropping their gooey guano on shrubs and stream banks . . . and sometimes on him.

"HhhWaterroot," whispered the wind sister, her breath now scented by the sea. "Hhhwe have arrived."

"So I see," answered Basil. "And what a journey you gave me, Aylah. I'll never forget it."

"Nor hhhwill I, little hhhwanderer." Her airy voice gusted like a storm at sea. "Nohhhw I hhhwill leave you again, stretching myself to the very hhhwidest to search for Merlin! Even then, it hhhwill not be easy to find him, in a realm so huge as hhhWaterroot."

"I want to go with you! To help find him." He shifted his broken wing only slightly, but that was enough to send a wave of pain through his whole body. "Please," he said through gritted teeth. "Take me with you."

"No. This hhhwill be faster! I must look over vast distances. Hhhwhy, he could be anyhhhwhere from the Geyser of Crystillia to the magical hhhWellspring of Mist. He could be south, in the Rainbohhhw Seas, hhhwhere the hhhwater shines like liquid rainbohhhws. Or he could be far to the north, in the lair of the hhhwater dragons."

"Water dragons?" Despite all the moisture in the air, his throat went dry. "There are *dragons* here?"

"Yes, and hhhwhile they do not breathe fire, they are hhhwoefully fierce." She swept around him, reassuring him with her airy embrace. "But they live far ahhhway from here, little hhhwanderer. You need not hhhworry."

"If you say so," he said doubtfully, as his eyes scanned the rolling waves for any suspicious shapes.

"Besides, little hhhwanderer, hhhwe have something hhhworse than dragons to hhhworry about."

"Right. Rhita Gawr."

"Hhhwherever he may be nohhhw."

She veered sharply to the right, sending up a spray of water. "I hhhwill set you here." Before he could say another word, she lowered him gently onto a gnarled piece of driftwood.

Hurriedly, he inspected this little floating scrap. Though only slightly larger than himself, it did seem to be stable. It rode on the waves, bobbing constantly, like another kind of whitecap.

"All right," he agreed. "Come back soon, though."

"I hhhwill," she promised. With a sudden swirl of spray, she departed.

"Good luck!" he called after her.

He adjusted his weight on the driftwood. The motion, however, jostled his injured wing. A new burst of pain, sharper than before, exploded in his shoulder, and he groaned in anguish.

Hoping to distract himself, he took another whiff of sea air. Salt, ever pungent, seemed to slap his nostrils. Seaweed deepened the smell, as did a sharp, silvery fin that rose briefly above the surface. Then a pair of wide-winged birds, as blue as the water, skimmed past, adding scents of wet feathers and webbed feet.

Just then two waves collided, sending a spiral of spray into the air. As the droplets fell, they sparkled like shattered rainbows. Vibrant purple, yellow, green, and red shimmered all around, raining downward.

My promise to Dagda! he suddenly remembered.

Before the shining droplets all fell into the sea, he stretched out his tongue and caught one. Tiny as it was, he knew it was the true essence of this realm—the magical liquid soil that supported all life. Pulling back his tongue, he swallowed.

I am water, announced a voice within his mind—a voice that roared and crashed like a distant waterfall, endlessly churning and splashing. *I am all shapes, all forms, all places: as soft as mist and hard as ice, as thin as a stream and wide as an ocean, as high as airy vapors and deep as the ultimate abyss. I am boiling, bubbling, pouring, rolling, and ever flowing.*

The splashing voice paused, as if listening to the continuous surge and swell of the waves. *Magnificent am I! Wild and pure, furious and calm, violent and serene. I am home to giant whales and creatures as small as aquatic dust. Gentle as a bubble yet powerful as a maelstrom am I, ever changing, ever flowing. For I am the sea, the storm, the river, the glacier, and the cloud.*

Once again the voice paused, then spilled and gushed these final words: *I am water.*

Gradually, Basil noticed something odd. The waves closest to his small shard of wood were calming, despite the constant motion of waves beyond. He peered closely, but the mystery only deepened. The water right around him was *flattening*—as if it were a small, quiet sea within the restless ocean. Soon his piece of driftwood sat motionless, fixed to the surface of the water.

A sudden splash—and he was rising into the air! Somehow the driftwood was being lifted higher. *What kind of wave is this?* he asked, stretching his neck to peer over the edge.

What he saw was no wave. Massive scales, the deep blue color of glacial ice, supported him—even as they pushed swiftly upward, rising out of the sea. The scales covered a huge, undulating surface that rippled like an ocean of muscle and bone. Rivers of water coursed off the scales, pouring down into the waves that receded farther below every second.

It's a tail! I'm on the tail of—

His mind froze as he realized the terrible truth. *A dragon.*

Slowly, steadily, the enormous tail rose above the waves, bearing Basil and his shard aloft. Aghast, he watched as— just ahead of where he sat—the scaly surface broadened into an immense back as wide as an island, narrowed again into a powerful neck, then swelled into a gargantuan head. Countless teeth, shaped like titanic blue icicles, gleamed as water poured out of the dragon's perilous mouth.

Higher and higher rose Basil, an unwilling passenger on the last creature he'd wanted to meet in this realm. Then, without warning, the dragon's tail tilted sharply. The shard of driftwood flipped, knocking Basil off. He skidded down the slippery scales, grasping desperately to keep himself from tumbling into the cold ocean where he'd drown—or be eaten—in seconds.

His broken wing shrieked with pain as he bounced and slid down the tail, fighting to grab hold. Water coursed over him, stinging his eyes with salt. But he kept flailing, digging his tiny claws into the scales.

There! One claw latched onto a row of barnacles that sprouted from a crack. Breathless, he dangled for a few seconds. With all his strength, trying to ignore the searing bolts of pain, he swung his body higher and pulled himself onto the barnacles. Just below, waves splashed against the immense tail, soaking Basil with spume.

Groaning miserably, he tried his best to make himself stay hopeful. *My wing may be useless . . . but at least water dragons don't have any wings at all. None that I can see, at least. So this fellow won't suddenly lift off and dump me into the sea. As long as he stays on the surface . . . I'm all right.*

He shook his head, having utterly failed to convince himself, let alone lift his mood. *Then he'll dive down and I'll die as soon as water fills my lungs. So after all this . . . I'll never get to warn Merlin. Or help Avalon. Or do anything that really matters with my life.*

Trying again, he forced himself to think of something else. *Aylah's coming back soon . . . I hope.* He caught a glimpse, as the massive tail swayed, of the dragon's enormous purple eye. *Seems to be looking for something. What, I wonder?*

All at once, another gigantic head lifted out of the waves only half a league away. Water flooded off its surface to reveal—

A second dragon!

The new beast, whose head was crowned with dozens of deadly horns, roared angrily. Then he slammed his titanic tail on the water, sending huge waves rolling across the sea. Basil's dragon turned and roared in reply, a sound so loud that Basil felt as if thunder had just crashed on top of him.

Barely hanging on, he wrapped his own minuscule tail around the barnacles. *Please, Aylah. Please hurry.*

Suddenly the dragon's tail beneath him pumped. It didn't strike the sea violently, but moved with mighty grace—and unfathomable power. The two beasts charged each other, a pair of armored ships sailing straight toward a collision.

Basil, soaked with constant spray, clung to the barnacles. Yet every sway of the immense tail loosened his grip. He started to slide off . . .

Roaring with rage, the dragons bore down on each other. Seabirds screeched and wheeled above, while schools of fish fled in all directions. Speeding to a crushing impact, the enormous rivals drew closer and closer.

Basil slipped off his precarious perch. Whipped by salty

spume, he hung on with just three slender claws. One tore loose. Then another. By the last tip of his last claw, he still held—just as the dragons came together in a slew of spray.

From each of their cavernous mouths came roars as deep as the ocean. And from their nostrils came jets of blue ice that slammed into each other with a shattering explosion. Bodies, ice, and waves all collided at once.

Basil broke loose. Helpless, he spun downward through the spray and flying shards of ice. He hit the surface of the ocean.

Cold water enveloped him, filling his mouth and ears, stinging his eyes, clogging his lungs. He tried to gasp for air, but only swallowed more seawater. A final, gurgling cry came from his throat.

Then he sank.

29: DEEPEST FOREST

Magic, I have concluded, is one part wisdom, two parts mystery, and three parts—now for the big surprise—well now, come to think of it, I'm just not telling.

The tip of Basil's snout sank beneath the waves. He disappeared, swallowed completely by the sea. No marine life took any notice: not the fast-swimming fish, not the gulls wheeling overhead—and certainly not the two battling dragons. Only a thin thread of bubbles marked the spot where he dropped into the depths.

It's over . . .

An intense, gale-force wind suddenly struck the water. Waves parted, briny curtains sprayed, and the drenched body of Basil lifted out of the sea. Surprised by the fury of wind and water, the dragons briefly paused to see if another foe had joined the fray.

Seeing no one else, they resumed their battle, hurling jets of blue-tinted ice and slamming each other with massive tails. Meanwhile, Basil's tiny limp form rose higher into the air. A warm breeze, smelling of cinnamon, carried him upward. At the same time, sharp currents of wind poked at his chest, trying to force the water out of his lungs.

Yet his eyes remained closed. His head drooped forward. He showed no sign of life.

"Hhhwake up, little hhhwanderer." Aylah sent the strongest gust yet into his chest.

Basil coughed, spewing seawater. His eyes opened and he shook himself dazedly. Again he coughed, and again. Then he vomited another gush of water.

At last, he drew a rattling breath. "Aylah . . . you . . . saved me."

"Only hhhwhat you did for me," she whispered, drying his body with her whirling wind.

Regaining his wits, he demanded, "Merlin? Did you find him?"

The wind blew chillier. "Alas, no! Hhhwherever he is, it's not this hhhwatery realm. Nohhhw hhhwe must try hhhWoodroot."

Basil tossed his head, flapping his ears to rid them of water. Even after the shake, though, they hung down from his head like a pair of drenched leaves. "What if he's not there?"

"Then hhhwe hhhwill keep searching until hhhwe find him."

"And what . . ." He winced and coughed again, though he wasn't sure whether that was because of the water still dripping down his throat—or because of the thought that had just occurred to him. "What if Rhita Gawr has already found the kreelix? And attacked Merlin?"

"Then hhhwe hhhwill . . ." She hesitated, unsure what

to say. Turning to the north, she flew faster. Her wind made a wake upon the waves, carving a path across the sea. "Hhhwe must hurry!"

Swiftly they soared, racing over the shining waters. In time, the brightness faded, as mist thickened around them. Though not as dark and dense as what they had found beneath the roots of the Great Tree, this mist still shrouded them. Like a vaporous veil, it fluttered and billowed, scattering the starlight. Hard as Basil peered into it, he couldn't see more than the veil itself.

Finally, the mist began to thin. Shafts of light tore through, shredding the clouds.

"There!" he cried excitedly. "I see Woodroot."

All he'd actually seen was a vague hint of color. But that was enough. For this was a color he knew well, a color he'd missed more than he even realized.

Green. All shades of green. The color of the forest. The color of his first home.

Slowly the mist revealed the rich green of spruce trees lined with moss, the golden green of meadowsweet sprinkled with fern, and the glistening green of rain-washed hawthorn, maple, and oak trees. Willows swayed gracefully as Aylah passed overhead, while tufted grasses bent their heads in greeting. Everywhere, birds fluttered, deer sauntered, insects whirred, woodland faeries gathered fruit, badgers burrowed under roots, and squirrels leaped from branch to branch.

Woodroot. Remembering that its elvish name, El Urien, meant *deepest forest*, Basil nodded. For nothing could better describe this place. Here grew all kinds of trees—trees so tall that they brushed the clouds, so transparent that they seemed almost invisible, or so liquid that their wood could actually be poured.

But Basil was scanning the forest for something else. *Let's hope*, he wished fervently, *that Merlin is here!*

"Listen," said Aylah suddenly.

Basil's ears cocked. Beyond the continuous rush of the wind across leaves and needles and stalks, he heard a different sound, a song so haunting he held his breath, straining to catch more. Somewhere in the glades below was the source of this soulful, sweeping music. But what was making it?

The trees themselves! Their whispering boughs, vibrating with the wind, made this soft, magical music.

"Harmona trees," said the wind sister. "The elves, I am told, are learning hohhhw to craft that hhhwood into lutes and lyres, flutes and hhhwondrous horns."

Instead of replying, Basil took a deep breath, savoring the smells of this realm. Smells he hadn't known, except in memory, for many years. He caught scents of ripe plums, spicy pepperroot, and larkon fruit—whose bright aroma reminded him, somehow, of starlight. He found a hint of the rare Shomorra tree, whose every branch produced a different kind of fruit. And then he caught a trace of an old favorite: the musty, murky smell of deer prints in a marsh.

Drawing another breath, he inhaled more smells—along with something else, something he hadn't expected. A tiny fleck of dirt, caught up in Aylah's wind, had risen into the air just as they soared past. And so, when Basil took that breath, he also took into himself some of the magical soil of this realm.

I am wood, spoke a richly resonant voice. It sounded like someone's breath blown through a leagues-long wooden flute. And to Basil, who had lived so long among the trees of this realm, it sounded, too, like the voice of a friend.

I am the circle, I am all—life into death, death into life.

I am fragrant as crushed spruce needles. Fresh as rain-washed maple leaves. Full as the ripest apples, the stream in spring flood, the doe carrying her yet-unborn fawn. And I am deep, very deep, as the memories of fallen boughs that have landed on my face, melted into me, and made a womb for countless new seeds.

My essence is a book, whose story is life, and whose language is time. The long, rounded notes of the wooden flute faded, echoing in his mind. Then they rose again for one final phrase: *I am wood.*

For a moment, he listened to the echoes of that voice. His broken wing didn't pain him; the search for Merlin didn't call him.

"This realm is your home, little hhhwanderer." Aylah's gentle breath stroked his ears, lightly brushing the small green hairs inside. "You should return here, after hhhwe . . ."

Her voice trailed off. He felt a cold shiver in the air around him.

"I see Merlin!" she cried with a sudden gust of words. "In danger—the hhhworst kind."

An ear-shattering shriek filled the sky. It came from somewhere in the forest below, stabbing at the air like a dagger of sound.

30: ONE LIFE

Dying really isn't so bad after the first time. But I still prefer to do it as infrequently as possible.

Aylah instantly veered in the direction of the shriek. She turned so sharply that Basil rolled onto his side, jostling his broken wing. Blades of pain sliced through him, cutting from his shoulder down to the wing's bony tip.

"Where is Merlin?" he called through the gusting wind. "What made that sound?"

Below, branches waved and tossed violently as the wind sister swept over the forest. But she didn't answer.

Just then Basil noticed something strange. Far ahead, on a ridge darkened by thick groves of spruce and pine, hundreds of birds took flight. Hawks, larks, terns, sparrows, geese, owls, and more winged creatures rose into the air like a ragged, feathery cloud. Screeching and honking, whistling and hooting, the mass of birds lifted out of the deep green trees.

Flying straight into Aylah, the birds were knocked in

all directions by the force of her wind. Feathers flew, while
birds squawked and piped and screeched in alarm. Yet she
didn't slow down at all, carrying Basil at gale speed toward
the tree-covered ridge.

"I still don't see him! Aylah, can you tell me where—"

His words halted as he glimpsed, through the mesh of
branches on the ridge, a wing—huge, jagged, and dark.
The kreelix! An instant later, the distant branches shifted
and covered the wing completely. Yet even though Basil
could no longer see any part of the monster, he could still
hear the echoing memory of Dagda's words: *a kreelix—the
greatest mortal foe a wizard can face.*

"Aylah, what exactly makes a kreelix so perilous? Those
wings?"

"No," she replied. "Hhhworse than its hhhwings, by far,
is its unique pohhhwer."

"Surely," he protested, "Merlin's own magical powers
can defeat—"

"They cannot!" she shouted. "They are hhhworthless.
Don't you understand? *A kreelix devours magic.* Uses its
ohhhwn terrible pohhhwer, *negatus mysterium*, to suck the
magic out of anyone, no matter hohhhw skilled."

Stunned at this news, he glanced down. Though the
wind made his eyes water, he saw, galloping away from the
ridge, a pair of golden unicorns. Their hides gleamed as
they sped away, fleeing for their lives. "Then how can Merlin possibly fight?"

"Hhhwith his bare hands, if he must. But never hhhwith
magic! Even his staff is useless for it, too, is made hhhwith
magic."

"So he can use only his mortal strength?" Basil shook
his head vigorously. "That won't be enough!"

"I knohhhw," she howled, racing over the treetops.

"Hhhwhen a hhhwizard is caught by a kreelix..." She whistled angrily. "The hhhwizard usually dies. And that is hhhwithout the interference of—"

"Rhita Gawr," he finished with a snarl. "Do you think that evil spirit is down there right now, helping the kreelix?"

"Hhhwe cannot tell."

Basil stretched his small head forward, as if he could make her fly faster. "What will you do once we get there?"

"Distract the beast, perhaps, so Merlin might escape. Beyond that, I am hhhwholly helpless."

"Helpless?" Basil blinked in astonishment. "But his life's in danger!"

"So is mine, little hhhwanderer. And hhhworse, I cannot even give my life to save his! For if any part of my hhhwind, even the slightest breath, touches the kreelix's fangs—all my magic hhhwill instantly vanish. The kreelix hhhwould barely feel my touch. And since my hhhwhole being is made of magic, hhhwhen I vanish...I hhhwill also die."

He released an angry growl, barely audible above the loud whooshing of the wind. "Then," he declared, "I will help him."

"*You?* Hohhhw?"

"I don't know, Aylah. My body's made of flesh and bones, not magic. So at least I can try."

"No, little friend, you cannot! You, too, are made of magic. I see it in the glohhhw of your eyes. Just one touch of those fangs and you hhhwould lose everything. Your magic—and maybe also your life."

His eyes narrowed. "Whatever magic I have is small—very small. Losing it wouldn't hurt Avalon one bit. But losing Merlin? That's something else."

"Impossible," the wind sister countered. "You cannot help him."

In a voice that seemed much bigger than his body, he replied, "Escaping from that windtaker—that was also impossible."

Aylah, racing toward the ridge, waited before answering. "All right," she said at last. "But this is beyond bold, little hhhwanderer. This is crazy."

"My specialty." The memory of the windtaker renewed his confidence, strengthening his small limbs. Then, as they reached the ridge, he suddenly saw the whole hulking mass of the kreelix. Instantly all his confidence vanished.

The kreelix, shaped like an enormous bat, towered over Merlin. Though the wizard's tunic expanded with the rushing wind, he seemed very small—a mere dwarf by comparison. Standing upright on the forest floor with its huge, hooked wings extended, the evil beast was forcing him back against a thick tangle of brush that grew beneath a massive old cedar.

In just a few more seconds, Basil could see, all Merlin's routes of escape would be cut off. If he went forward, it would only be into the kreelix's fatal embrace; backward, into the impenetrable brush. And if he used any magic at all, it would be instantly swallowed. His wizard's staff lay useless in a patch of ferns, having been cast aside.

As the kreelix slowly advanced, moving with the adeptness of a highly intelligent killer, its leathery wings whipped at the air and its bloodred mouth snarled. Within that mouth, three fangs arched toward Merlin. Saliva dripped off their sword-sharp tips, gleaming like deadly poison.

The dream! All at once, Basil remembered it—the

wings, the stench of death, his own helplessness and despair.

So it was true. All true. Merlin is going to die . . . here and now.

The terrible reality paralyzed him, clutching at his heart. All his blood ceased flowing. His lungs stopped breathing. If it weren't for the persistent ache of his broken wing, he wouldn't even know that he had a body at all.

Wait, he realized. *That ache . . .*

His wing really was broken. He *did* have a body, a life, of his own. And he had something more, as well: the choice of how to use it.

He took a slow, ragged breath. Aylah, meanwhile, circled the area, whipping the branches with her wind, trying to distract the kreelix. But the monster paid no heed. It continued to advance on Merlin, rustling its dark wings menacingly.

Suddenly Basil understood something else. It was those wings—so huge and terrifying—that he'd seen in his dream. Not his own! And if the kreelix's wings meant deathly attack . . . his own wings, even if they were small and wounded, could mean something different. Very different.

"Aylah, bring me closer!"

"Are you sure, little hhhwanderer?"

"Yes. Do it now."

Swirling madly, the wind sister lowered him toward the confrontation. Merlin's sleeves fluttered, while the assailant's leathery wings billowed like sails. Yet neither the wizard nor the kreelix seemed to notice. They continued to glare at each other, watching for any weakness.

Basil's mind whirled like the wind, trying to decide what to do. *How can I help? I can't fly, can't stop that thing. I'm just one person, just one life—*

His thoughts halted, caught by that final phrase. And he remembered what Dagda had said at Merlin's wedding: *One life, no matter how small, can make a difference.*

The old cedar creaked loudly as it swayed above Merlin's head. As if in answer, the kreelix let loose another shrill, ear-piercing shriek. The horrible noise made the wizard stumble back another step, so that his back jammed against the wall of brush. Thorns tore at the cloth of his tunic, while branches raked at his hair.

"Nohhhw he is trapped," wailed the wind sister.

"Drop me, Aylah!"

"But little hhhwan—"

"Drop me *now*!"

With a final gust to guide him toward Merlin, the wind sister released him. Suddenly he was plunging downward, spinning as he fell. Air rushed over him, whistling in his ears, but it was not the warm, embracing air of his friend. Instinctively he tried to spread his wings to slow himself, until a sharp pain erupted in his shoulder.

Down he tumbled, unable to aim where he might land. Confused images spun below him—a bloodred mouth, a tattered tunic, a tangle of brush, a daggerlike fang that dripped saliva.

All at once, he slammed into something hard. A branch of the cedar tree! Taking the impact on his back, he struck with such force that all his breath burst out of him. He heard the crunch of his broken wing even as brutal pain shot through his whole body. Needles, brittle and sharp because the old tree was on the verge of dying, sprayed into the air and jabbed against his scales.

Through the cedar's branches he plunged, smashing into bark, twigs, needles, and cones on the way. Down, down, down. At each new impact, he flailed his little legs, trying to grab hold, throwing his back into the effort despite the painful throbbing of his wing. But he kept falling through the old tree, bouncing from branch to lower branch with a cascade of dead needles.

Finally, he hit a bough squarely on his underside. With all his remaining strength, he squeezed tight with his legs, hoping to straddle the branch. But he started to slide off sideways, rapidly losing his hold. Just before he lost his grip and slipped over the edge, he swung his tail up, throwing his weight in the opposite direction.

It worked. He lay atop the bough, stationary at last. Panting with exhaustion, aching all over, the little green fellow who had fallen from the sky peered cautiously over the side.

What he saw made him want to freeze—or, if he moved at all, to crawl away and hide somewhere. The kreelix stood right below him! Just under the end of the branch, the beast's mouth opened wide, exposing its three murderous fangs. Its eyeless face seemed to be laughing, gloating in triumph.

Meanwhile, backed against the brush at the base of the tree, stood Merlin. His face showed an expression Basil had never expected to see on a great wizard. Fear. Heart-wrenching fear. Merlin's long black hair brushed against his shoulders as he swung his head, searching desperately for some way to escape. Yet no way existed. Between the wall of thorns and the kreelix's wide wings and hooked claws, he was completely surrounded.

An idea burst into Basil's mind. As dangerous as it was desperate, the idea instantly took hold. *I can't defeat this monster—or even hope to harm it. But I can buy Merlin some time! He might still escape.* His brow furrowed. *Even if I won't.*

Ignoring his painful shoulder and wing, he started to crawl farther out on the branch. Hard as he tried not to lose his footing on the slippery, warped bark, he nearly slid off when a twig supporting one of his hind legs suddenly snapped. Then, just when he'd righted himself, the kreelix released another terrible shriek. This time, Basil knew, the kreelix intended the cry to be the last sound its prey ever heard. The force of the shrill cry shook the cedar's branches, almost knocking Basil off his perch. Barely, amidst the rain of needles and cones, he clung on.

Not for long, though. Even before the shriek ended, Basil saw that the kreelix's mouth was open to its widest. And he knew that the moment for his idea had arrived.

Gathering all his strength, he dashed a few steps farther on the limb. Then, without a second's hesitation, he leaped. Through the air he plunged—right into the mouth of the monster.

He tumbled between two of the deadly fangs, just missing their gleaming tips by a hairsbreadth. As light as a twig, he landed on top of the kreelix's bloodred tongue. And then he did something no twig could have done.

He bit the tongue. Hard! Clamping his slim jaws on the soft flesh, he squeezed with all his might—so ferociously that one of his tiny front teeth cracked and broke off.

A new shriek erupted from the kreelix. The noise, for Basil, was deafening, echoing all around him in the cavernous mouth. But he barely noticed, since he needed all his concentration to stay focused on one goal: hanging on.

The kreelix writhed and shook its head madly. All the while it continued to screech, and also to wag its tongue, bashing Basil against the roof of its mouth again and again. Soon he felt dizzy, as well as nauseous from the overpowering stench of the kreelix's breath, something like curdled vomit.

Still he hung on. Biting with every last morsel of strength, he endured the shrieks in his ears and the assaults on his body. His shoulder and back stung with excruciating pain; the smell made him gag; his jaws felt ready to explode.

And still he hung on. He didn't notice the blood pouring down from his broken tooth, nor the fact that he could no longer hold his wounded wing against his back. The wing, now just a mass of broken bones and ripped flesh, slapped lifelessly whenever the beast's tongue moved.

And still he hung on. Darkness seeped into his mind, like poison polluting a stream. He began to lose awareness of where he was, and why. He even forgot, as the darkness stifled his thoughts, what had caused him to sacrifice his one life.

At last, the darkness overwhelmed him completely. His battered body finally relaxed, slumped lifelessly in the mouth of the kreelix. Even then, however, some of his muscles remained rigid, so firmly fixed that no force in Avalon could possibly budge them.

His jaws still held tightly to the monster's tongue.

31: A Missing Tooth

Funny thing about awareness: What is right there in front of our eyes is often harder to see than what's missing.

Ugh . . . what a terrible taste!

When Basil formed that thought, the first one to enter his mind in what seemed like a very long time, he did the best thing possible. He spat. Out of his jaws flew a large hunk of raw, bloody meat that smelled even worse than it looked. It was the smell, as putrid as decomposing flesh, that fully revived him.

"Yuck!" he exclaimed. "That tasted as bad as—"

He stopped, both because he was at a loss for the right word—and because he had just opened his eyes. The sight that greeted him suddenly flooded his mind with memories. And also with questions.

He was still in the forest of Woodroot. Towering trees, draped with moss, grew everywhere. Rich aromas of cedar and spruce and lute's neck fern sweetened the air. A flock of summer geese honked enthusiastically as they flew overhead. But something even more wondrous captured his attention.

Gazing down at him was a strong, clear-eyed man with a thick black beard. Long locks of black hair fell to the man's shoulders. His open hand, which held Basil, felt both sturdy and gentle at once. This was a man Basil recognized immediately, a man he could never forget.

"Merlin! You're alive."

"Only thanks to you, my little friend." The wizard lifted his hand, examining the small creature closely—so closely that his prominent nose, as pointed as the beak of a hawk, almost poked Basil's side.

"Yes, now I'm sure of it," Merlin proclaimed. "We have met before, haven't we? Twice before! At my wedding—and then atop a cliff in Stoneroot."

"Why . . . yes," mumbled Basil. "But how did you survive? I mean, the kreelix—"

"Is dead," finished the wizard. "Because of your bravery." He smiled gratefully at the tiny creature in the palm of his hand. "And so I am in your debt twice over. For the life of my son, whom you saved from being crushed to death by a sleeping giant." His dark eyes danced with amusement. "Though Shim, to this day, puzzles over whatever happened to that honey." Then his face grew serious again. "And now for my own life, as well."

He regarded Basil fondly. "Tell me your name, little friend."

"First tell me what happened! The kreelix—the tongue—all that shrieking . . ."

Merlin spun around. He tilted his hand, revealing the new scene. But the instant Basil saw what lay on the forest floor, he shouted in surprise and leaped into the air, flapping his small wings wildly. The realization that he was flying again, painlessly working his wings, shocked him almost as much as the sight Merlin had shown him: the lifeless body of the kreelix. Struggling to comprehend, Basil flew so erratically that he barely managed to land back on the wizard's open hand.

"What—my wings . . . when? And the kreelix! It's . . . it's all—but . . . well, errr, but *how*?" he sputtered.

Amused, the wizard stroked his fulsome beard. "Shall we take your questions one at a time? Or shall I attempt to answer them in that same fashion?"

Still in shock, Basil merely stared at the hulking form of the dead kreelix. It lay crushed beneath a toppled tree—the old cedar where Basil had first landed. The beast's wings, once so powerful, were now utterly lifeless, just contorted folds of skin, no more dangerous than discarded rags. And its mouth, only partly open, dribbled blood that stained the needle-strewn ground dark red. Just one look at the mouth was enough to make Basil shudder in revulsion.

"Hmmm," said the wizard thoughtfully. "I take that as a request to go one at a time."

Stepping over the hooked wing tip of the kreelix, Merlin explained, "Your courageous gambit—sweet Dagda, you actually *leaped into the mouth of a kreelix!*—totally distracted my assailant. For just a few seconds, mind you. But that gave me time to escape from its trap. And then to call for help."

"From the hhhwind," breathed a familiar, airy voice.

"Aylah!" shouted Basil, flapping his wings ecstatically. "You're here."

"I hhhwas never far ahhhway, little hhhwanderer."

Sweeping closer to Basil as he sat in the wizard's hand, she encircled him with warm air. Above all the fragrances of the forest, he now smelled the scent of cinnamon. "You are even braver than I thought."

"Crazier, you mean," he replied. He grinned at his invisible friend, revealing his missing front tooth. Then he turned back to the body of the kreelix. "And this tree?"

"We pushed it over, Aylah and I." Merlin walked over to the fallen cedar. Gently, he placed his hand upon its rippled bark and stroked the ancient trunk. "Though it was near the end of its days, we still asked its permission to die for this cause. It agreed—and most grateful we are for its sacrifice."

For an instant, Basil thought some of the cedar's dead needles actually moved, quivering ever so gently. It could have been merely a breath from the wind sister . . . or maybe something more.

He looked up at Merlin and spread his small, bony wings. "And these? You healed the broken one?"

"Broken, torn, shredded, and pulverized," corrected the wizard. He nodded with a hint of pride. "You challenged me considerably to fix that one. Is it stiff at all? Skin too tight?"

Basil rustled the wing. "Supple as a new sapling."

"Good." With a wave at the corpse, the wizard continued, "The hardest part, frankly, was removing you from that mouth. It wasn't the kreelix who made it difficult, either. It was you." He turned his hand to look into Basil's face. "Although you were completely unconscious by then, *you simply would not let go.*"

A touch of pink colored Basil's normally green eyes, then melted away.

"In fact, I had no choice but to cut you out."

Again, Basil shuddered. "So that piece of meat in my mouth . . ."

"Was part of the kreelix's tongue." Seeing the little fellow's frown of disgust, Merlin reached into his tunic pocket and pulled out a sprig of greenery.

"Here," he said, handing the sprig to Basil. "Sweetwater mint. I always carry some to freshen my breath. Especially," he added a bit shyly, "when I'm about to meet Hallia." He gave an encouraging nod. "Go ahead, chew it. Even the terrible taste of a kreelix is no match for fresh mint."

Cautiously, Basil bit off a strip of one leaf. As soon as he began to chew, a burst of cool sweetness exploded in his mouth, as if he'd just taken a drink from a river of mint. He gladly took another bite, and chewed avidly.

"Excellent," remarked the wizard. Abruptly, his face fell. "Sorry about your front tooth, though."

Basil stopped chewing. Probing with the tip of his tongue, he felt the gap at the front of his jaw. "You couldn't fix it?"

"No," replied the wizard. "You need a specialist for that. I do bones, skin, even internal organs. But not teeth."

The lizard in his hand shot him a mystified glance.

"It's true," Merlin went on. "I can fix all manner of bones. In your case, twenty-seven! But teeth—that's a different matter. Someday, I predict, there will be a certain type of healer who will only do teeth. And only by appointment. Dentists, they'll be called."

Basil shook his head, a bit worried about the wizard's sanity. Then, pushing his tongue into the space between his teeth, he announced, "Truth is, I rather like this little gap." He grinned. "This missing tooth is, in a way, a reminder."

"A souvenir," agreed Aylah, ruffling his wings with her breath. "From your battle hhhwith the kreelix."

"Right," said Basil with a chuckle. "If any dactylbird attacks me in the future, I'll just flash this gap at him! If he has any sense, he'll flee for his life."

The wind sister gusted merrily.

Suddenly Basil's expression changed. Glumness showed in every wrinkle on his snout. "That's only fantasy, I know. After this day, I'll still be a scrawny little . . . *whatever*. Tempting prey for dactylbirds, unless they want a full meal instead of half a bite."

"No," declared Merlin. His dark eyes gleamed. "You are much more than that."

Hefting the tiny creature in his hand, he went on. "How someone so small could accomplish so much is, indeed, a mystery. And yet . . . do you remember hearing these words at my wedding? *Just as the smallest grain of sand can tilt a scale, the weight of one person's will—*"

"*Can lift an entire world,*" finished Basil. He nodded at Merlin. "I remember. And I suppose that could be true. You know, I never thought I'd really feel this way—but maybe . . . I'm just about the right size, after all. For me."

Waving a wing at the kreelix, he added, "After all, if I'd been any bigger, I couldn't have jumped into that thing's mouth."

"Couldn't have hhhwon against the kreelix," added Aylah, her breeze buffeting his face.

"And couldn't have saved my life," declared Merlin.

Feeling strangely content, more than he'd ever felt before, Basil gazed thoughtfully at the fallen beast. He looked at the huge head, the slack jaw, the crumpled black wings. All of a sudden, he noticed an odd vibration near the fur at the base of one claw. The air in that spot quivered, distorted, throbbing like a wound.

Peering closely, he concentrated on the source of the vibration. All at once, his vision cleared. He could see without any distortion. And what he saw confirmed his worst fears.

32: A NEW THREAT

*Some words, I've found, carry more weight than others.
There are even words that, like literary oxen, bear enormous loads of meaning and metaphor. Yet there is no
word, in any language, that carries more weight than
this one: friend.*

A leech, swollen and dripping dark red blood, crawled
out from the lifeless folds of fur. Although it was
twice the size it had been when Basil last saw it, he guessed
that the leech would have been even larger by now if its
only goal had been to suck the kreelix's blood. Instead, as
Basil knew all too well, its primary goal had been to tap
into the bloodstream of the monstrous beast—and to add
its own evil energy and purpose, enough that the kreelix
couldn't possibly fail to kill Merlin.

And yet . . . it had indeed failed.

Instantly, the leech started to scurry away over the needles, twigs, and other debris on the forest floor—but not
before it turned to meet Basil's gaze. The blood-drenched
creature shot him a look of intense malice, full of hatred

and vengeance. Propelled by dark magic, it struck Basil like a body blow.

Groaning in pain, the little lizard reeled and staggered sideways, almost falling off the wizard's hand. He tried desperately to speak, to warn the others, but could only make a hoarse, choking cry.

"Hhhwhat is it, little hhhwanderer?" asked Aylah, suddenly concerned. She spun so fast in the glade that the surrounding trees swayed and clacked their branches as if caught in a sudden storm.

"Tell us," demanded Merlin. His bushy black eyebrows arched in concern. "What's wrong?"

"Over . . . there," Basil croaked at last. He drew a ragged breath, as the evil spell began to wear off. Still weakened, it took all his strength to jab his wing toward the spot. "The leech! Rhita Gawr."

"Rhita Gawr!" exclaimed Merlin, as the wind sister wailed overhead.

"He's . . . here," Basil said hoarsely. "Saw him before. On Dagda. Tried to warn you . . . too late! He's . . . here, Dagda said, to conquer . . . Avalon. Then to use our world . . . as a stepping-stone. To conquer other worlds—like Earth."

Merlin winced at his words. Then, as quickly as a hare, he bounded over to the place where Basil had pointed.

"There," said the lizard hoarsely. "In the needles! By that claw."

The wizard pounced on the spot. Setting Basil down on a branch of the toppled cedar, he started sifting through the needles with his hands. Furiously, he searched for this foe from the Otherworld. He worked with both speed and care, inspecting every twig, cone, and scrap of bark before tossing them aside. Meanwhile, Aylah swept across the ground, turning up ferns, broken roots, and clumps of velvety moss. The forest floor seemed to bubble with motion.

But they found no sign at all of the leech. The wizard's hands dropped to his sides, and the air in the glade fell still.

"Gone," the wizard whispered.

Grimly, Merlin raised his head and turned to Basil. For a long moment, he studied the small figure on the branch. At the same time, Basil raised his leafy wings as if to ask, "What now?"

"This bodes ill for Avalon," Merlin said at last, tugging on his beard. "Yet now, at least, we are warned. That gives us a chance—just a chance—to prepare for whatever is to come." He sighed. "And for that I am grateful."

"Hhhwe are all grateful," whispered Aylah.

The wizard rose to his feet, strode over to a nearby patch of ferns, and picked up his staff. Its runes glowed subtly green, much like Basil's eyes. Grasping the gnarled top of the staff, Merlin announced, "From this day forward, we must be on guard. All of us."

He raised the staff high. In a ringing voice, he commanded: "Spread the word far and wide, to every creature of every realm! Avalon faces a grave new threat. *Rhita Gawr has entered our world.*"

All around the companions, trees swayed and rustled, their branches creaking ominously. At the same time, a great horned owl, seated on the highest branch of a spruce, hooted in its husky voice and took flight. Smaller birds, too, took up the cry, fluttering from tree to tree and wheeling overhead. Squirrels chattered in the boughs, a grass snake hissed as it slithered through the ferns, and a lone possum piped a warning cry while padding across the needles.

Even a pair of orange-backed beetles, perched on a twig beside Basil, opened their wings and leaped into the air.

Seeing all this, Merlin lowered his staff and looked directly at Basil. Speaking with quiet intensity, he declared, "And from this day forward, Avalon also has a new defender. A courageous warrior who, despite his size, possesses remarkable gifts."

He stepped closer to the small winged creature who had saved his life. "I still don't know your name. Or how you have lived your life so far. But with all my heart, I call you . . . my friend."

The wind took up his words, carrying them through branches and treetops, bearing them high into the clouds. And so, throughout the seven realms of Avalon, the twin messages spread: An ancient enemy from the Otherworld had arrived—even as a new defender had appeared.

33: A LIFE WORTH SAVING

I don't mind being corrected. Not at all. Except, of course, when it happens in public or in private.

Basil," the little fellow said in his small, crackling voice. Seated on the branch of the fallen cedar, he ruffled his leathery wings and hopped toward Merlin. "My name is Basil."

"Hmmm," said the wizard, stroking the curls of his beard. "I'm not so sure about that."

Puzzled, Basil cocked his head to one side. "What do you mean? I know my own name, don't I?"

Merlin knelt down on the needle-covered forest floor, so that his face was directly opposite Basil's. "That can wait. First, tell me this. What can I possibly do to thank you? Today, to save my life, you dived into the very mouth of a kreelix! Surely there is something I can do for you."

Immediately, Basil felt tempted to ask for an increase in size—a longer tail, maybe, or a bigger back. After all, adding even just a little length would be a great improvement, making him equal in size to something truly enormous—say, a sparrow or a chickadee. But he merely shook his head. "No thanks. It's enough to see you safe again."

"Tell me the truth," pressed Merlin, pushing some stray locks of hair off his brow. "Surely there is *something* you desire in your heart of hearts."

Basil's scaly tail quivered. "Only," he admitted, trying his best to sound lighthearted, "to be bigger than a broken twig. Are you handing out longer tails? That would be nice."

Merlin merely sighed. "That sort of magic, I'm afraid, is beyond my reach. It would mean changing you into a different kind of creature than you are."

He paused, a slightly guilty look on his face. In a whisper, he added, "Not that it hasn't occurred to me on occasion. How delightful it would be to turn a mosquito into an eagle! Or, for that matter, the reverse. Or what about turning a young boy into a fish or a goose? Now, that would be true magic." He tugged at his beard. "As I said, though, such skill is beyond me. Someday in the future, as an elder wizard, I may know how to change creatures' kinds. But not today."

Basil shrugged as if he really didn't care. "Right. Anyway, that sort of thing only happens in those tales the faeries tell their young."

"Not here and now," agreed Merlin.

The little fellow nodded. He stretched his wings, appreciating their breadth, their lightness. It felt good to spread them again, to know they could carry him skyward, even without Aylah's help. Sure, he would like to have a bigger chest or a longer tail. But then these wings probably couldn't lift his weight. Truth be told, he could be a lot worse off than he was now.

And yet . . . Part of him had hoped, for just a second, that Merlin might be able to change him into something a bit bigger. Something a bit more, well, *frightening*. To dactylbirds, at least.

The wizard suddenly scrunched his nose, pondering. "So tell me, one-who-calls-himself-Basil. What kind of creature *are* you? In all my travels, I don't believe I've ever seen anybody quite like you."

"My good hhhwizard," breathed Aylah as she brushed past, swishing Merlin's long hair, "that is because there *is* nobody else like him."

"She's right," Basil agreed, sounding less than joyful. His round ears drooped. "I'm one of a kind."

"But what kind is that?" the wizard wondered aloud.

"I don't know." Basil blew a long, slow breath. "I really don't."

"And yet," said Merlin softly, "you must have wondered."

"Oh, from time to time, I suppose."

"Only hhhwhen he is conscious," teased Aylah, blowing across Basil's brow. "And then only four or five times a day."

The lizard shifted uncomfortably on the cedar branch. "How do you know so much, Aylah?"

"Ohhh, I just listen to hhhwhatever is on the hhhwind."

Merlin, still kneeling, edged closer. Gently, he stroked the small green scales of Basil's tail. "Can't you tell me anything more? Any clues about your kind?"

"Only that Dagda said I'm not a dragon. *You are not a mere dragon* were his exact words."

At this, Merlin's tufted brows lifted. "Anything else?"

"Well, I'm not a kreelix." He glanced down at the lifeless hulk that lay sprawled under the old cedar. Dark blood from its mouth continued to seep into the ground, soaking the needles and cones nearby. "At least . . . I hope not."

"You are definitely not a kreelix, my friend. Anything else? Where were you born?"

Basil shifted his weight on the branch, thinking. "I hatched from an egg. A green one. Here in Woodroot."

"I knohhhw," whispered the wind sister. "I hhhwas there."

"Yes!" said Basil, bobbing his head brightly. "I remember, Aylah. You were right there."

The wind swept through the glade, tossing boughs of spruce and cedar, lifting shards of bark off the ground. "And I hhhwas also there, before you hatched, hhhwhen you came floating dohhhwn the River Unceasing in Lost Fincayra, hhhwhen you hhhwere carried ahhhway by a falcon, and hhhwhen you fell on the Forgotten Island."

"The island!" exclaimed Merlin. "You were *there*?"

Basil tilted his head, unsure.

"He hhhwas," assured Aylah, "though still in the egg. Just as he hhhwas there hhhwhen a certain young hhhwizard planted a magical seed—a seed that grehhhw into a hhhwondrous nehhhw hhhworld."

The wizard pursed his lips thoughtfully. "And how did you know, good wind sister, to look after this particular egg?"

"You have guessed already," she whispered, stirring the branches around them. "Dagda came to me in a vision, asking me to hhhwatch over this creature. He never said hhhwhy, nor hhhwhat kind of creature he might really be, only that this hhhwould be a life hhhworth saving."

"A life worth saving," repeated Merlin. With a decisive nod, he stood up. "Now I've heard more than enough to confirm my suspicions. For a long time, my friend, I have puzzled over your abilities, and over that green glow in your eyes. At last, I know what kind of creature you are!"

Basil's heart leaped. "You do?" He waved his little wings anxiously. "Will you tell me?"

"Better than that," he announced. "I will *show* you."

Planting his staff firmly in the carpet of needles, Merlin met Basil's gaze. "While I cannot change you into someone you are not, I *can* change you into someone you are truly meant to be."

His voice deepened. "With your consent, I can accelerate your growth, giving you whatever form you might ultimately have. Let me warn you, my friend, that nothing may change. I could be wrong; you might already have the form of your destiny."

The wizard's eyes gleamed. "Then again, you could have a little surprise."

Basil drew in a full breath, trying his best to stay calm. Could he really be something more than he seemed? Placing his small feet firmly on the branch, he declared, "You have my consent."

"Good. In that case, I shall give you a body as great as your heart."

34: GREAT HEART

Like starlight, a person's soul can be hidden by a seem-
ingly endless storm—but never really extinguished. All it
takes is one good wind to clear away the clouds, and the
light will be revealed.

Standing in the center of the forest glade, Merlin placed
both his hands on the gnarled top of his staff. He
waited, watching a lone cedar needle drift slowly down
to the ground, twirling in the tree-shafted light as it fell.
Then, gazing skyward, he started to chant:

> *Powers unborn,*
> *Powers to be,*
> *Grant us the birth of a destiny.*
> *Sprout now the seed,*
> *Welcome the child.*
> *Bring forth enigma, mystery wild—*
> *Under the secret,*
> *Over the sight,*

Honor the soul of emerging light.
Beginnings shall end,
New ends begin:
Free now the future that dwells within.

Three times he spoke the chant—first in the language of Avalon, then that of Fincayra, and finally that of the Otherworld of the Spirits. With every word, the sky overhead grew darker. Dense, heavy clouds gathered. The air buzzed with electricity, lifting strands of the wizard's flowing hair. But no lightning, which could have released the tension, blazed overhead. The electric tension continued to swell.

The surrounding cedars, spruces, firs, and pines began to quiver. Their boughs trembled, knocking more needles loose. Yet this was not movement caused by wind. No breeze at all stirred the glade. Wherever Aylah might have been, she remained utterly still.

All the while, the electricity grew. Tiny sparks ignited in the air, crackled briefly for an instant, then vanished. Tree bark sizzled and popped, as drops of resin exploded. The soil under Merlin's feet started to vibrate—gently at first, then steadily gaining force, until the very ground was humming.

Seated on the branch of the toppled cedar, Basil felt the swelling energy. He felt it in the air, the quaking branches, and in the vibrating ground. Sparking with electricity, the loose scale on his neck slowly lifted toward the darkening sky.

Most profoundly, though, Basil felt the growing energy inside himself. Not only in his bones, which felt steadily warmer, or in his eyes, whose vision seemed increasingly blurred. Most of all, he felt it in the deep, untouchable depths of his soul.

Something is happening to me. But what?

All at once, a great bolt of lightning exploded, searing the sky. A powerful blast of thunder erupted at the same time, strong enough to make Merlin stumble and nearly fall over. The lightning flashed downward, but it didn't strike the tallest tree around. In fact, it didn't strike any tree.

The lightning struck Basil.

With a brilliant flash of light, the potent bolt hit the little fellow on the back, right between his ragged wings. The green scales on his shoulders sizzled and briefly burst into flame. Basil's eyes glowed brighter than ever before.

Simultaneously, the sky above opened, illuminating the forest. Heavy clouds melted into mist and then disappeared. The trees ceased quaking, as did the ground. Air moved freely once more, freshening the grove.

Basil, however, didn't move. He simply sat there on the newly blackened branch, as if nothing unusual had happened. But for the intensified glow in his eyes, he seemed completely unchanged.

Then, inexplicably, the torn scale on his neck twisted and broke off, tumbling down to the needles on the forest floor. Another scale, behind his head, suddenly bulged and popped off. Another one, this time on his stubby left foreleg, did the same. Basil turned his head to see what was happening to his body, yet his face didn't show concern. Rather, it showed anticipation.

One by one, with gathering speed, the scales all over his body burst away, falling to the ground. In their place shone new, vibrant green scales that gleamed like polished emeralds. More amazing still, the scales started growing, swelling in size—along with every part of his body.

First to expand was his head. Swiftly it grew, larger and larger, until its massive jaws could have swallowed a whole village. Within those jaws swelled a huge, green-tinted tongue. His eyes grew into luminous stars, radiating green. His once-tiny nose also expanded, until his nostrils became enormous black archways. And his small, cupped ears stretched so tall that a full-grown man easily could have stepped inside.

Teeth by the hundreds grew in his jaws. One row was not enough: The sharpest ones, rising like mountain pinnacles, sat three rows deep. Only one place lacked any teeth at all—the spot at the front of his mouth where he'd broken his tooth biting the kreelix.

Basil's neck, back, and tail expanded, so rapidly that his swelling frame knocked over trees, pushed aside boulders, and completely crushed the remains of the kreelix. Merlin leaped out of the way to avoid getting flattened by the burgeoning chest. And when a towering spruce, uprooted by the giant shoulder pressing against it, fell on top of Basil's back, he barely noticed.

His gargantuan legs rippled with powerful new muscles. Perilous claws sprouted from his feet. Meanwhile, his wings, no longer as little as crumpled leaves, swelled in size, extending their reach so far they could have covered the surface of a lake.

Basil's tail grew longer and longer and longer. When finally it stopped, it reached deep into the trees of the surrounding forest. At its very tip, the tail widened into a massive, bony club that could have knocked another dragon out of the sky.

For Basil had, indeed, become a dragon. Or, at least, something that dramatically resembled a dragon—one larger and more powerful than had ever lived in Avalon. The fierce dragon Gwynnia, who had almost destroyed him at the wedding, who had shown him no more respect than a man would show a mosquito, would have fit entirely inside his cavernous mouth.

"Well, well," he thundered in a deep, resonant voice that shook the trees. "Look at me now!"

Merlin, brushing himself off after his dive into a holly bush, answered with just one word: "Indeed."

Grabbing his staff, the wizard paced slowly around Basil's massive head, inspecting this truly gargantuan creature. Finally, he stopped beneath one of the enormous, green-glowing eyes. Peering up at the radiant pupil, he said, "Now you have the body you were always meant to have."

"A body," whistled Aylah as she swept around the glade, "as hhhwide as your dreams."

"A body," echoed Merlin, "as great as your heart."

Basil started to wag his tail triumphantly, but stopped when three tall spruces came crashing down with an explosion of broken branches. An angry flock of wrens took flight, screeching at him for demolishing their homes. And a family of badgers, their den suddenly exposed by uplifted roots, shrieked in surprise and ran off. Yet as chagrined as he felt for having caused so much damage, Basil felt even more amazed. *That was me who did that. Me! With my own tail. My own body!*

"Sorry about that," he muttered to the wrens, his voice now only as loud as an average thunderstorm. Yet somehow he didn't sound too remorseful.

Aylah breezed by his great green head, bending the tip of one of his ears. "Dagda, for all his hhhwisdom, hhhwas hhhwrong. He said you hhhwere not really a dragon. And yet here you are, the most hhhwondrous dragon I have ever seen in all the hhhworlds."

He gave a satisfied grunt, but kept his tail stationary. Still, he glanced behind to make sure no more trees had been toppled.

"Not true," announced Merlin, pounding his staff on the ground. "Dagda was perfectly correct."

Basil's massive snout wrinkled in puzzlement. Aylah ceased flying and hovered in the air, awaiting the wizard's explanation.

"Dagda said, *You are not a mere dragon.* And so you are not!" Leaning closer to the sweeping jaw, Merlin added in a quiet voice, "The crucial word in that sentence is not *dragon*, but *mere*."

He raised his staff, gripping its shaft, and pointed it at Basil's eye. "That green glow, do you know what it is?"

"No," came the answer, echoing among the trees.

"That, my friend, is élano. The essential, life-giving substance of the Great Tree. The sum of all seven sacred Elements. The most powerful magic anywhere."

He paused, allowing his words to sink in. "From the very moment you hatched, you possessed an extraordinary amount of élano. Like my staff here, Ohnyalei, you have always glowed with the light of that magic."

As he spoke, the staff's seven runes swelled in brightness. Basil could see them all clearly: a butterfly, for the wizard's power of Changing; a cracked stone, for Protecting; a sword, for Naming; a dragon's tail, for Eliminating; an eye, for Seeing; and a star within a circle, for Leaping.

All these, Basil knew, Merlin had gained on his Quest of the Seven Songs, a favorite of wandering bards. He decided to ask Merlin someday to explain the runes' meaning—especially the dragon's tail.

"And so," the wizard explained, "you are no mere dragon. You are, in truth, a unique kind of creature, a dragon with a remarkable amount of magic. You are an *élanodragon*."

Basil, not sure he deserved such a name, furrowed his great brow.

"Ahhh," breathed Aylah as she flew across his enormous neck, "that is hhhwhy your body has taken so long to develop, and hhhwould have taken longer but for Merlin's help. Nohhhw, at last, you are grohhhwn."

Merlin turned his head, looking from the very tip of Basil's snout, down his long neck, over the massive wings, and down the tail that vanished into the trees. Adding to Aylah's comment, he said, "*Fully* grown." Then, looking up at Basil's eye again, he chided, "And you wanted a bigger tail!"

Basil laughed out loud—a deep, full, mirthful sound that might have come from the immense harp strings strung between the clouds of Airroot. Merely the force of his breath was enough to break off dozens of branches, along with moss, cones, and several birds' nests. Then, to tease Merlin back, he reached out with his tongue and, with a tiny flick, knocked the wizard over backward into a patch of ferns.

Merlin picked himself up again. Spitting out a frond of fern, he grumbled, "What ever happened to respect for one's elders? You may be as big as a mountain, but I'm at least twenty years older than you."

"And I," said the wind sister, swishing through the

spruce boughs, "am at least several thousand years older than you both."

All three of them burst into laughter. Basil's mirth exploded, shattering more branches and spraying needles and cones everywhere. Aylah's bubbled and seemed to tickle the very air. And Merlin's came so gleefully that he lost his balance again and nearly fell back into the ferns.

Steadying himself, the wizard stepped closer to his gargantuan friend. With the top of his staff, he tapped lightly on the gleaming scales of an oversize knuckle. "Hmmm," he said, listening to the vibrant echo. "I believe these scales are infused with élano. Which should make them impervious to any attack, including fire." Almost as an afterthought, he added, "Which is good, since you probably don't have the ability to breathe fire yourself."

Basil grunted in surprise. Twitching his ears as if he'd been insulted, he drew in a titanic breath. Narrowing his eyes, he made a deep, rumbling noise in his throat. Then, with a look of pride worthy of a fire-breathing dragon, he opened his gigantic mouth and exhaled with frightening force. Out of his mouth came air, saliva, and a deafening roar.

But no fire.

Lowering his hands from his ears, Merlin gazed up at Basil's huge eye—which, for the first time, showed a hint of disappointment. "As I thought, my friend. No dragon whose egg hatches in the realm of Woodroot can breathe fire."

The wizard shrugged. "Part of Dagda and Lorilanda's overall plan, you see. Keeps the trees from burning down every time two dragons have a little spat." Glancing up at Basil, he went on, "You might not know this, but the dragons of Waterroot also don't breathe fire. They breathe—"

"Ice, I know," Basil rumbled like a landslide. "Blue ice. Useful in a fight, but still not as impressive as fire." He heaved a sigh, cracking more branches.

Merlin placed his hand on the gargantuan knuckle. "Even if you can't breathe fire, you more than make up for that with your great size. And great magic."

"And something more pohhhwerful yet," added Aylah as she flew between Basil's ears. "Your great heart."

Circling closer, she continued, "You are the bravest creature I have ever knohhhwn—the only one in history to defeat a hhhwindtaker as hhhwell as a kreelix. And you accomplished those feats hhhwhen you hhhwere small, as small as a frail-hhhwinged butterfly."

As she swept past his ears, brushing against the greenish-yellow hairs that grew along their edges, Basil released a low rumble of appreciation. His eyes no longer showed disappointment, but something more like gratitude.

"And now," declared Merlin, with a sweep of his arm. "About that name."

He strode a few paces away from Basil, so that he could see more of the immense face. "No longer shall you carry the name Basil—a name quite fitting for a tasty little herb, or perhaps even a feisty little warrior. But not for a dragon! And certainly not for Avalon's only true élanodragon."

The wizard raised his staff and announced: "From this day forward, your name shall be . . . Basilgarrad. A most worthy name! Be sure to say it properly, with the accent at the end—garr*ahhd*—as it would be said in the Fincayran Old Tongue. For in that most ancient language, your name means *Basil the Great Heart*."

Above Merlin's head, Aylah whirled through the trees, whistling her approval. *Great heart, great heart, great heart*, the wind seemed to say. Tousled by the gusts, the treetops nodded in agreement.

Though Basil's mind spun with delight, he made no big show of emotion. He merely grinned, just enough to reveal the gap of a missing tooth.

35: New Adventures

And now, my friends, a dragon's toast! Here's to life's little blessings: wars, plagues, and all forms of evil. Their presence keeps us alert—and their absence keeps us grateful.

Merlin lowered his staff. Drawing a full breath of forest air, replete with the resins of spruce and cedar, he looked into Basilgarrad's gigantic green eye. When he spoke, it was in the voice of an elder wizard, with celebration and sorrow, hope and longing.

"This world of ours is a truly wondrous place—full of great mysteries and great contrasts. Chief among those mysteries, I am afraid, is how a world with so much beauty and richness could also be home to greed, arrogance, and intolerance. How can a world that produces abundant fruits, inspires timeless poetry, builds lasting friendships, and creates chances for us to realize our dreams also contain the horrors of war and religious hatred? That is the greatest challenge of our time, my friend: to tip the world's scale, to find hope where there might be despair, to help all living creatures live together in harmony."

He paused, gazing into the unblinking eye. "Whatever his plans, Rhita Gawr will seek to worsen those horrors— for as they grow, so will his power. But as they shrink, so will his chances of conquest." Gravely, he nodded. "And so, Basilgarrad, will you join me in this quest? Will you be a true guardian of Avalon?"

The green dragon's first thought was, *Does he really need to ask?* But he gave his answer in one word.

"Yes," he bellowed. His thunderous voice echoed through the forest, shaking the trees with its force.

"Excellent," answered Merlin after the reverberations died down.

"Hhhwonderful," added Aylah, flowing breezily among the boughs. Then she asked, "Hhhwhat do you knohhhw, Merlin, about his ancestry?"

The wizard looked up into the waving boughs above his head, then back at Basilgarrad. "You are the only élanodragon ever, which explains why you started life looking different from any other dragon in history." He paused, measuring his words. "But that doesn't mean you don't have any kin."

The enormous eyes widened.

"Because your egg first appeared in Fincayra, on the River Unceasing, I would guess you are a direct descendant of the most powerful dragon who ever lived on that enchanted isle. His name was Valdearg—meaning *Wings of Fire.*"

Not bad, thought the young descendant of that dragon. His chest, already as big as a hillside, swelled some more. *Not bad at all.*

"Which means," Merlin continued, "you are also related

to Valdearg's only other surviving child. The dragon named Gwynnia."

His chest squashed down like a popped pastry. "That irascible old fire fanny?" he protested. "She is my *relative*?"

"Your sister, to be exact." Merlin did his best to hide his chuckles, though without much success.

"Ahhh," added the wind sister playfully, "but the best part is all her hhhwell-behaved children! Since birth, they have only set fire to half of Stoneroot." She swooped closer, tickling the enormous ears. "Young as you are, you are nohhhw their hhhwise old uncle. You can teach them some hhhweighty lessons."

"Starting with some manners," he declared. His eyes narrowed as he thought back to how one of those fledgling dragons—at that moment more than a hundred times his size—had attacked him at Merlin and Hallia's wedding. "It will be a pleasure to meet them again."

"A pleasure for you," said Aylah, gusting with amusement. "But they might not feel the same hhhway."

"Whatever relatives you might have," said Merlin, "you have your whole life ahead of you. And as a creature of great magic, it could be a long life indeed."

Fingering some of the longer hairs on his beard, he twirled them into a tight knot. "Why, you could live for a thousand years or more!" His eyes, as dark as his hair, opened wide at a new thought. "It's even possible, I suppose, that you might someday meet my own descendants—the heirs to my magic."

As soon as he spoke those words, his face clouded and he said under his breath, "Which may not include my own son."

Straightening his back, he walked up to Basilgarrad's

prominent jaw. Rows upon rows of mighty teeth gleamed above him. Taking hold of the bottom end of his staff, he stretched up as high as he could reach, so that the top of the staff touched the dragon's lower lip. Firmly, he rapped three times on the lip—a blow that would have bruised any man, but that Basilgarrad barely felt.

Wizards can be totally bizarre, Basilgarrad thought while this was happening.

"There," announced Merlin, lowering his staff and holding it as he normally would. "Now, thanks to the magic of Ohnyalei, we are linked, you and I. You can call to me with your thoughts at any time, from any distance. And I can do the same."

With a sly grin, he added, "So remember that now I can hear your thoughts . . . in case you ever feel like calling me *totally bizarre*."

The dragon's brow immediately furrowed.

"Don't worry," the wizard added. "I can't hear all your thoughts. Just the ones that pertain specifically to me. Such as any new adventures you might be planning for us. And I hope there will be many!"

At that moment, a pungent odor drifted into the glade. The air reeked of decaying flesh mixed with vomit. Instantly recognizing the smell, the wizard's face went pale. Whirling around, he shouted a word he'd hoped never to use again.

"Kreelix!"

Planting his feet on the dry needles of the forest floor, he braced himself for another attack. Beads of sweat appeared on his brow, then slid down his temples. A look of pained regret on his face, he tossed his staff aside so that its magic would survive even if his own did not.

From behind, he suddenly heard a deep rumble. He

spun around again, and all at once realized that it wasn't the sound of a kreelix attacking—but a dragon laughing. The rumble grew into a great, rollicking roar as Basilgarrad lifted his mighty head and laughed so hard the ground trembled. Cones tumbled off the trees and branches swayed as the wind sister joined in. Soon, it seemed, the whole forest was sharing in the laugh. Except for the wizard.

Merlin glanced nervously over his shoulder, then back at Basilgarrad. He sniffed the air, which was quickly returning to the fresh scents of the forest. "You?" he demanded. "*You* made that smell?"

"Why, yes," his huge companion replied, still mirthful. "Not so appealing as that honey smell I made for Shim, but just as effective." He chortled quietly, like a simmering pot of stew. "You may be able to hear all my plans, but it seems you can't hear all my *pranks*."

Shaking his head, the wizard started to push his way into a thorny bramble to fetch his staff. "Why, dear Dagda, does a dragon need a sense of humor?"

"Hhhwe all need humor," reminded Aylah, flying low enough to add the scent of cinnamon to the glade.

"I suppose so," grumbled Merlin as he fought to extract the staff from its bed of thorns. "But . . . really!"

"You cast spells," declared Basilgarrad. "And I cast *smells*. Seems only fair."

Merlin's scowl finally melted away. "I suspect, my oversize friend, that our adventures have only just begun."

The great dragon thumped his tail on the ground in approval. This jovial gesture caused tremors that rattled the forest for leagues around, sending deer galloping, squirrels scurrying, and birds flying.

Taking his staff, Merlin spun it slowly in his hand. Then, peering up at the immense eye of Basilgarrad, he said qui-

etly, "I am glad we have met, truly met, on this fateful day."
He sighed. "And now, alas, I must go. There is some trouble brewing in Fireroot. Something about underground caverns, flaming jewels—and wrathful dragons."

Basilgarrad cocked his tremendous head. His voice a resonant rumble, he asked, "Would you like a ride?"

Merlin raised a bushy brow. "Are you fast?"

"Not as fast as the wind . . . but I'll do my best."

The wizard's whole face brightened. "Then I'd love to have a ride."

Avalon's only élanodragon tilted his head so that his ear, itself taller than Merlin, flapped down on the ground with a spray of bark and needles. Quickly, the wizard clambered up. Holding tight to the edge of the ear, he managed to hang on as Basilgarrad straightened his head and lifted higher.

Merlin stood atop the dragon's head, clasping the huge pointed ear. Now as tall as the trees, he looked out across the forested hills, surveying the richly layered landscape. In the distance, a flock of bright yellow butterflies, their wings shimmering like stars, settled on a dark green spruce. Nodding, he said, "I think I'm going to enjoy this view."

"Hhhwait," breathed a gentle voice flowing past. "Before hhhwe part, I have something to say."

"Come with us, Aylah," the dragon bellowed. "You and I can stay together! Fly together. Just as we've done for so long."

The air swirled across his mighty brow, tousling his ears, as well as Merlin's tunic. "No, my friend," the wind sister replied. "Hhhwe have already stayed together for a hhhwondrously long time, much longer than I have spent hhhwith any other being."

Currents pressed closer, filling the air with the smell of cinnamon. "A hhhwind sister must fly, hhhwith no thought of sleeping or hhhwaking. For I am as hhhwatchful as the stars, and as restless—"

"As the wind," finished Basilgarrad.

"Ahhh yes. Hhhwe have flohhhwn far, you and I—to all seven realms of this hhhworld, hhhwhose magic you have tasted, and to the very edge of the Otherhhhworld."

She swept around his head, caressing his soft ears, his glowing eyes, his massive mouth, and even the gap of his missing tooth. "But before I leave you, I hhhwant to say this. Hohhhwever far you may fly, you hhhwill alhhhways have a friend."

Somehow, as large as his throat was now, Basilgarrad couldn't make any sounds.

"I may never see you again," she continued. "But I hhhwish you hhhwell, hhhwherever your hhhwinds may blohhhw."

She encircled him one last time. "And even though all the hhhworld hhhwill knohhhw you as the great Basilgarrad, slayer of the kreelix and defender of Avalon—to me you hhhwill alhhhways be . . . my little hhhwanderer."

With a swirl of wind, she departed. For several seconds, both Basilgarrad and Merlin remained motionless, as still as a day without a breeze. Then the green dragon's ears quivered as his eyes scanned the distant horizon.

In a deep, resounding voice, he declared: "All right. Time to fly."

Epilogue

To Drink

In all my years as a dragon, what have I learned?
*   What you don't know, don't see, and don't expect—*
that's usually what kills you.

Year of Avalon 45

Struggling to take another step up the stony ridge, the sheep tried to keep her head high enough to see the mountain stream just a few more steps up the slope. The stream glittered invitingly, emerging from a jumble of rocks that, until recently, were covered by snow. Even now, she could hear the water's muffled burbling from under the rocks. And the satisfying splash as it broke free, tumbling into a pool.

She licked her parched lips. But her tongue, like her lips, was as dry as a sand-filled gulley.

Water, she knew, would save her. Restore her strength. Then she could rejoin the flock—and, most important, her young lambs. All three of them.

She bleated mournfully, blinking her glazed eyes. How

many dawns and starsets had passed since she last saw them frolic? Since she last licked their small furry ears, or nudged them away after a satisfying drink of mother's milk?

Too many.

Like all mountain sheep native to upper Malóch, she had adapted to living in these high, arid ridges. Unlike the tangled jungles to the south, or the treacherous marshes to the north, these lands harbored few predators. In her many seasons, she had never seen a fierce jungle tiger, and had only once met a marsh ghoul—glimpsing its shadowy form as it stole into the flock's nighttime hideaway and captured a lamb.

She took another laborious step. It took all her strength to lift her cloven hoof over a sharply angled rock. Never, in all her years, had she felt so weak. Or so thirsty.

Not that she hadn't known thirst before: This region was very dry. Especially in the months after all traces of snow had melted, these lands became a high-altitude desert, a place of cracked soil and bristly grass that craved water. Yet this particular thirst was more extreme than any she'd ever known.

Weakened by her aching thirst, the ewe hadn't been able to keep up with her migrating flock. She had continued to fall behind, slowing her companions. Because she knew their traditional route so well, she had urged them, over the loud bleating of her lambs, to go on without her while she searched for a mountain spring. She would certainly catch up with them after her strength returned. Only freshwater could do that . . . and now—at last—her goal was in sight.

Yet her steps grew steadily more difficult. Even her heart, it seemed, was laboring to pump enough blood through her body. Her eyes couldn't quite focus anymore. But she could still make out the shining pool of water just ahead.

With a supreme effort, she took one more halting step. She could hear the water splashing into the pool, even if she couldn't see it through the swirling shadows that pressed closer all the time. Gritting her teeth, the ewe lifted her wobbling leg and—

Collapsed. She died at once. Her heart, brain, and the rest of her internal organs all ceased to function. And yet, as dry as her mouth and throat were, she had not died from thirst.

She had died from loss of blood.

From the base of her neck emerged a bulbous gray leech as big as a man's fist. Fresh blood dripped from the edges of its mouth, running down its sides like anguished rivers; wrath smoldered in its bloodshot eye. Its belly distended from having gorged on the ewe's blood over so many weeks, drinking more than her body could replenish, the swollen leech fell to the stony ground. There was a sloshing sound as it landed, for it still had its most recent meal to digest.

And digest it would, in short order. For this leech, unlike others of its kind, needed to drink blood not just to sustain its body. No, it needed blood mainly for a different purpose—strengthening its own dark magic.

Magic truly worthy of the immortal warlord Rhita Gawr.

As it heaved itself into the shadow of a rock, its shiny gray color shifted to black—not the rich black that was the color of ebony or obsidian, but the empty black that was really the absence of light. Why bother to disguise itself anymore, blending into the sheep's woolen folds, now that she had died? Twisting its wide, bloodsucking mouth, the leech silently cursed the fallen ewe for failing to deliver it all the way to its ultimate goal: this realm's haunted marsh.

Still, she had done as well as any of the unfortunate creatures who had unwittingly carried the leech over many leagues of land and air before they, too, perished. For eight long years it had traveled, step by halting step, to get here. And it had, before that journey began, ridden other creatures, as well—including an uncooperative stag and a slow-witted kreelix. It had stayed with the kreelix for several frustrating weeks, guiding the beast's every move, hoping to destroy a miserable wizard called Merlin.

An angry hiss escaped from the leech as it thought about that cursed man who had caused so much trouble over the years. And about the reckless green lizard who had helped him by destroying the kreelix. Annoying as that green beast had been while still small—when he'd warned Dagda about the leech's presence—now that he'd grown to the size of a dragon, he'd become a true menace. How lovely it would feel to suck all his blood straight out of his heart!

The leech worked its mouth hungrily. One day, perhaps, it would have that enormous pleasure. Right now, though, it had higher priorities. Far higher.

Starting with traveling the remaining distance to one particular part of the haunted marsh. Once it had reached that remote, desolate place, the engorged leech would swiftly become more dangerous. Its size would swell, along with its strength. For by then it would have begun its primary task here in Avalon—to suck not blood, but something far more vile.

Far more tasty.

And far more powerful.

What the leech would find there was the most potent drink imaginable. A drink made from distilled terror, hatred, and death. A drink that would enable it, at last, to conquer this miserable world—and other worlds, as well.

T. A. Barron writes novels, children's books, and nature books in the attic of his Colorado home. Explore his website: **www.tabarron.com**.

BOOK TWO IN THE
MERLIN'S DRAGON TRILOGY BY
T.A. BARRON

NEW YORK TIMES BESTSELLING AUTHOR

T. A. BARRON

The Merlin Effect

Kate Gordon accompanies her father on a quest for a sunken Spanish galleon that contains a priceless treasure—a mysterious drinking horn that legend states may have been responsible for Merlin's death. Now, to save her father's life, Kate must enter an undersea world of bizarre creatures and terrifying foes, and succeed where Merlin failed.

penguin.com

T. A. BARRON

The Great Tree of Avalon
The Eternal Flame

The wondrous world of Avalon is about to be destroyed—for the warlord Rhita Gawr, now a wrathful dragon, is bent on conquest. With an army of deathless warriors under his command and a corrupted crystal of unimaginable power in his possession, Gawr has nothing to stop him—except a trio of unlikely heroes.

"A satisfying conclusion."
—*Deseret Morning News*

"Combines adventure with a deep appreciation for nature."
—*The Oregonian*

penguin.com